Just As I Am

Just As I Am

Maurice Senior

Copyright © 2017 by Maurice Senior.

Library of Congress Control Number: 2017913054
ISBN: Hardcover   978-1-5434-4633-3
         Softcover   978-1-5434-4632-6
         eBook   978-1-5434-4634-0

All rights reserved. No part of this book may be reproduced or transmitted in any form or by any means, electronic or mechanical, including photocopying, recording, or by any information storage and retrieval system, without permission in writing from the copyright owner.

This is a work of fiction. Names, characters, places and incidents either are the product of the author's imagination or are used fictitiously, and any resemblance to any actual persons, living or dead, events, or locales is entirely coincidental.

Scripture quotations marked KJV are from the Holy Bible, King James Version (Authorized Version). First published in 1611. Quoted from the KJV Classic Reference Bible, Copyright © 1983 by The Zondervan Corporation.

Any people depicted in stock imagery provided by Thinkstock are models, and such images are being used for illustrative purposes only. Certain stock imagery © Thinkstock.

Print information available on the last page.

Rev. date: 08/25/2017

To order additional copies of this book, contact:
Xlibris
1-888-795-4274
www.Xlibris.com
Orders@Xlibris.com
543022

Contents

Introduction\Inspiration vii
Dedication ix
Content xi

Chapter 1	They that Wait...	1
Chapter 2	God's got you..	4
Chapter 3	In the eyes of children	9
Chapter 4	The call...	13
Chapter 5	The return call	18
Chapter 6	The price of happiness	24
Chapter 7	Mind over matter	32
Chapter 8	Fatherly figure	37
Chapter 9	Sinking Sand..	43
Chapter 10	He who is without sin	47
Chapter 11	God is standing by...	51
Chapter 12	"My heart never had an Hero"	55
Chapter 13	Children at play...	59
Chapter 14	The inner cry	64
Chapter 15	The Dinner	69
Chapter 16	Bon Appétit	74
Chapter 17	The intentions..	80
Chapter 18	Play ground	85
Chapter 19	Lord I give you my heart...............................	91
Chapter 20	The prayers	97
Chapter 21	No Match..	103
Chapter 22	Don't judge me	110
Chapter 23	Who feels it knows it	117
Chapter 24	Leave my child alone	124
Chapter 25	The birds and the Bees	130
Chapter 26	Unwelcomed visitor.......................................	140
Chapter 27	Visitor #2	147
Chapter 28	Butterflies in the stomach.............................	155

Chapter 29	What if God was like man?	161
Chapter 30	Basic skills	167
Chapter 31	Delilah	176
Chapter 32	Trust	183
Chapter 33	The Sermon	191
Chapter 34	Bridge over troubled water	200
Chapter 35	"Where do we go from here".?	210
Chapter 36	'How to make it work	218
Chapter 37	The four Seasons	224
Chapter 38	A conflict of interest	230
Chapter 39	Break-Even	236
Chapter 40	Dirty little secrets	244
Chapter 41	Love is coming at you	254
Chapter 42	Be a man about it	261
Chapter 43	'What I need from you is understanding"	267
Chapter 44	How deep is your love	276
Chapter 45	How to control the home	283
Chapter 46	Heart and Soul	291
Chapter 47	The road to happiness	297
Chapter 48	Trials are training	302
Chapter 49	Too close	307
Chapter 50	Tell it all	313
Chapter 51	Working Together	319
Chapter 52	Mindful thinking	326
Chapter 53	The truth about love	330
Chapter 54	A Parent and a Leader	336
Chapter 55	I am coming home	343
Chapter 56	The water is trouble my friends	348
Chapter 57	Have You Forgiven Yourself?	356
Chapter 58	"What circle are you in?"	364
Chapter 59	"The judgement of mankind"	371
Chapter 60	The verdict	381
Chapter 61	"Wedding Jitters"	386

Introduction\Inspiration

Growing up with a Stepdad who was Christian minded. Much like Paul in this story. Myself and my siblings had a front seat view of watching faith and hope at work in our household and daily lives.

Our mother Sharon who was a believer had ensured that we went every Sunday.

Now that they have both passed on. I honor the love they showed to each other and to us as children.

Like Paul Glenroy met Sharon with kids of her own. I was one of four. He took on the battle of taking care his own kids merge with hers and displayed his great faith in God. Not only were we inspired by the trails they went through as parents but the fact that they have always taught us that there is Hope.

Growing up in Rockfort Kingston, Jamaica was never a bed of roses.

But with two powerhouse parents, esteem role models then and now (their memories) have inspired such phenomenon, that with God's grace I was able to put together this powerful sequel. (look out for the other two books) in their divine memories.

Dedication

To:

God for making me a shining example of his bright yet humble light.

The off springs of Sharon Elizabeth Henderson and Glenroy Brown.

Everyone who believes in and God.

Everyone who had ever had a doubt in their life. Here is another reason to try Jesus.

Everyone who believed in me and encouraged my writing talent.

Content

This book contains 61 short story chapters that will hopefully; intrigue you, teach you, inspire and motivate you to have faith and never give up. You may find something of value that may help you along the way.

Share it with someone, share God's love.

Chapter 1

They that Wait

"I'm sorry Mrs. Johnson our investors have pulled out".
"Ms. Johnson".
She corrected him.
He continued sounding firm.
"We are no longer able to keep you on staff". "We have tried, I am sorry our hands are tied". Said Mark Taylor CEO Hepdart Insurance.

A company that newly appointed Evangelist Johnson has spent 5 years with and gave it her all.

"Look it's 2015,". "I can give you a glowing recommendation", you're good!",
"I'm sure you will find a job in no time". Mark Taylor continued.

She took a deep breath. Wondering if he knows what it is to fight for five people to survive.

At home she has four mouths to feed. Because before she met the man called God, She was nothing. She has always told herself this. Her past was a jungle filled with poison Ives. She drank, smoked and gambled.

The reason she was true to her calling was because she was not afraid to say who she was and have been. For sure you can see who she is now. "Glory be to God". She said.

She was hoping God would have sent her a proper husband by now. To help her raise the kids. A 16-year-old boy, Peter, With the desperate need for some man handling. A pair of loveable but sneaky 13 old twin girls, Natasha and Natanya. A full mouth, know it all. 10-year-old Justin.

The birth papers bore all three different last names. How she pulled herself together with all the chaos only her prayers could answer this. Now she is faced with unemployment at age 40. With kids in school and their fathers, (Oops wrong word) and the 'seed bearers' She can't be bothered to even think of them. But she was very sure like at least sixty percent of Jamaican women, let's say around the world share the 'Tale of fatherhood.'

She would have really love to have had someone to come home to, and one who she could relate to at this crucial time.

She takes her kids along with her to church and hope that they will learn to love and accept the faith and love of God. She was in doubt of her next move. All the stress and frustration has now just piled on her. Her neck felt tight and her back was aching. As she walked she felt dizzy. Even though she had eaten a perfectly balanced meal she had made from home.

She boarded the bus, her journey from New Kingston to Harbour View. Where she lived on Poinsettia Drive. She paid rent monthly and in a leap of faith, she had just paid this month's rent two days ago. She still gave God thanks because it could have been worst.

She had to make it out somehow.

She bought a Star and read the classified, to see if there was anything she could apply for. With a certificate in Secretarial Skills, A few CXC business subjects, She still had further to go. She fell asleep before she could properly browse the newspaper.

The noise from two women quarreling woke her up. After she was having this lovely day dream of having a decent husband and living in cherry gardens. And all her kids were well accounted for.

She is not the type to meddle in other people's affair but she reached out to one of the ladies and asked her to stop.

The lady continued for a while and eventually stop [stopped] after Evangelist Heather Johnson started singing in a low tone.

"For I know redeemer lives". Slowly scattered voice pitched in and before you know it she could have directed a choir.

This was making her feel better about her own situation and felt the presence of the almighty around and about the place.

(1st Cor. 10:13.)

This came to her mind. She has never ministered before openly on a bus. She was hoping for some 'Divine Intervention'. For the spirit to lead her. She prayed.

"Blessed your name oh Lord and all that is within me bless your holy name". She repeated it. As the bus song along waiting for her to minister the word to their sinful souls. But she waited upon the Lord to lead her and guide her tongue. That every word will be according to his way. That doctrines and denominations will not hinder the growth of his love for it goes on from generation to generation. She waited upon God.

And then she spoke.

"For the wages of sin is death but the gift of God is eternal life".

"Amen".

Said a decent looking mid age dark skinned man at the back of the bus. They made eye contact, and she could read him if the spirit allowed her. Because it wouldn't be good Christian values if she did, but she could tell by the words he was pure in heart.

Chapter 2

God's got you

She continued her inward thinking as she stood facing the people. She was not yet potent with a sermon. But once God is in the midst it shall be blessed and the words came to her.

"Men shall not live by bread alone". (Matthew 4:4.) "Nor the furniture", "nor the house and land that he has acquired".

She paused.

"But by the words of the almighty."

Her confidence was building.

"Amen"
scattered confirmation came from the occupants of the bus.

But for sure a few of them sat there-even a pick pocket. Who never raised his head to make eye contact with her. Because she was elevated and could tell on him. But wisdom is a special gift. It should never be confused with knowledge because not everyone knows what to do with acquired knowledge. The ones who do have both in their spectrum, Especially the divine input from God through prayer, faith and experience that nurtures understanding.

These people should shine brightly. And because she is humbled. Today God has chosen to exalt her and raise her above her circumstances. She shouted.

"Praise be to God".

She encouraged the people going to their whereabouts.

"To seek ye the kingdom of heaven and all will be added to their lives".

"Sign up for recruitment and fall into line". "Like in the army", "each man has a number he is next to the guy with the number that follows his and the one that his number was followed by".

"This means every person has his own life", "number and time".

"In the army, there are rules and restrictions". "If you want to be the best you can be!"

. She said.

"Then follow the rules don't be left behind or caught up".
"You could lose your place".
"You Lose your life and your soul".

"Let's bow our heads in prayer".
She said.

As she prayed for the children who are mercilessly slain, raped and abused. The women who shared the same faith of pain and injustice. She plead for mercy and that God may ease their pain. She prayed for the unemployed, the employed and those in need and the hungry. But her biggest and loudest prayer was for God to touch someone. To change one person so that when he or she the walk through their door at home, They would be shining example.

"Amen".

She closed.

She was close to her stop, unaware of where the night's dinner may fall from. She sat wiping her sweat when a lady handed her a hundred dollar bill and then a man and money kept coming though she did ask for it.

But she said it before when she quoted. (Matthew 6:33). She collected at least over a thousand dollars. Not a lot but enough for a few nights dinner. She teared up and thank her provider.

As she exited the bus, the man she observed got off too. He said "Good sermon".
She replied.
"Thank you".
"Are you a Christian?"
. She asked him.
"What will make me a Christian?".

He asked her.
"To be baptized and accept God as your lord personal savior".
"The bible is your weapon".
"Use it!", "know it!

She said in calm but passionate tone.
"How long have you been a Christian?".
He followed up with the conversation. "About three years". "It's been hard". "But god is great".
She answered him.

"Nobody ever said living a Christ like life is easy". The man said.
He continued.
"Before I forget my manners". "I am Paul"." Oh, like the apostle".
She smiled and He smiled genuinely.
"Not really I am not that close to the lord it's not something I'm proud of".
but I am not the worst of person".
He said in a very polite and grounded tone.
"I am Heather".
She said reaching out to shake his hands. With a pleasant and confident smile. He could tell she was not married because she wore no ring. But he was adamant that her love for God had enough grace to keep her afloat.

Just As I Am | 7

Her flesh was not weak. Her mind was determined he can tell because she is so poised in the name of the Savior. She can't say this out loud but she found his countenance to be very interesting and it was a ease having a conversation with him.

"So, what you do for work?". He asked her.

"I am", "Well I was a secretary and lost my job today".

"Wow".

He said.

"You don't look a bit sad or worried".

Paul added.

"Because the God I severe will take me from good to great and from better to best".

She responded.

"I am not a big bible person".

Paul added.

"But isn't that when God would have said thy faith that's made thou heal?".

"Oh, that's the lady who touched the hem of his garment and Jesus said that to her". "It's your faith that made you whole.".

He said.

"I will have asked around in my work place for you".

"I am carpenter or just say handyman", "I work at wharf".

"I will see if they have any office jobs and let you know".

"Thank you kindly".

She said.

"This is where I live".

He turned into a nice yard just ten gates away from hers.

The garden was well kept and the picket fence was a lovely carpentry display.

"Can I have your number to call about the job?".

He asked politely.

"Can I have your number and I will call you?". She asked.

"Sure"

He said.

Writing his cell phone number on the piece of paper she handed him.

They bid farewell.

When she got home as tired as she was she had to make dinner. Peter was not home from school as yet. The third time this week he has been messing up. He knew his job was to see about his siblings until she got home. She had to display the tough love method because just before she made the full view of her gate. The twins ran off inside and they were with two older boys that made off quickly before she got to the house. She had warned the girls several times to pay attention look around and see what's happening. She felt all alone with raising and providing for them. And the attitudes sometimes displayed by the teenagers including Peter was a case that needed its own prayer.

For a good weight of 180 and a very great pleasing face she was blessed with the fine assets of a woman that made her look younger than forty years. She had to make dinner before disciplining the girls. The rod may not come out so easy. But she won't be nice about it and when Peter gets in that's another opportunity to kick off her daily harsh routine of being a mom and a provider but for her the motto is "God is able".

Chapter 3

In the eyes of children

She waited until after dinner to confront the kids. Two at a time as they shared room in the three bedrooms flat they rented. Dinner was simple sailfish, butter beans and rice and some mix veg.

It's more than enough to give thanks because she had to pay the shopkeeper what she owed her up to this point.

Luckily, they grew up together and shared a nice friendship. Until Heather became Christ like. But they still talk and exchange ideas as friends.

"When you coming to church Marlene?". Heather asked her as she served her the items for dinner three hours earlier.

"I put two pieces of fish in there extra for my God daughters".

"And let me tell you this", "The Malcolm boys line your gate a evening time!". "Try and warn them girls", Marlene cautioned her.

"Ok I saw them running from my gate today". "That is why I came to shop myself".

"To see if I meet any of them and warn them off my little young chicken them". "Because I think they must be over 18 or so".

"Soon 18". "And those boys drive their parent's car so you won't see them walking!". Marlene answered with that motherly stance that she always took with Sasha and Dimitri. Her 12 and 15-year-old girl and boy respectively.

She was trying to hide from the church going story.

"Ok I have to go cook so talk to you later". "You a Come a church with me Sunday?"

"Ok I will try". Marlene responded.

"Mommy a come!".

The twins said to each other. Hiding the cell phone, they were using to text the Malcolm boys. Trey and Trenton as the names suggests one lead the other follows. They were 4 and a half years older than these girls and already they had some serious unhealthy connections between the four of them.

They had been secretly advancing in relationships over a month now. It's not sexual but if someone doesn't intervene it will be. The girls are losing faith and are buying into the lures of the Malcolm riches.

These boys have the Latest version of everything. They are twins as well, luckily that's why they are bounding their mother thought. When she first saw them.

Now they have brought the girls a cell phone and that's how they keep connected.

The boys are waiting for their cars to arrive for their 18th birthday. The girls will be fully fourteen in May which is 3 months before the boys turned 18. They like the attention from the boys. The little necklaces and bracelets that their mom can't afford the boys can and more. Like the other day when Trent Bought Natanya a book for class values at $3 grand Their mother Heather was clueless because they don't wear these things around her. Except when they lie about studying and went to the sovereign mall to meet the boys. The plan was to say they were going to library for a research and then they will change clothes in the mall washroom.

And really look like the world wanted them to. And do what the world demanded of them.

Peter the older brother to the twins was not aware of everything that took place. Either he was busy chasing a 25-year-old school teacher who is showing him more interest in personal development classes. Then she should. He was tall and good look like his father. With the real dark Jamaican skin tone. He stands close to 6 feet for just being 16.

And his maturity was sometimes too real to be true.

Janet Jennings a gorgeous, brilliant, dark skinned young lady. She carried a sweet innocent smile. She just started teaching at his high school about three months ago. They seem to have a lot in common until the day she bought him lunch and sat with him under the tree in open play area. He told her about the dreams he had she knew exactly what he was talking about. She dropped him off at his home that evening.

"Girls I notice the Malcolm boys are coming to gate often". Heather said in a concerned tone. The girls looked at each other. Natasha the bolder of the two spoke. "Mommy you know they are friends with Peter". "I don't think they are interested in Peter". she said sharply. Natanya gave out. "Mommy man again about the sex talk". She was not as bold but very to the point. "Yes." their mother added "Because when that happen kids like you happen and there is no money around to take care of them". "I can take care of you guys much more grandkids" "Mommy we say hello to them but nothing like what you talking about". Natasha said. "Ok! Heather said, "I am going leave it there". Good night and say your prayers.

She went to the boy's room. "Who was that young lady who dropped you off today? ". She asked Peter. He was busy sharing his daily activities with his 10-year-old brother.

"His girlfriend". Justin yelled out.

"Boi shout your mouth". Peter said firmly.
"She is my biology teacher mommy".
Peter said putting on his humble face.

"How old is she?". Heather questioned.

She could tell by the way he talked that something was brewing.

"She is not your age I am warning you!". "Do not start nothing there and furthermore you are not ready for something like this!".

"You're sixteen why your hormone raging like this?". His mother stormed at him. Justin was laughing and she chased him out of the room that host a bunkbed a computer table but no computer, a small barrel with some curtains and the small wooden cloth holder that was sectioned off by huge piece of clothes

Heather was not well grounded in raising boys and even with girls she was just going through the motions her parent taught her. During teenage years, or young adolescent boys need more positive male role model such as a coach, pastor, older family members. They have to be of good moral standings and or equally balanced to face the world that men and greed has Peter should pursue a unhealthy relationship Like this one. He may see women has the breadwinner instead of meeting her halfway or taking on the responsibility

If, he may not learn independence, he may become a womanizer and more importantly if and when the older lady is finished with him. There will be this hate void that may damage how he views all other women. She was thinking about all this. She was hoping all other single mom's or dad's will share some tips somewhere of how to raise these hormones that will be become the men and women of tomorrow.

"Do have your own place?" she asked him. "No". he answered.

"Ok can you send yourself to school?".
"When last you read your bible Peter", "hmm when last you prayed?".

"Wake up and pay attention Peter," pay attention to your school work ok?". "As long as your life in my house you will play by my rules".

She said and left him standing with several things on his mind. One of them was that he felt he was too grown to be spoken to like this.

She left and Justin came back in jeering peter.

After she had a long prayer and felt overwhelmed, she picked her phone and called Paul.

Chapter 4

The call

Paul picked up his Nokia 3310 cell phone promptly, unaware of who the caller was. When he heard the "hello" and recognized the voice he was near shocked. After all he was not expecting her to call at all, except for the job he had promised her to ask about at his work place.

He had been a single man for about 8 months now. His ex-wife had left him for a number of reasons including he was too reserved. She wanted to have her party ways and this lead her to cheating on him. They were together for 14 years. They have had their ups and downs. Like any other couple. Because she was used to the abuse in earlier relationships. She was expecting him to slap her around to put her back into place. Because he was not that type. She mainly stayed around because of the kids. She was having like a double life thing. Waiting for him to put her out or caused the breakup. He refrained from having intimacy with her. She slowly drifted away and left 8 months ago. Like most Jamaican man would do try and slap her into shape. He was not raised like that and hitting a woman is never the right thing to do. He was a type that idolized women. He could have been a womanizer if he was more robust and out in the world. He was tall. Had neat muscular body. A look that's a mix between Anthony Evans who sang (let it rain) look this song up it will bless your hearts. And Jai Kingston.

"Hello".

He said back it was close to 10 pm that evening and he had just showered after tending to his pet fish and was about to watch the 10 o'clock news.

"I hope I did not wake you up". She said.
His response was very intriguing.

"You can feel free to call me anytime".

She smiled and then caught herself.

Because she shouldn't be feeling a little jittery about a man's voice on the phone especially one she didn't know that well.

But it's almost been five years since she had spoken to male on the phone which was not her pastor or a church brother. But speaking of church brother. She did have her eyes on brother Roy Williams. She can't seem to forget the day he song. Amazing grace acapella and blessed her soul. She had always wanted to ask him out or say something to him. But she was following the golden rule. 'That man should make the advancement. Whosoever wrote that rule is same giving authority for families to be Separated and wars to start.

Because not every car that can start and run at the same speed. There are racing car and there are just movable cars. If you want something ask and it shall be given

(Matthew 7.7)

She was asking God for a husband. But she wasn't asking brother Williams. Maybe he too had notice her and was shy to make the date move. Yeah, they said hi, hello and howdy. But never! Had he said let's go out. Or never did she ask.

Opportunities only presents itself at the moment when you can have snatched them. When God knows it right for you. 'Now brother Roy is going out with sister Ariel'. Who as she saw him said hello got his number and she talked to him. There was nothing rushed no sins committed. And no intimacy just time spent together. And Ariel was 39 and Roy was 40 years old.

Now she was thinking long and hard. How she had let that moment slip away. But sometimes you have to wait.

"How is your night?".

He asked her in a sweet raw Jam-down accent. Keeping her in tune to him.

"It's a little frustrating you know with kids and being teenagers and all".

"Yea I understand I get my share on weekends and holidays", "a 13 and a 14-year-old". "two bad boys", "but I can't call them that to their face because they would grow into thinking that who they were meant to be".

She laughed for the first time in a long while.

"What so funny?".
he asked her. "Nothing". She said caught up in the moment.

"Well it's the hormone thing, right?" He asked her right off the bat. "Yes, how did you know?".
She asked him. "It's their time". "We all were the same if not worst".

He sounded like she had known him forever.

"We just need to guide them", "let them know we love and respect them". "Show them the right and also the wrong".

"Don't ever compare other kids or people to them". "Let them be themselves". "But more importantly let them feel comfortable talking to you about anything".

She listened as he sounded so passionate about what he was saying. And for sure she had made a few mistakes just going by what he said.

"Would you like to come to church with me Sunday?"

She asked him.

"Yeah I can do that I just have to wake up a bit earlier". He answered sounding confident.

The girls were giggling and it was becoming annoying.

"Hold on".
She said to him.

"If any of you girls let me come round there you would know where water walk go a pumpkin belly." She yelled out to them.

Of course this drove them into hysterical laughter. They had to cover their mouths and laughed because they have their own meaning for this Jamaican proverb.

She went back to the phone and he was laughing too.

"What's so funny?"
she teased at him. He flipped the script back to her.

"A weh water walk go a pumpkin belly?" (what route water takes to get to the belly of a pumpkin)

He played her to her own tune.

"Through the vine".
She answered

"You could be right you know", "why you sound so doubtful?". He answered.
She rested her head on the pillow in her room with the pictures of her whole life. A queen size bed, a dresser, and a chest of drawer. She was very modern and kept up with good tasting fashion. She knows how to manage money and make it stretch to feed the family. Hoping something will turn up soon. Even one the kids father could send something to make the ends meet. Because if the end of the month should ever come and meet her in this predicament. It's would be like where the tree falls there shall it lay (Ecc 11:3).

She was hoping that she was not being selfish in wanting to be happy. She was praying for her moment to come. Laying up in her bed alone every night can be devastating. But she tried to remain humble and trust God.

Paul was making quite an impression on her. He spoke well and he was very knowledgeable about the raising of kids.

"I am running out of credit".

She said. Sadly as she was listening to his broke up story.

"No problem". He said.

"I will call you back".

Chapter 5

The return call

Paul returned her call as quick as she could hang up. He sent her a $100 credit. Though she did not ask for it. A kind courtesy she somewhat appreciated. In all truth it was needed at this time.

"Thanks"
She said seeing the text regarding the credit. But she was not very happy to be taking stuff from him so early like a sponge ready to soak up all the clean water and you will have to squeeze it to get anything back.

She wasn't even sure if this is what God wanted for her. She search inside herself for answers.

"What colours you like?". He continued to asked her.

"Red and blue". She said. "Depending on the mood".

She smiled

"So I guess you are moody?".

She can tell he was smiling because he held it so well in his voice. Just his voice alone could set her at ease from her earlier depressive mood.

"What are you doing?".

She asked him.

"Sitting on my lazy chair watching the news". "Seeing how the rain mashing up some places".

"I barely watch the new'. She said. "It's too depressing".

"I know but now you have a new friend to talk to I can break it down easy for you". Like fill you in on the good news

"Do you read your bible?". She asked him.

"Yes man something especially when I am in fear of making a difficult decision".

She paused.

"Don't worry I'm not looking for much in return".
He said.
"Just friendship".

She was relieved to hear this. This was something she could work with. 'Is it against the church if a member goes out for casual meeting. with a non christian?'. In her mind it should be ok. But it's the thoughts that one carry in the mind that will cause problems in a cause like this. Not to mention what people would say about newly appointed Evangelist with a uneven yoke.
(2 Cor. 6:14).

She was more afraid of the judgment will be mostly based on the people, the society and not so much own morals. Because she knew herself. She was trying to search back in her mind where she could find it in the bible that you should not keep a casual friend.

She cannot force him to be baptized just encourage him. There is a saying 'See me and come live with me are two different things.
She had her kids to think of. Herself and he had his responsibilities.

"What are thinking about?". He questioned her. "Just life". she replied and he could tell she had a heavy mind.

"You need to let go of all the stuff that weighing you down?". He encouraged her.

"The failed relationship," "the things you didn't get to do". "And put yourself right where you are now". And either you're going pull yourself forward or backward". he said.

"I know you're a woman of many prayers". "But do think you just pray and god just answers?". "You will have to mean it and be on your way to get it". "If not physically", "then in your mind. You have claim it. "That's the only way it will be given unto you".

"Sounding like you would make a great preacher Mr.?. She tried to get him to say his last name.

He laughed a little.
"Why didn't you just came out and asked me my last name.". He toyed with her.

"Maybe I thought that would be too forward Mr.?. And she did it again.

"Your strong". He said. And you will hold onto your point of view"." That's good". He complimented her.

"You are not easily lead". She began to laugh now. He paying compliments to her one her weakness as what she considers her strength.

She was too strong in some cases. For example work. Though there was flexibility she would always chose to firm to point where it became an addiction. It's her way wish is the old way and If you do it any other way. Your work will be highly scrutinized and picked apart with a fine tooth comb. Usually she will find one and two mistakes and you be shown and corrected. She was not aggressive or rude about it. But she let you know you made a mistake. Which sometimes feedback is a gift. That's how we learn, grow and become Olympic stars. Bobsled winners. Preachers and educators. Farmer and correctional officers.

Looking at her profile against Paul's. It's easy to see two human beings who were capable of making mistakes at anytime. But one has A saviour,

A Guide, A System, A King. A God to honour in her doing. She should exemplify him in every way possible.

Talking to Paul may not be the ultimate sin. If she lust or allow her feelings to go ahead of her, ahead of time. Thus might be considered the the downfall. Her focus should not shifted from the almighty and the work he called her to do. But at the same time he knows there troubles of the flesh. 'Not just the intimacy'. But the physical need to belong to a relationship. 'To have some semblance to your life', her mom may have said her or someone. Long time ago heaven rest her soul.

"Your are stubborn too". She said. "Because you have not said your last name yet".

"Phillips" he rolled off his tongue. "Paul Patrick Phillips". "That's my full name" He stated.

She was listening attentively. If she should ever go back on anything he said then there will be a rainy day in Kingston.

"And you what is your?". "My name is Heather Jennifer Johnson"

The girls were giggling because they were listening to her conversations at the doorway.

They started up again and she was not having it.

"Hold on!"
she said. She quickly rushed through the little passage more like a door about(Roundabout.) To other room knocking twice before the girls open it

She said loudly.

"Can you giggling girls show a little respect", "I am on the phone and this is my final warning". The moment she left the room they were quiet because they know what may come next.

Peter was in an upset mood. He was thinking long and hard about what is mother at said. Know the relationship has not gone very far he was still having mixed feelings towards his teacher. She showed him so much attention and care to a detail point they claimed Akon 'Nobody wanna see us together' as their team song. He felt as if he owed her something.

Could he be too far in, to be brought back to reality?. At the last football practice they had a cordial kiss from her. He scored a goal. She is now giving him love trinket for good deeds done. His emotions and hormones are now fused into one. And one knows what happen to young pulls who are put out to fight too early.

Inside Peter is a mama's boy. He was just caught up in the streets the wrong friends and the music. He may have had one or two puff of the green bush that will make think faster than his mind can contain. His downhill spiral begun after his dad went away. The relationship between his mother and father was not the most Pleasant. They quarrelled. Fought and cheated on each other and he we was right in the middle of it all, as far back as he can remember. He wouldn't know how handle a relationship without proper guidance. The street is too rough and rigid to teach love, brotherhood and peace. Survival can be learnt and some street slangs. All the prior ingredients he will need from home. If He was thinking of hitting up her place and spend sometime there.

While next door his sisters were making plans to see their boyfriends."

"What if we went all the way on their birthday?". Natanya joked.

Natasha said. "what all the way. "Let him wait remember what Judy at school said", "we have to get all we can and give very little!". "I want my own phone tired to share!". Natasha said. As they look out the window for when the boys will come back with Macdonald they promised. Estimated time a around 11pm. Usually when mom fell asleep.

Unfortunately she did not tell them she had lost her job. And she had company on the phone tonight. So she may not fall asleep as early as they hoped.

The phone conversation was moving along and what they like in a person came up.

"Say if you were looking for a husband?". He asked her. "What will the ideal man be like?", "and give details". he said.

Her eyes rolled over and she smiled.

Chapter 6

The price of happiness

"I am looking for a down to earth person". "Who have a great head on his shoulders". He was smiling.

"Also be very good with kids and a hard worker and family man". "I preferred if he believed and willing to accept Christ as his Lord and personal Saviour".

"Sounding a bit like me man".
He replied Sounding shy.

"What are you looking for?". She redirected the question to him.

"Someone who knows how it is to have a good life", "good positive relationship without the hand ups". "I don't do this", "I don't like that". "And all the drama of make up and break up".
She listened attentively.

"I have passed that stage of my life". He said. "I just want to raise my boys and be happy". "Get married to right person if she comes along". She listened to him.

In Her mind she was thinking she could get to know him better. It could work better if he was baptised. But them again. There are those who are walking with the name of the Lord but not in the name of the Lord. Not that she is giving herself justification. But if there is one thing she displayed well was honesty.

"What do you do for fun?". He asked her progressing the conversation to better and deeper ground.

"I sing on the choir", "I like leading worship and I like teaching Sunday school".

Ok he said. "An outside of church".

"I like to cook", "bake a little and observe nature".

"I like nature too". He said.

She heard a car braked at her gate and decided to peek through the window. But her bedroom was facing the opposite side of the street. She listened selectively, though he still spoke on the phone.

She was taking on the role of a private investigator. Or call her inspector Gadget. But she was making rounds for the times she had to just come home, cook and go to bed. Her efforts to keep a neat house sometimes goes unnoticed once all her kids are home.

"What's going on?".

He asked her noticing the lack of attention he was getting.

"I am not sure yet?". But I hope it's not the Malcolm Boys them outside enuh".

"What would they want at this time?". he asked concerned.

"They are after the twins". "But them do let me catch just one a dem".

"What you going to do?"

He kind of teased her. Then she remembered her calling.
"
I will give them a good talking to and a bible to read".

The both chuckled.

"Well go and check and let me know if you need backup".

"Ok I soon call you back".

she replied. Almost with a smile in her voice.

He hang up first. She tiptoed to her door and open it. She was close to 5 feet 8 inches. A light to fair complexion. Her background was a mix of Maroon and Scottish Indian. She was of a good body structure and bless with perfect femininity. She can rule with an iron fist at times. Hence her kids won't readily come to her with anything.

Just last week she shut down one the twins who wanted to asked her a feminine hygiene question. She might have been upset because the pardona lady had sent for her money and she didn't have it earlier that day.

She tiptoed slowly down the hall almost off her feet. She walked by the boys door and heard Peter playing is music. It was moderate but the content she was not too impressed with.

He just made it on her hit list again. Just after she cracks this case wide open. She didn't hear the girls since she heard the car, she crept up to their closed room door listening.

She was careful to stand far away that she did not cast a shadow under the door.

She listened carefully, she heard male voices. It's could be Peter with then they are close sometimes. But she listened further. And there were two different male voices.

With her eyes popping out of socket and head pounding and her mind racing she bang on the door and tried to open it. It was locked l. Seemed to be doubled locked too.

"Open the door now!".
she yelled.

"Natasha open the door!". She banged on it". "Natanya open the door!".

They refused the noise must have startled Peter who came out of his room as well.

"A what mommy?".

He asked her.

She was too upset to answer. Then she heard the car start again. Then it drove off.

"Ok as of today this door is coming off as a matter of fact all the door coming off!".

She banged and the door again. While Peter went out the front door to see if he could make out what or whose car it was.

The boys have sped away in their parents Lexus Rx 350. He knew the jeep. In Fact the last time they went to a party he drove them home. They were too drunk to drive. As a way of saying thanks their father asked his butler or Houseman to drive him back home. So now he is in good with the Malcolms.

She finally pushed again and the door was opened both girls sitting on their beds like saints and wearing their innocent and pity faces.

She grabbed them one in each hand and shook them. Her anger so raw, real and in the moment. That she could just slap them nonstop.

(Ephesians 4.26)

"Who was in here?". She yelled trying to reach for a belt or something she could use to wapp them.

Peter came in a pulled her off them. Because he had never seen her this angry before. Except for when she was not walking with the lord. These three years have been the best years of their life so far. Luckily the twins had spent over three four years alternately bouncing between their dad and Heather.

"Mommy ease dem man I beg for dem!". Peter bargained for the twins.

Where is that food smell coming from?". "I said who was here" she fussed still in anger.

The girls still acted like they didn't know what time it was. But deep inside they are terrified. Because they know she is on the chill pill call 'Jesus'. Other than that she would have giving them some good old jamaican slaps already. She searched the room for the food, she was smelling so strong.

"Peter through this food in the garbage", She snapped.

"Macdonald!" mmmm Macdonald?". "for Macdonald", boys can climb through my window.". "So if should be a grandmother now it would be for Macdonald?".

She wanted to make them feel ashamed to their core.

The girls wanted to laugh internally but they felt dirty. But looking at what she said from many variations was funny. Peter took the bag and looked at both girls with disgust because if their mother haven't busted their big dinner deal he and Justin wouldn't have gotten none. Justin knows better than to come out of the room when someone is getting disciplined. Because one look from his mother and he knew exactly what to do. She wished still worked on these teenagers.

"Get me the hammer and some nail. And you see the piece of board on the drum top?". "Meet me at the window outside with it".

Peter just like to do thing and avoid the conversing. Because she always came up with some past issues that still held pain for all of them.

Her cell phone rang out.
She got it on her way outside it was Paul. "I did hear from you so I just called to check in". He responded. Sounding concerned.
She let herself go and told him exactly happened. Almost to point of tears. I am sorry he expressed his empathized with her.
Peter turned back and sat on verandah waiting for her to end the call. Then she announced help was coming.

"Ok don't do that yet let me come and help you". He offered.

"My son is here and he will help".

He interrupted before she finished.

"I said I am coming", "please wait. He said with great care on the phone.

"Ok hurry if you're coming".

"Let me just get my tool kit". He said.

When he arrived at the house and he knew which one because he counted them. He met Peter sitting on the grilled up verandah of the huge two sided house. He was assuming the landlord lived on the other side but the place was needed of proper lighting and some repairs.

"Hi Good night". Paul greeted him. "Is Ms. Heather inside?".

"Who are you?". Peter asked. Then the good night dropped from the back of throat.

"I am Paul the guy she is waiting on to look at the window".

"Mommy!". Peter yelled out. And she came rushing out.

Overlooking Peters insolent behavior. Paul looked up at her. She looked radiant. Even for her seeing him all shaved and in a more fresh setting. He was appealing.

"Thanks for coming ". She opened the grill and let him in. Peter got up.

"I guess you don't need my help anymore". He said walking into the house.

"You can still come enuh peter". She tried to comfort his ego.

He frowned not in a rude way but more like a it's ok upset shrug.

Peter was revisiting his pain. From his father's standpoint for abusing and beating on his mother.

it's was the same on both scales he thought. whenever they were both drunk.

They kicked the doors down made the police came. He is reminded each time he sees the scar on her hand. How he will always protect her. He never wanted to relive the pain again. (1 Peter 5.10)

'Here comes another friend the girls thought'. As they listened to them talked outside the window.

Natanya rushed into Peter's room.

"You don't hear to knock before you come in here!".

Peter lashed out at her.

"A hope you don't throw my food in the garbage enuh".

She pouts and shakes and is nothing short of an attitude.

"Don't come talk to me like me and you a size man". "And the food under cupboard". "Worthless "he said hissing his teeth and pointing her out his room.

"Worthless like you, little teacher lover".
She snapped back him.

At the window, Paul measured and quickly made a nice design to keep the boys from coming in. He accomplished this by allowing the window to open just a half of its usual width. She was a little embarrassed as mother. About everything, the girls, Peter mannerism, the only hope is, was and forever be God. For he is her strength and her shield. (Palms 28.7) He has it under control. 'Where are the good morals she taught them'. 'Are these really the kids I work so hard for?' she was even thinking if they are really her kids.

But Paul understood this type of behavior. It's in the schools. The lack of dual parenting. The lack of talks instead of slaps. The absence of a male figure to respect and love. The stress of mommy doing and solving everything.

'You can pray for them.'. She thought 'but you can't save them'. Since her three years of faith, She has been chasing them to be baptized. "You can't force them". Just keep encouraging them". Pastor told her.

They behave well when needed. But lately they are changing and she find herself slipping into the person she use to be. But she knows he will not let her stumble. (Palms 121.3)

When he was done. He changed several light bulbs. In and around the house. Shedding light on the what one hidden by darkness.

"Do you care for a cup of tea or a drink?".

she asked him while he worked.

****

Patwa key

Dem - them
Enuh- make sure, for certain.
Partna - money pot, susu, saving ring.
All that I am

Chapter 7

Mind over matter

"Have you ever wonder why men were meant to be sociable beings?".

Paul asked her while he was sipping on the cup of mint tea he had been offered earlier.

"And how is it that animals in most cases respond to each other better than we do?". He continued.

"For the earth is the lord and the fullness there of".
(Palms 24.1)
She responded.

"Everything is done to his glory".
"And he said if man won't serve him."

She raised her voice so her kids could hear the gospel.
"Then he let animals and things serve him" (Luke 19.40.)

It was close to 11pm Thursday
She wanted her landlord to hear too. She was so much concerned is money and don't ever repair the place. Now Paul had to come. and brought light to the house. And some sense of manliness.

32

"So all who don't want to pray and get to know him for themselves". "Seek out a little church and settle their and life for him no one forcing anyone here".

She explained to him in the form of a prayer and sermon.

But this was good for him to hear the word of God as well as she her personality up close. For at that moment she was a Christian lady upset about what her girls have done.

She is venting he got that much.

she was wondering if her landlord had already send out the telegram that she had man over. For the first time in three years of living there. He having tea at that. Her landlord. Mrs. Reds. Like to gossip. Very nosey, everyone knew her. Loudmouthed type. She would be last person one want to tell or share anything personal. Her husband died four years ago. You could see the fight in her to cope. But she was an easy personality to handle if one was not strong.

Heather was calming down gradually. And her true self came breaking through.

"I may have to leave soon".

Paul said nothing the time.

"Or you have may have to call me and wake me up at 5am so I won't be late for work". Said in a playful way.

"I can do that"
she said.

She felt easy and comfortable talking to him. He came the next home Sunday after church and made her a small garden to corner where the landlord said she could plant up if she wanted. She made dinner for everyone. She set up small table and everyone sat down to eat.

"This is my friend Paul".

She formally introduced him to them. Sure they have seen him doing stuff around the house but no formal introduction.

"What does this mean?"

Natanya the smaller of the twins lashed out.

She had nice brown eyes, like her mother's. She was strong built and active and promising child.

Natasha smiled.

"This mean he is our stepfather?". she asked. With some innocence.

She was the one who bigger and more hefty both in personality and structure she could be easily mistaken for being older well both girls were. She had a mix of her dad and mom eyes giving her a lighter and darker brown eye. Like her sister she had high cheek bones and good natural hair that get plaster with styling gel to get their desires styles. Heather wasn't a fan of this as long as they don't put cream to it. That's tolerable.

Paul answered while Peter was busy texting on his phone.

"Can you put that phone down?". Heather asked giving him the eye.

He did after eyeballing paul.

"I am just a friend of your mother".
"If she needs help or anything and I can I will".

"The same for you all too".
The girls eyed each other. Like is he serious if he don't see the mess he is getting into. Like there is the big caution sign staying trouble ahead divert. They looked at him speaking

Peter asked." "So what let you think we need help?".

Heather cuts him off before he could answer.

"Peter would like to pray for dinner. She asked him?".

"Ok," No problem" He said.

Let's pray.

"Father in your name we thank your for this food you have provided".

they held hands and bowed their heads and closed their eyes. The reason for this to avoid all distraction as she had taught them. That when they are before God in prayer they show reverence always.

"Lord I pray that you may fulfill all our needs". "Be it love", "money", "or stability". "Lord I thank you for our mother and the battles fights for us"

The twins were impress by the length and the merit of his prayer. Though already the have classified him as a little mama's boy.

He continued

"Lord protect us from wolves in sheep's clothing". Hinting at Paul.

"Amen" he said.

They got down to eating rice and peas and chicken. Their blessings came from the handy work of Paul. Who raised white chickens just as a hobby and sold them to close friends. Who shared his conscious idea about not eating the injected chickens.
The ones that are are grown in mass production and mature way too fast to feed the blowing up population.

The peas was also and vegetables were also from his garden. They were having a dinner good conversation. People can talk while eating. She remembered being taught a seminar. It's just important that when you decide to speak your mouth is empty and chose only light and pleasant topics.
Paul had discussed ahead of time with her how to help the kids.
He raised the topic at the dinner table.

'What do kids want from parents?'

"To be left alone!".
Natanya said almost in a serious face.

But when her eye graced her mother's. she withdrew her statement.
"Sorry"
she said openly.

Peter answered."

"For parents to be open enough so kids can talk to them".

Justin added. "For parents to listen before they beat". The girls agreed.

For the first time Heather was quiet and listened to what they had to say. They were finding it odd. They saw that Paul her friend may have had a positive impact on her

The outside critiques were taking notes of how often he had been there. And how often they can be seen together. Not that the temptation didn't came and knocked. But she tried to avoid them.

They had a good dinner and conversation. Until they individually found there own niche.

Heather and Paul was left on the verandah. He invited her out into the springing garden area and showed her the blooming of the first roses.

"What do think of me so far he asked her?".

Chapter 8

Fatherly figure

That Monday morning Paul had to go to work. she got up early and made himself some salt fish fritters. Crispy and dry with the cornmeal in it, little scallions and thyme flavors. She asked Peter to ran it by his place.

"So early mommy?". He said barely waking up. She had no choice she wanted him to have something to eat before and at work. 'That what a wife do for a husband right'. She laughed within herself. Because she has not reached that point. A friend can do that for a friend as well'.

'Is she liking him?'. 'Yes she was that only natural' But she can't go too far out into her emotions. (Cor.3 vs 4-8.)

Though Peter was reluctant. He did went and delivered the food. Any to distracted her from seeing about his misses.

"Oh thanks man", Paul said. "but your mother did not have to do this".

He gave Peter some food items he gathered from his garden. Including bananas that had just started ripping. The smell was so pure. When he took Peter around the perimeter of the garden. He saw why Paul had food all the time. Because he plants them.

"It's hard to grow all these". He asked him.

"No not really," "I just plant them on water them". Paul responded.

"But there is a time when I have to plant them".

"And a time when I have to reap them"

"Each crop has its season".

"Just like people and life". (Ecc. 1-9).

Paul spoke like a noble poet.
The He turned to Peter.

"What you taking in school?". Paul asked him.

"Well I just started electrical technology".

He responded moderately.
A bit surprised because no one really asked him about school. Except for his mother and it's only when there is a turmoil and she is giving all of them a tongue lashing.

"Aww that good man". "I did electrical installation in my time so if need any help let me know". Paul responded to him.

"Ok I will let you know". "Thanks".

He he said to Paul. And made his way back home to get ready for school.
He realize that Paul was someone he could talk to with ease. But still he needs time to be more familiar with him. To unload some of the things that was happening in his head.

He also wanted to confront the Malcolm boys about his sister and disrespect they brought to the home. He didn't even knew it was this serious among them.
But he was their friend. (Galatians 4.16).

On his way back his cell phone rang
It was his teacher girlfriend.

"Do you want me to pick you up this morning?". She asked him.

"No I will just take the bus". He answered poorly.

"Why from yesterday you keep acting like this?". She yelled at him through the phone.

"I just need sometime ok?".
He said to her.

She responded. "Are you seeing someone else!?". She blazed at him.

"Don't let me find that out!". She yelled.
Then went calm again.

"Peter I love you".

"You mean alot to me".

She added.

"Baby please let me come pick you up".

He was just silent on the phone

A little overwhelmed. This new relationship with the family and Paul and now she is demanding so much of his time. His youth. She as overlooked the wrong in in the situation.
Because she was wronged too.

Ms. Jennings as a child was mislead into the concept of having her youth ripped away by a family member. Who secretly bullied and tormented her from ages 6 to 10. She was subjected to a great deal of fear. She had to do all that was asked of her except sexual intercourse. But what she asked she did. This lowered herself esteem. Kept her silent afraid to try new things. Didn't want to go out in public. Would have given up her last meal for a sense of freedom. Always she feels someone as to be in charge of her. She gives kind gestures now as adult to feel better about the love she didn't get as a child. Now it's easy to hate any member of her family just one tug and she is could just pull away for good. But when Peter told her she was beautiful. When Peter kissed her lips. She felt alive. Like she had her youth back.

"Ok you can pick me up at the bus stop as usual".".

"Ok baby,". "I will bring you breakfast".

Talk about needed and controlling Now the cursed has reversed she now wants to control him with gifts and car and shopping sprees and trips. He wants to resist but

1. Peer pressure

He was at the peak of attention in third form at school being a star athlete his friends expect him to date big. Roll deep. No preacher kid nonsenses. He had reputation to uphold. He has got name to live up to. "King cobra" they called him. After he slap the sense out a fourth former who rubbed him the wrong way. His anger is built in but it's too deep and when it's rattled up he spurs venom. He has a reputation to protect.

2. He hustles for his family too.

Often times he would foot in on gas or groceries and a few times gave his sisters lunch money. He would get money off his misses if things got stiff. His mother would have to tell him. He would just figure this out.

3. Unstable love at home.

He need to find or have a nursing place where love is neither bought nor sold but is natural and pure and free.

She was his perfect match on a psychological scale. He was looking for someone to love and protect and she was looking for someone to love and to have control over.

Situation like these don't just happen in life when we see someone dating out of their wave length whatever the mix maybe there is always some psychological issue that binds to two ingredients. Though looking on the outside it is wrong but to the people inside it makes perfect sense. There needs are being fulfilled.

Paul's day at work was refreshing he kept coming up with new ideas to get Heather's attention. He knows he can't asked that forward question.

He need to get himself in line first. He knows the church rules marriage before sex.

He is a man and he has needs but will be patient enough to take the wait.

Prior to Heather being his friend. There was this nice lady Tracey that use to come by his place. He didn't have a formal farewell party with her. He has been dogging her calls here and there. Not much of a player but he was seeking something more stable than what Tracey had wanted. He was looking for life and not just fun. She was sweet very good where it counted but a future was not forthcoming.

Now she wants to pay him a visit to see what's been going on because he had once told her she was the only one he was seeing. Also because he was kind and courteous to her she cannot forget this. And hoped no one had ventured into her sweethearts life causing him to lack her out.

The twins are behaving well this morning more calm and the giggles weren't as frequent. It would be this evening that Heather will pay these boys parents a visit and let them be aware of what their kids are doing.

She wants to make it look as serious as possible to avoid recurrence.

After work Paul met up with her to accompany her to the Malcolm's Residence. He thanked her for the food and showed off how he enjoyed it.

"How do you feel about me?". He asked her out of the blues.

Trying to gain insight of her feelings for him.

"Good"
she responded smiling.

"But we have a long way to go". She literally teased at him.

For him to asked her this heartening question at this time and making her have butterflies and a smile that she can't contain.

And for him to have that cute little smirk on his face like a rabbit looking sideways. It's that not enough sign to they that they have a connection for each other.

She ran off a little, hiding her shyness. He chased her down, just a little, he caught up with her. As they laughed. She turned around and just hugged him. So warm they embraced.

A few people saw them as they walked by and early the next morning she answered a call from her pastor. (Provb. 26.17)

Chapter 9

Sinking Sand

"Why are you playing at hell's gate Evangelist Johnson?". Pastor asked her. As she met with him at the church.

"Why are members of the church seeing you running around with a man that's is not of the faith?". "Nor are you two wed".

"Pastor there is nothing serious going on we are friends". "Just as how I would give my church brothers a hug". That's the same way I gave him a hug", "He has been a big help to me and I am just paying my respect and gratitude. (Mark 12:31)

"Because I know that I cannot lay with a man of uneven yoke".

"Calm yourself down Evangelist".

"Pastor pardon my outburst but I am just tired of people who play hypocrites". (Romans 12:9) She responded.

"If I am seeing with a man". "I must be sleeping with him".: Have I not enough sense to know that I can't do that". (Matthew 7:1-6.)

"Why didn't the church did get together first and prayed that I don't fall before condemning me into a pit".

She continued not angry but very strong in her stance. (Genesis14:1-24)

"I am not afraid to do the work of the Lord pastor even if it is by his will that I may make mistakes I will follow and trust him". (Job 13: 15.)

"Take heed Evangelist and get this man out of your life".

"His name is Paul and he is learning to love God".

"I am patient and obedient that whatever God has plans for me with or without Paul as a friend and maybe a future husband". I will wait upon the lord pastor". Heather said letting her words be heard.

He quoted (2 Cor 6:14-18).

In this case reminded her of how the Malcolm parents had behaved. Like everything is wrong on one side and ok on the other.

"It's teenagers at play".

Mrs. Malcolm said.

She should have know better a pediatrician and that's her only augment. Mr. Malcolm was more balanced. Telling her he was sorry and will talk to the boys. It was what he asked that had made her so furious.

"When are your daughter going to be 18yrs old?".

He asked her with a smile on his face.
She told Mr. Malcolm that if she ever saw boys near is girls again. She was going take legal action. She stormed out because they took it as a daycare joke.

Paul finished up by saying.

"If anything else like that happens remember we know where they live!".

"Is that a threat?"

Mr. Malcolm asked him.

"Does it sound like a treat?".

Paul replied and closed the grill.

"Those boys!". Mr. Malcolm turned to his wife.

"What are we going to to do with the them?".

"That's the third complain about girls since last week".

"Enrolled them in the national youth service Programme for summer".

"Or find a church and send them". "Give them some God".

"Because you know your side don't have no god in them that what these boys are so bad".

Mrs. Malcolm lashed out at him.

They were busy making more money on what they already had.

The house was so huge with a helper and the property gated. Nice well cared lawn and pool and play area. Three storey, it was the talk of the community. Brightly painted in Yellow black and green symbolizing the Jamaican dream.

The mix Indian couple with some hint of Portuguese blood. Were doctor and business owner respectively.

With no proper time for their boys they were raised by home nurse. Travel to Miami on summer holidays and some Christmas. The money is never the problem it's the time and the mentorship that's important in these boy's life.

At home Paul and Heather were discussing a amicable solution to the situation. They know they can't stop the girls from seeing these boys but the frequency was way too much.:

"Maybe we should fence round our side". Peter added.

The girls were at 'extra lessons'
So they wanted to do it behind their backs.
"Ok that's not too bad but I have check with the landlord?".

Heather added.

Put at the same time Peter had his story on his mind because his girlfriend wants to have a sleepover this Weekend at her place in portmore. A lovely place. She bought two lots and build her own thing. He had been there before and felt like a king when he did. She catered to him. She was stern on smoking and drinking but that he does with his friends.

This weekend might be the curtain closer or something special for both of them. She was contemplating going all the way. Peter wasn't sure yet. Not that he was foreign to situation he wanted to take his time.

But she can be so persuasive and all he wants to do is make her happy.

Tracey had boarded her bus and was on her way from Windward road to Harbour View. Her outfit was quite the highlight of her evening's adventure.

Every was tight fitted. Her hair well done and her makeup was very nice. She looked good.

She looked around his house and yard and he wasn't not there.

The nosy landlord was on her way to the shop. When she was asked by Tracey, if she knew where she could find paul.

For sure the landlord had turned back to take Tracey to meet Paul at Heather's house.

There was a knock at the door and Heather got up to answer it.

Chapter 10

He who is without sin

Heather opened the door, and this lady One she sure didn't not have any form of encounter with.

One who just started cursing.

It was just 4pm that Tuesday afternoon. And the devil was at her doorsteps

Ranting, raving and carrying on like a fierce bull.
She was loud, vulgar and ordinary.

People started coming out of there houses and the gossips starts to spread.

"What are you doing over here!?".

Tracey cussed out at Paul. With her hands in the air, so much neck movements, and shaking and attitude.

"Stop disrespecting the lady's house and come and talk to me at my place".

Paul responded in a serious manner to her.

A couple of people had came out out of their houses to get a first hand look at the grand spectacle. And if needed, cast the first stone. (John 8:7)

"She is a Christian what is she doing with man in her house?"

Tracey yelled and tried to get inside the house. Paul pulled her and directed her to leave.

Tracey was fueled by words of a well informed bystander.

The group most of them not of the faith laughed and cheered on the evening's entertainment. For a while nothing this big came about.

She asked him to leave peacefully and take the crowd with him.

Now she is of little hope that he was ever the one for her. Now her mind was telling her to forget about her own happiness and just live for her kids. (1 Cor 7:13)

Seems like when it rains it pours at her address. First it was the girls and the Malcolms and then her pastor and now this. Then the girls are coming home for dinner.

She was thinking this is exactly what church wanted to hear of her the devil was hard at work on her mind. How sooner could a warning come.

She closed the door and went to her room. While Paul tried to pull Tracey along with him. She was so caught up in the moment and surely wanted to make a point. So all other ladies will take their eyes and now hands off Paul.

Should he have at least told Heather about his little fling?. He was having a mind warfare. Because the stability was there. They needed more time. But this catastrophe may damper any future growth.

"What you did was not right".
"Why didn't you call me and let me come and meet you".

He asked Tracey calmly.

She was about to be loud.

"Don't raise your voice he said to her". Your out of place. He said letting her be aware of how bad it was.

"The lady is an Evangelist".

"She could be my friend or whatever".

"You had right to do what you did".
He nailed Tracey with the piercing truth.

"But the landlord told me that is everyday you up there". "And you're not answering your phone".

Tracey tried to explain her actions.

"I don't think we belong together". He told her right off the bat.

Sending her into spirals of shock.

"What do you mean?".

"It's like four months now I am having feelings for you?".

She replied in the form of a plea.

"I don't think so". "You come around only when it's my payday and when you are broke".

"The fun we had was ok but I just don't want that anymore".

He answered and stood firm. Just standing in the middle of his living room. While she sat on the couch.

She had him in her mind as a soft one. One she could have manipulated easily. Like the times she hit him up for money and never showed up after she got it. She took his kindness for weakness. (Luke 6:38)

After your drink you can see yourself out. She knew he was serious. She had never seen him like this before. She was confused a bit scared even. He went into his room. She heard the door closed. She left.

He texted Heather "I am sorry please forgive me".

She didn't text back.

The twins had came home in the midst of the squabble and was wondering what going on.

"Is this the mother who was suppose to set example for them as well as ward out the Malcolm boys?". For all they saw it may be an hoax. The more thought of things getting better the worst it got. They were getting use having Paul around and he talked to them and make jokes and made their mother laughed. Peter was learning so much from him they built the rabbit pen together. And decide to get the rabbits the next day.

Peter has been drawn to nature and caring for things and watch them grow. He was finding healing through planting and taking care pigeons geese and chickens. He helped Paul on his small farm at the back of his property.

In Peter's mind was big picture of Paul becoming a father figure to him, to all of them. Now this. Which left him in doubt that good will ever come. No one is who they are said to be. Is this what Paul wants him to think of him. A womaniser and a cheat. It's obvious that he liked my mom Peter played out in his head so why not let go of the other lady. He can't come to an agreement.

Just the same in Heather's head only that she had the better picture. Because she had taken a vow to her king.

She took her situation to throne of grace.
Heavenly father she prayed for your have seen me through may storms and we arrived victorious. Lord you're the master and I am the clay mold me out of situation. Put me where you want. Use me lord. She knows sometimes testing may come in many different ways and the will rattle her ship but she has a new captain and he have set her sail. And she prayed and prayed.

Her phone had rang so many times during her prayers.

She checked it was Paul and her Pastors. Missed calls.

Chapter 11

God is standing by

Heather hang in her pain. She returned pastor's call and she had to go see him the next day.

She was contemplating whether or not to return Paul's call.

The embarrassment had just socked in.

When she walked out on the street and they group up and talked about her.

She knew because the pointed and stared.

When she went to prayer service and no one laid hands on her. Or prayed with her.

She felt as if she was carrying her own cross. But still she knew the reason there was only on set of foot print everywhere she walked. Was because she was being carried by her God. (Isaiah 46:4)

The way people lashed her with their tongues and trampled her name to the ground. But she is opened and willing to forgive them. Because that earth's operation not heavenly. The same as everyone wants to go to heaven but no one wants to die. Let there tongue fly free because this may be a part of her testimony.

She had sent out a number of resumes and still no reply. It's been almost two weeks now and there is rent coming up as well she has to have food for everyday. Her prayer have not gone unanswered. She went off in a hymnal. They that wait upon the lord. Her voice was powerful sweet sounding like those old time singers. Who when they start singing that alone is a testimony.

All this time Paul was trying to call and text her. She was not responding. Is only hope is to try and get Peter to continue help him around the farm. Maybe for a little fee. He can always get food from his farm for the family there is plenty to go around. He had asked about the position as secretary for Heather. But she just has to hold the fort for two more weeks. One of the secretary Stacy was due for maternity leave. That's the post she would be able to fill or if something else came up. She doesn't know this yet that why he was calling her. And also to apologize.

"How is your mother?". Paul asked Peter as he came by his place after school to see about the rabbits.

"I am not sure which one you would like so I bought one black and one white they are a pair".

Peter smiled.

"Everything in nature seems to be paired".

"You're right". Paul answered. "But sometimes it's hard to find your perfect match".

"Listen I just want to say I am sorry about what happened the the other day". "I didn't know that Tracey was still pursuing me".

"I kind of understand like this teacher". He caught himself. "This girl at school won't stop trying to take things to the next level".

Peter said. Well Paul could tell that he was frustrated his voice had given him up.

"Teacher or girl"

Paul asked him. With just a friendly kind of voice.

"Well teacher but promise me you won't tell mommy?".

"I can't promise you that". Pauled laughed.

"That is if your mother ever wants to talk me again".

"Well everything takes time man".

Peter continued very poised and thug like in his mannerism. But he was getting his point across.

"And wasn't you the one who taught me that for everything there is a season".

"She will come around man".

Paul listens and found confidence in the youngsters voice. By the sounding of his voice and his diction you can tell that Peter had lived way beyond his years. A man trapped in a child's world.

"I just don't want her getting in trouble with church" Peter added.

"That place changed that lady so much". "If it was ever one time she would give that Tracey more than she bargained for"

He looked up to the sky.

Paul listened with a conscious look on his face. but still inside he wished he could have undone the clock.

She was ready for whatever God wanted to happened to her. Because he his the author and finisher of her faith. (Hebrew 12:2).

She also will make a surprise visit to the the kids schools. Just to make sure her labour was not going in vain.

For in trouble times I will be there. The lord had said I will never leave you nor forsake you. (Hebrew 13.5)

She sat and pondered what for dinner. And her mind was lost for thoughts and there came Peter with food items from Paul's place and a envelope in his hand.

Paul said to give you these. He gave her the bag. And the envelope. She opened it. It read in very good cursive handwriting.

'Dear Heather,

For I do know much that there is a God who forgives. I am hoping he is the same one who made me took that bus that you preached his word on. So coincidence we got off at the same I am hoping that is same god that had caused this to happen. So I can miss your friendship like the way kids like to play. It's not typical of me to write to a nice and godly person like you. So forgive me if I leave out any formalities you stop a few hours after talked and became friends.

I like the part of the our father prayer that says. "forgive us our trespasses as we forgive those who trespass against us".

Please forgive me and call me please
Your friend Paul.

+She read the note and went inside her room. Still she was festering inside.

She picked up the phone.

Chapter 12

"My heart never had an Hero"

She picked up her phone and checked the time and put it back down. Should I call him was not really on her mind the note was cute. She liked it.

Thinking back her heart has never really had an hero. Someone she could use to mirror what a real man a ought to be like.

She fondled around in her memories to see if there was ever such a person.

Except for the bringing her to grade six in primary school she was yet to have had any other fatherhood. Though she can't blame her mom for wanting to be alone in this man made world. Because she watch it happened to her mom. Looking for the right person and ending up with wrong person's baby.

She was venturing into the past.
(Philippians 3:13-14)

The twins were having the same experience one she did want them to have. My children should never go through the things I went through she thought to herself. But she needed to get all in order before she can present them with that possible male figure. (Proverb. 22:6)

For sure got up early the that Friday morning acted like all was a normal day did her morning worship. Prayed. Set the kids off to school. She knew what her plan was.

She was going by her pastor first where as she arrived there was a table and member of higher rank of the church. She noted each face and addressed then accordingly.

Evangelist Johnson we gathered here today to make a decision of whether to dishonor you of the title of Evangelist.

"What are your reasons Pastor?"
We did not say we were going to".

"We said we were considering".

"Is there proof of my judgment?". She asked openly.
(1 Peter 4:5).

The Revent spoke.

"I have read through the list of things the Evangelist is accused of". There is no solid findings.

"I don't see even the need for this meeting".

"Most of this personal".

He pointed to the paper.

"Evangelist take a look at this list".

He continued

"And If there is anything true on this paper".

"And I will believe in your words".
"Because if God did not see it fit he would not have raised up and appointed you to this post in his ministry.

She read the list.

*Engaged in street brawl regarding housing another female's common law husband.

*Seeing hugging and playing with said male.

*Male visits the household regularly and seems to be living there as a provider and mate.

* Children are unruly and have cars coming by all hours of the night.

This detail information sparks interests because only her landlord could have provided such a report.

"I find most of these to be personal and still not true to the point. "Paul Phillips the man in question". She paused.

"Only visited my house on four occasions"."
"The first to helped me secure a window to bar out the Malcolm boys who seemed to have interest in my daughters".
(1 Timothy 3:4-5.)

She was very direct but not rude. SHe held her head up and kept eyeing contact with all four men.

"Secondly we had dinner and invited him he never slept over once". "Should I go on".

She asked.

She knew the relationship she was having with Paul was not physical She knew like the bible said. (I Cor 7:1-4)

"No ". The Reverend stop her.

You have all heard for yourself let's pray this sister up.

Pray for your needs Evangelist Johnson and don't ignore the answers that God giveth. Bless your soul he walked over and hugged her.

She had already prayed and declared her victory over all manner of disgrace. Shame and judgements. She had the faith of a mustard seed. She knew he would come through for her. Like he always did.

He said her farewells with a smile on her face. Basking in the grace of God.

She heading to the girls and Peters high school.
This is one of her random checks.
She is at gate walking in.

The school was in recession and she saw the Malcolm boys well just one at the gate in the car. She tried to get over the other side to speak to him. But he drove off.

She headed inside the school just to see Natanya walking towards the other one. She called out to her and Trenton ran off. A surprised Natanya came up to Heather.

"What are they doing here she asked her?".

The bell rang.

Come take me to all your teachers Heather said firmly.

Hoping the results was not reflective of what she saw just by entering.

At work Paul was wondering if he had made things worst by sending her the note. He was hoping she would call soon are just need is help in anyway so he can at least see her again.

He too had a prayer in his heart. Hoping she would respond to him soon.

Chapter 13

Children at play

The teacher showed Heather Natanya and Natasha rap sheet. Absences were among the pile of dirt that was dished out on their records.

She could have chosen to embarrassed them. But she listened and gave them both the eye. The same eye that got us straighten when we misbehaved as kids. The girls were ashamed. But not as much as surprised.

She has done a random check before but things weren't as bad as it seemed now. How can they be absent. With less than a half hour ride on the bus. She was thinking of not sparing the rod this time. There is a lot of money invested in their schooling.

School fees, uniforms, lunch and bus fare. It's is not fair that they choose to waste there time playing around with boys much older than themselves and boys who may not even remember then five years to come.

It's funny how children toy with the opportunity they are given. She has seen a number of students loitering along the corridor and stairwells. No sense of urgency and bell had just rang about 10 minutes ago.

In her school days she had to walk to and from school close to five miles and she better make that lunch trip home and back to school on time.

Now they say it's years of technology she argued in her mind they making smart cars. Smart phones and smart robots. "So we don't need people to be smart anymore?". She asked herself.

Natasha and Natanya have the same classes.

They are in second form. They were pushed ahead because of their good grades. But now she is wondering if they can maintain those grades for a scholarship.

The last call made to the girl's father made him more furious than ever. He wanted to take girls from her and raised them with his present wife. Dave Lawrence. An sales clerk at a pharmaceutical company. He made ok money. But he is tied up with a wife that only thinks of herself and the one son they have together. Talk about control she has him by his collar and because she was blessed with good looks. He took like it is to please her but the bible said that a man is the head of the household. (Ephesians 5:23). It's not that he is a softy but her family they can be controlling and once you're in there is hardly a way out. Or it could be just how he is. One of the planters but not a nurturer. You best believe that when it's reaping time he will be there.

"But if one does not provide for himself or his household".: He is worst than an unbeliever. (1 Timothy 5:8)

She went to Peter's form teacher.

"Peter is not a bad student".
She assured Heather.

"He is too big on athletics".

"He needs to spend a little more time on his academic".

"Only then we will have some vast improvement".

She did not get to meet the famous Ms. Jennings. It was her class time. But she is not too worried about Peter or Justin the girls were more of her concern. Since Peter has been hanging out with Paul he was gradually changing. His mannerism and choice of words. Heather had been noticing the changes.

She was aware that all she has is here time and now is all we have on earth. And what you reap is what you have sown.
(Galatians 6:7)

She was investing a lot in her kids for the children are the future if it was this rough. She was worried what there future may look like if they did not study to make thyself approved unto god. (2 Timothy 2;15)

On his ride home from school with girlfriend Peter told her he would like to go school.

"Despite this relationship is not the norm I don't mind the studying, the hang outs all that is cool. He sat there in the car at the Harbour View Shopping center. She looked at him.

"Why are doing this".

Janet asked him.

Looking like she had just lost her mind.

"I need sometime. He said to focus on school".

"It not like you have not done this before"

She tried to push him.

"I never said I didn't". "But if you care about me like you said you did you will wait until I'm ready".

He said in a low but firm tone.

He hopped out of the car.

"I will walk the rest of the way home".

"Thanks for the ride".

He said to her.

She couldn't believe what he just said. She slammed on the horn in a rage and startled a set of nesting dark coloured pigeons that flew in a circular motion across the skin.

He stopped by Paul like he did most evenings. He told him of his mom surprised visit to their school.

Then he proceeded to tell him what happened between himself and Ms. Jennings.

"Did I do anything wrong by telling her to wait?". Peter asked him.

"No not all". "How did she respond?".

Paul asked him.

"I don't think she take it so well". "But it's not like it's a breakup".

"I just need some time to be a youth".

"Yuh understand what mi saying right".
Peter asked paul.

He knew he felt as if he had hurt her feelings. What Paul he fears next is that she may not know how to process this and saw it as rejection and came at Peter with some form of vengeance.

"No you did the right thing".
He said patting Peter on the shoulder.

"If later on in life you both of you feel the same way about each other then you guys can proceed".

"Well I can always be her friend", "just not her boyfriend," "just not right now".

"She is always over my shoulder is like I can't breathe". "But some how I do care about her".

"I just think what she want right now is too much for me".

Peter's phone was going off like crazy and it was always her.

He ignored the call.

"I guess because she bought me this phone she will call it now as many times as she wish"

Peter said as he gazed at the ringing phone.

"How about you did mom call you as yet?".

Peter asked him.

"No she did not call me yet". "I Am giving her time".

"Ok well today is the day".

Peter said smiling.

He dialed his mother number on his phone and she answered. He said.

"Mom hold for someone please".

He handed Paul the phone.

Chapter 14

The inner cry

She said hello. This caused him to smile and Peter taken a clue. Stepped away.

"Hello Heather".

his warm voice beat through the phone. She was a bit taken aback. When she realized it was him she had to take a seat.

"How are you?".

She asked him.

"Hanging in there".

He responded sounding in control of things as usual.

"I am sorry for what happened the other day".

He generally makes no hesitation to apologize for his wrongs.

"You're already forgiven".

she added.

"So why haven't you call me". He asked her with concern.

"You're time would have come".

She said to him. In a voice that held his attention.

Meanwhile she was planning on not sparing the twins the rod. Peter knew this and was hoping Paul could've distracted her.

He finally mustered enough courage to confront the Malcolm boys. He saw that this was making his mother Miserable.

His approach was to get them to meet him half way they live at the end of the opposite street a 10 minutes walk. The Malcolm's house has the biggest east Indian mango trees. They ripen to a plummy red and yellow and are the juiciest in the entire harbour drive area. Peter can attest to that all because some day he survived on those mangoes.

He and his friend Odane. Who drop out of school because his mom had passed away. He haven't seen him in a while. But heard he was second in line for Don man ship in the neighboring town.

He was walking around in the small farm.

"When can I see you?".

Paul asked Heathe. As their conversation continued.

"I am not sure I am a little busy straighten up the kids".

Ok maybe we can meet when you're free he said feel like he is intruding on her time. She sensed it and gave a better solution.

"Why don't you call me later on your own phone".

She said with the usual smile in her voice.

"Do you still like mint tea?".

He asked her.

"because am sending a fresh batch your way". he said with the usual smile in his voice.

Yes please she smiled and Said call me on your own phone.

At church a new brother had just joined the minister. DAVID JONES. He was transferred from the branch in St James. His assets includes preaching singing, public speaking and he was single. A tele marketer by profession and master at words and he was easy on the lady's eyes slick and very adoptable.

The church hoping this may filled the need of any untied hands that may be waiting to be unionized.

He was supposed to be making an house visit that includes Evangelist Johnson house.

She was made aware of the arrangements just a few hours ago and she was marking sure all was in good standing before she meet this man of God because cleanliness is godliness. Psalm (51:10)

She had all good intentions in meeting him to learn about his ministry and maybe learn a few things from him.

David Jones she have heard that name before but wasn't he married to the head treasure Michelle. She was thinking wow they were like the lovebirds of that church group. How life can change and all so sudden she thought.

She reflected on hearing Paul's voice and it's eating away at her inside to not invite him over for dinner after all he has been footing dinner the last few evenings.

She found it very odd to invite and feed David without Paul being over and having a meal as well after all he is just a friend.

Mrs Jennings is not on the better half of her spirits. Since Peter had be trying to avoid the intimacy she picked up a bottle are two of strong stuff. She has resorted to her usual hobby. She calls it numbing her pain. She has been calling and he answered a few times.

'Hey". He answered.

"When are meeting up?". She asked him.

"I am studying".
he said.

"Didn't you see my mom at school today?"

"A student told me she was there". "Why didn't you have her see me?".

"For what?". "Are you joking?". "She will never approve of this". He scolded her.

"That means you don't know me very well". "I always get what I want".

She responded almost in a threatening whisper.

"You belong to me you know that".
She drilled him with fantasies of how it could be with just the two of them.

"My family is in a bind I can't leave them". He announced to her.

At this point he was home and the twins had just came home and his mother was waiting for them.

With the leather belt she had not taken out in about two weeks now.

Dinner was ready and the aroma filled the house. In a few minutes he knows they may be crying.

No sooner or later the first slap was heard. And word, "hold your hand out".

The second twin cried out.
He knew it was an accumulated whipping from months back they had been riding on high waves. Not that he considered himself any more safer but he wasn't at the bottom of barrel of today's complaints.

It sounded like six lashes in total three of each. He saw the girls rubbing their hands with the green bee bush. To prevent the slaps from reddening their hands. He won't intervene now because it would be awkward to see she turned on him. Based on past experience.

The twins were settling down and their little fesh up and plea for sympathy was going unnoticed

He heard her on the phone giving direction to David. The 40 year old Christian fellow who Peter was waiting to read into and see about his intentions.

'Why haven't she invited Paul?'. Peter questioned himself.

Shortly after she took up her phone and called Paul.

"I am having a Church brother over for dinner I feel bad not offering".

"Would you like to join us for dinner?" she asked.

His response was a resounding;

"Yes".

Chapter 15

The Dinner

Something told Paul to take a nice clean shave, showered up and all was looking neat and clean from his angle.

Of course she know he would be there early and she didn't mind seeing him either.

His brut Aftershave lingered everywhere he went and when he knocked the door and she opened it.

Her eyes were blessed. He brought her a perfect bunch of yellow roses he had cut them fresh from his garden.

(Solomon 2:1)

"I am sorry".

He said again.

As she opened the grill and gave him a friendly but firm hug.
That's of the past she said with a Crack in her voice.

She looked flawless too. Her natural hair was a beauty and her light skin was like velvet lining a jewellery box.

Her smile was a welcome curtain drape across her gorgeous face. Her spirit was so gentle and she did not wear elaborate jewellery or makeup.

(1 Peter 3: 3-4)

"How have you been?".

Looking at him like he was foreign to her eyes.

"I have being good".

He answered.

With his smile so bright it could light up a small house. His straight face and masculine features were on point. She could tell he exercises and his strength showed in his muscular built.

Peter was glad to see him as well. As he shook his hand.

"Welcome".
Peter said.

"Nice to have you over sir". He said with this polite look and a healthy smile upon his face.

They girls were still playing the sympathy card and acted like it would take a crane to get them out of their sobbing abist. But once they heard Paul's voice they began to get themselves together and prepared for dinner. They knew Heather would just leave their spaces blank at the table and when the guest(s) had left. They may be some hard questions to answer.

The Malcolm brothers were texting them like rain in August. Unaware that they had a clipped wing situation. Hence they got a little and low moods to text back.

'What going on princess?'

Trenton texted in for Natasha respond but she sent a sad face.
Same for trent from Natanya

"Man these girls into games man"
Trenton said to firing up Trent. As usual he is the firecracker and trent his side kick

"Let's go pay then a visit man" Trenton gave out.

"Look like you don't hear what they said about their mom". "She don't play!".

"We have been hearing that a while now". "Furthermore we have been taking care of these girls". "When is our payday?". (Genesis 29:30)

"This sound like Jacob and Rachel".

"What you start reading the Bible now?" Trenton asked Trent in a surprised tone.

"Well I want to make an impression on their mother I really like Natasha I won't lie"

"Ok since you want to make an impression who is Rachel?" Trenton Waited for an answer.

"She was the wife of Jacob, who was actually his cousin and she was the mother of Joseph and Benjamin". Trent reported profoundly

"Wow man you sound serious like anytime soon a marriage will take place mmm my little brother?".

They laughed

"We are just two minutes apart enuh no one is bigger"

Trent teased back at Trenton.

They are closely knit as brothers and had a very good relationship. They cover for each other and are like peas in a pot. What sets them apart is that Trent was slightly fairer and favors his mom with a close view. With interactions it was easily discovered that trent has a big heart and a lot of love to give. Regarding attitude Trenton is the more rowdy and outgoing. Together they are two of a kind. Girls are there weakness. Well they never had to really work for anything, so what's there to think about.

"Well if she play her cards right anything can happen".

Trent continued"

"Trenton do you love Natasha?"

Trenton reported.
"It was too early for love", "it's not even three months yet ".

He added.

"You too easily to love man".

He toyed with trent.

"Maybe later we can try and visit them". Trenton said.
While at Heather's house a sumptuous Curried Goat and Snow White Butter Rice would soon graced the table. Some tang and shacka -Berry kool-aid made it passed the drink requirement. If not a cup of might tea would be perfect, Paul had brought fresh mint.

The time was drawing close for David to arrive.

Heather briefed the kids to be on their best behavior and to only asked relevant questions.

The black Toyota Venza
Pulled up to her gate twenty minutes after. And out step a nice pair of shoes classy. Like a Hush puppy. Peter was hoping to get one of those in brown it would have been a great look with his khaki pants.

Then David came into full view. Dapper looking. Fresh like he haven't worked a day in his life and his Steve Madden suit seems far fetched from the humble dwelling.

"Hello".
He said.

"You must be the wonderful Heather Johnson".
he reported upon seeing her pleasantry. He walked up to meet her.

It took a while for him to see Paul. He had to come all the way up the stairs to have a full view of whoever sat on the verandah. He was introduced everyone and when he got to Paul he froze as Paul had his hand out waiting for a handshake.

"I am her friend paul".

Silence hit the atmosphere louder than a scream would.

Still Paul waited for a handshake.

Chapter 16

Bon Appétit

Finally David shook Paul's hand.

"Are you of the faith?". He asked him.

"I think you would have asked me how I'm doing?"

Paul answered not trying to avoid the question but ensure that all protocols was observed in his respect.

"I am David". He introduced himself.

"Ok".

Paul answered.
Leaving David enough room to express himself. His confidence announced itself. Maybe just a little bit too early.

His watch was a Calvin Klein. The girls took note. He was nicely shaved and his clothes were dry cleaned they could tell by the neatness.

'So refine'. Heather thought. His nails cleaned and cut not a hair out of place.

He spoke eloquently with a no nonsense persona. He used an extended vocabulary.

Peter observed him looking at the way talked with confidence and self poised.

Seemed like he was having a hard horn lock with Paul.

"When are you going accept to Jesus as lord and personal saviour?".

He asked Paul.

"I read my bible and pray in my heart I know there is a God". "Maybe I have not had enough courage or I have not seen too much examples.

"Only since I met Ms. Johnson" I am open and willing to learn".

Paul continued.

"Unless the lord build the house they labour in vain that build they that build it". (Psalm 127)

Paul gave him more than an answer.

"What do you do for work"?.
"if you don't mind me asking?".

Peter quickly pulled out a change to the heated conversation.

"I am sales manager. I manage the sales of pharmaceutical items online or over the phone.

"Sounds interesting".
Peter said hoping someone else would take the baton.

Heather did.

"Do you have kids Mr. Jones?".

The air was cool and the delicious smell of the curry pot was tempting

"Yes one daughter".

He answered. As she looked at him.

"Let's go inside she invited them".

He walked into her bumble home. Looking around at the three piece couch floral patterned. It hardly look used. The small center table nice and clean. Small but comfortable, the walls brightly painted in a half white colour and everything kept in order and clean.

Paul had helped her with the table setup early and she placed the vase of fresh flowers he had brought her on the kitchen table.

The twins were busy whispering to each other.

"He smells like foreign".
Natasha said.
"Look like foreign too". Natanya whispered back.
They have been corrected many times by their mom regarding this action hence they got the look.

'A wonder why he is single'.

Peter questioned himself.

Paul too was reading into David's countenance.

Looking at the way he looked at him like a competitor. But this look sure says he had the upper hand on him.

But Paul was not worried neither was he afraid. (Isaiah 41:10). He knew he had messed up and just like a sinner his sins had been forgiven. (Luke 17:3-4)

They all sat down to eat. She prayed and let God and all in the hearing of her voice knew how thankful she was.
She blessed their soul.

Dinner was served family style in large bowls. Paul whipped up a fresh garden salad with ingredients from his small garden. That was a surprised to Heather. 'Whoever said men can't cook!. 'They haven't met paul'. She thought.

As the salad bowl was being passed around and they helped themselves. (Psalm 127. Vs 5)

"What are you girls taking in school?".

He asked them to open up a dinner conversation.
Kind of awkward if one should remember what happened earlier that day.

"We didn't pick our main subjects yet that will be next year but I like the sciences"
Natasha replied.

She is usually the spokesperson of the two. She was a fast thinker and in most cases the brain of the two. She was more robust when it comes to emotional situations and sometimes live in her mind.

"So what do think you want to do?".

"I like business".

Natanya said.

Natanya was a contender all the way. One who was more to listen, observe and then act after. Maybe it's her mom's genes or a mix of both. But she was a gem and sweetheart of kindness.

"My daughter Alison is about your age she plays the piano". "She is head of the 4H club and the debate team".
He said while consuming some well need curried goat. It's been awhile since he had a great home cook meal. Begin single don't allow him the advantage.

David Jones wasn't the man he used to be when Heather first met him. He was more based. Not so concerned about material things or flaunting his well known rise from the lower ranks.

Her whole conception of him was that he was a little bit too cocky for her liking. She believed that children of God should be humbled and wait for their exaltation. (Matthew 23:12)

"So I heard you're looking for work". He just said out referring to Heather.

She was not really happy with discussing this in front of her kids. For all the girls thought she was on leave of something. But Peter had already read into her moods and saw that she was jobless but never hopeless or without a prayer.

"Well with God help something will come along".

She answered scanning the faces quickly for any negative reaction or doubt. Because if it was one thing she had taught them was never to doubt themselves because when they do they are doubting God. Who never fails. He may not come when you want him to. But he will be there at the right. (Jeremiah 29:11-13)

She has also taught her girls that they should see themselves as equals with their male counterparts in terms of going for their goals and being the key to the happy home they will lead as mother's.

Paul seized the opportunity to inform her of post to be filled when his coworker goes off on leave. She was elated. Her smile was a lit candle in a dark room and her eyes glowed as she looked across at Paul and how well composed he was.

"I should have told you from the other day". "But that's when we". He paused.

"That's when we what?". David edged him on.

"That when she was busy with the kids."

Lucky save Peter thought.

"These are some nice flower."

David announced not too believing in Paul's last speech.

"Thank you". Heather responded.

'They were a blessing from paul".

Kinda leading him in the frame of thought he wanted to escape.

"Can I ask a personal question?".

He gave out kind of feeling like his intentions were not yet established enough.

"Do you have feelings for each other?".

Chapter 17

The intentions

There was a awkward silence at the dinner table.

She was shocked at his outburst with little Justin being there, she almost lost it. Her mind, not her salvation.

"May I be excused for a moment". She asked.

"Can see outside Mr. Jones?". She said in a kind, clean tone.

"Sure". He said. He got up from the table slowly. He was probably too proud to see that he had just asked an inappropriate questions in front of the kids.

"Why would you asked such a question in front of the kids?".

She asked him.

"First let me apologise for the question". "But I was of the impression that you were single". "Based on the advice I got from the Church"

David responded in a polished tone.

"What advice you got from the church?".

She folded her hands and listened to see if this is really the church's responsibility. To find her someone who is kind. Passionate and loving or was it by the will of God and the person putting in his/her own efforts.

"The giss was that you were looking for a husband one of the faith".

"I am single and I was hoping to get to know you better". He paused and looked at her.

"This is how you get to know someone better?".

"By putting them people on the spot and try to humiliate them in front of their family and friends?".

"So are you saying that you and this guy." She cut him off."

"His name is Paul and I think he is an amazing person". "He just not of the faith as yet". "That's does not mean he does not deserve the same respect?". "And what about me I am of the faith and that's the respect I get?".

She continued and one should be mindful that she leaves no wrongs unright.

"People are people saved or not and how are we to convince them to join our train".

"Which Is for for the better good of their souls." "If we can't exemplify what it is to be Christlike".

"Please watch your diction around the kids".

She advanced her vocabulary and showed him that she too can speak eloquently.

She continued to put him in a dress down frame of mind, attitude and a subdued ego.

"Gaining riches and losing your morals is like having a sailboat but you don't like fishing".

"You see the sailboat is just the an empty vessel without the right captain to navigate it.

"It will just drift in the wind".

"To answer your question yes I do have feelings for him. "I won't go in detail but we have a very good friendship". (Proverbs 18:24)

"As Woman of God she won't lie because she knows that; "Lying lips are abomination to the lord but he who truly is his delight".
(Prov 12:22)

He felt powerless to her words even though she was just relating. The fact that she said she liked Paul had floored his ego.

'What's there to like about Paul'. He thought.

She knew an apology was forthcoming.
But he had to stretch the capacity of his ego and hold on tight to his emotion. Like most male counterparts of deep dark skinned but rich and vigorous roots.
After a few he fumbled around in his mind. He came up with something she could call an apology.

"I may have started out on the wrong footing Heather". "Can I start over again. Can we start over as friends.

"We can always be friends". Heather stated.

"To be honest Heather the church see it fit". "I see it fit to know you and see if you would accept my proposal for a marriage".

She chuckled. She was not all shocked. She had seen something like this before in her first year at this church when Juliet was dealt the same deal. They chruch saw it fit for them to wed. Juliet never felt like it.

Five months later the marriage ended.
It was the perfect fit.

Though Heather knew nothing was perfect in life. She also knew that God does not give anyone more than he can bear. (1 Cor 10:13)

"So the church wants you to marry me?". She investigates because she was not aware of this plan.

She continued not in anger but a little annoyed.

"But do want to marry me?" do you even know me well enough?". She asked him.

"I know your intentions are good and well". "But I don't think this is of God's doing". "I suggest we pray about it".

She continued.

"In the meantime let's have a civilized dinner with respect for all who sits around the table".

She allowed him to lead the way in.

At the six seater table with an additional chair added to host little Justin. They all were thinking his she going to send him away.

The girls again talked low among themselves and they all understood what was going on.

"I prefer Paul".

Natanya said.

"We need more time to get to know both of them".

Natasha added.

As for Peter. He knew his mom is strong enough to make the right decision. Even though they don't always see eye to eye on some issues. He highly respected her decisions. Before he was warned by her about Ms. Jennings and now the same things she warned him about is coming to past.

Justin was just giving blank stares maybe that's a ten year old way of internalising a fatherless life.
It's a while since he saw his dad.
Paul was the closest he has been to one in a long while.

They went back to the table after less than five minutes of talking outside.

"I hereby apologize for the question I asked earlier". David said as he sat down.

No one had a word to say and dinner continued on a low key.

"I like the vegetables". Justin said. Breaking a three minutes of silence.

"Thank Paul" Heather said.

"Thank you Paul". Justin repeated.

"Your welcome"

"How is school?" Paul asked him. Because he hardly opened his mouth at dinner or at any time unless a direct question is asked.

Not bad he said with a sad face and his head held down.

"Hold your head up and speak politely" Heather said.

He held his head up but with a eye filled with tears.

"Is something happening at school Justin".

Paul asked.

Justin got up from the table and ran to his room.

Chapter 18

Play ground

Heather was about to get up and chased after Justin.

Paul asked her to just sit down

"I will take care of it".

He said gently and calmly.

Everyone was wondering what's wrong with him.

A couple days ago he had a bruise on his arm and Peter asked him about he said he fell down on the playground.

However Paul used charm and smarts and questioned him.

"If I should come to your school who is nicest teacher I would meet".

Paul tried sought out where was his happy place and what makes him sad with the mention of school.

"Mrs. Beckford she is one of the good teacher. All my teacher are OK he said wiping away his tears.

"So what happens at play time?".

Paul asked him. He saw the fear in his face. (Isaiah 35:4)

Then one drop of tears came. Justin stop talking.

"OK Justin we can talk about it whenever you're ready".

"No I want To Tell You Now".

"There is this bigger boy from upper grade".

"Who keep fighting me at breaktimes". "He took my lunch money and tell me if I talk he will beat me up more".

He sobbed and looked pitiful.

He showed Paul the bruises. On his hand and then back.

"How long has this been going on?"
Paul asked him.

"Since Three weeks ago". He answered. Tear drenched, Justin was almost shaking.

"We have to tell your mother?.

Paul encouraged him.

"She will be mad?". Justin announced.

"She can't be mad Justin".

"Do you know the story of David and Goliath?".
(1 Samuel 17.)

He told him the story. Paul went on to say.

He said to him. "It's OK not to fight back if the fight is bigger than you".

"It's OK to ask for help".

"You can't always fight fire with fire".

(Hebrew 12:29)

"It OK, Paul assured him.

"Do you want to finish eating Justin he asked him no I'm too shy to go back out there".

Heather came in with a tray with. The rest of his dinner and a cup of milo.

She indicated to Paul to and he gave Justin a head rub and left the room.

Dinner was almost finish at the table and desserts would have been Ice-cream.

"Anyone for Ice-cream after dinner?".

Paul announced to cheer up the gloomy dinner diners.

The twins said yes for sure just after he Paul said

"Don't worry he is going to be ok?".

David gave out.
That's good". He finished up his plate. The girls watched him.

While in Peter mind he was hoping he didn't have to go put someone in check if that person is picking on his little brother.

Because for sometime now he has been his brothers keeper. And brother to him despite his age has been his listening ears for things he can't tell anyone else.

(Galatians 6:2)

Justin has always been quiet and just do what he was told. Not a child that will play randomly on the playground and is very selective about who he drew into his circle of friends. He was the easiest child to please as he made nothing around him affected his quiet and humble nature.

Because of this some, student saw him as being too soft geeky or nerdy. Where among the names they called him.
Ever since he got his glasses for being near sighted.

The names wind screen and plasma were the new tags to him.

Jermaine an overgrown child. With an obnoxious behavior. Even the teachers didn't have enough methods to control his trifling behavior.

Reds they call him or Big Red the playground bully. Has taken little Justin lunch money away as well as his speech freedom to be himself and freedom to coexist in what should have been a godly world.

No Stranger than fiction was the plot that Big Red is from a very dysfunctional home. With many siblings, his new stepdad is just over 8 years older than himself. He was in grade six. A chubby brown skinned kid, who bullied whom he could for lunch or whatever snacks they could offer him.

His mother could barely help the situation she was in.

She was labeled as being worthless and she has accept it she even called herself the name.

Not knowing that what cometh from the mouth defiles the whole body. (Proverbs 18:31)

Now she has several kids with the same report in school. Because they have been bullied at home. They show what they know.

When Justin told Heather this, she broke down almost in tears because her cup was being filled to brim. And it was not with joy love and peace. Now she has to pray for these to return to her life in the form. of blessings.

She laid her hand on his hand and she anointed him with short prayer.

"Father when there was darkness you turned it into light". "Cover him under your blood lord". "Make some changes in this house".

She cast the devil out. Be she knew everything was a form of temptation for her to lose her sanity and even her salvation.

She bind all principles of darkness like fear, depression, anxiety and sickness to find another place to make their nest.

She prayed for her children.

She ended and song the hymail.

"Is blood will carry me all the way"

When she returned dinner was finished. Paul and the girls were washing up the dishes. David was about to leave.

"I didn't want to disturb your prayers but I wanted to say thanks for dinner".

"And please do not mention to the Church what I said to you about the wanting to marry you".

"I tweaked it a bit and hopefully I was hoping we could get sometime to talk more". "But it seems you're busy.

"It's was nice to see you again". David she said to him as they walked out on the veranda.

"I know in my heart that I am the fit for you".
He said looking up and down her nice house dress.
"I won't give up".
"I want to get to know you better"
David. said.

She listened but she did not respond to him.

He stepped sideways and and leaned in and whispered in her ear.

"I won't give up".

"Have a great night" He said.

Paul glanced out from the small kitchen window and saw what seemed to be like a close encounter. He was hoping it was not what it appeared to be. And it was just a fragment of his imagination.

Ms. Jennings was on the phone with peter. She was telling him if he don't come back. in a full on relationship with her she going to hurt herself.

He was trying to bargain with her. But she was emotional and irrational. She wanted any little attention he could have spared her.

The twins are not too much texting and talking to the Malcolm boys since they got disciplined.

The boys are getting tired of waiting and planned to make a move tonight.

They sat out on their journey to visit the girls.

Chapter 19

Lord I give you my heart

The twins received the text that their friends were on their way.

They sent back "No not today".

This has been the text they have been sending for the last two days and it's driving the boys over the edge.

So much that even though they were banned from driving their parents car. They did anyhow because they fear that someone else may be seeing the girls.

They are being very disobedient they are tempted by lust.
(John 1:14-15)

Heather was thinking to go and confront the bully or bullies parent. But when she figured out in her head who the parents were. It made no sense. Before she started to judge the parenting skills of the other mother she rather to pray for them. Because she was thinking of circumstances that could have lead the boy to such weakness as bearing on smaller boys.

David had made so much mess in her head. Even used the Church's name to get what he wanted. The church did mentioned that she was single and they might be a good fit. But no one had suggested that he be so forward about it. An act of greed she thought. (Proverbs 23: 4)

She could have seen through his materialistic facade. He wanted a wife to show and tell. (Ephesian 5:25)

Paul has been a rock and she had been praying for him to come to lord. So he can be blessed and if God want them to have a future according to his will. She would give it her last breath. (Jeremiah 29:11)

It was a sad hard time for the poorer class of people. It was coming on to summer and the heat was on. It seemed like the more the heat poured out the more the troubles rained in. Like the bible said 'Perilous times' where men will be lovers of themselves, boasters. Children will be disobedient to parent.
(2 Timothy 3.)

Ms. Jennings had gotten the attention of Peter and she had him concentrating on her. They have been on the phone about an hour. She kept him at bay by using some manipulation tactics. Being older she know how to play his sixteen year old mind.

"I just want you to love me".
she stated.

"We talked about this already".
He tried to get her off the topic.

She sidetracked him.

"But I love you she said look at all I have done for you". "It's because I knew you are the one for me".

"Your are moving too fast". He argued with her.

"I just need love".

She said sitting in front of a bottle of Scotch.

"Have you ever tried reading the Bible?".

He asked her.

Copying what his mother would have said. Whenever he went to her with boy problems.

"It's been a while".

She said. Looking at it across her night stand. It's ironic that it's so close to where she was given another chance. Every morning to wake up. But the last thing on her mind was to pray.

"A little god is good for the souls sometimes" he advised her.

"See your turning back on me again".

She said using the saddest tone known to her.

"If I give you god I give I give all you will ever need". (John.14:8)

"When are you coming over?".

She asked him.
"I am helping mom with something".

He told her.

"My little brother is being bullied at school and I need to pay the bully a visit".

At this time he heard a car pulled up a couple meters from the house and there was total silent again.
he wasn't sure who it was put he peered through the cracked blade of the window. But was unable to see.

Usually the twins will be moving around in there their rooms. But he did not hear such movement because it seems the girls never expected the Malcolm boys to really show up.

There was this light tapping sound. Like raindrops on parched soil. And then a loud cracking sound. The girl had opened their window.

Heather and Paul were still talking on the verandah. there attention was more focus on what happened with David and a little about little Justin. Like a couple they are already solving problems together.

"Don't go to the parents yet". Paul advised her. Go to school.

"I have been to the school recently".

Heather responded.

"No one mentioned this not even Justin."

She held her hand to her heart. Lord I given my heart"

"So you can give me strength she said with one hand held to the sky. Knowing this is only where her strength will come from.
The boys sure can't get in so they are talking as low and as cautiously as they can. They house is a corner house and with the front facing on one street and the side and back on the next it difficult to keep tabs on everywhere.

The boys were conversing with the girls and a little giggles could be heard.

"When are you going to be mine forever?".
Trent asked Natasha.

"When you free from this prison". She smiled.

And then a cell phone went off. Their parents was calling, regarding the car.

Heather heard it and it was one she had never heard before. Are not one she would entertain in her household. The lyrics uncensored. No wonder our children think and act like the things that motivate them. The music not all but most of them she listened and the sound stopped.

"Excuse me". She barely breathe out as she moved quickly inside.
Because her countenance had just became heavy and the devil has set cramp around her dwelling place. First she has to deal with the physical side of it.
She rushed passed Peter's room and rush into the twins room. She had removed the locks from the previous incident.
Behold she saw the Malcolm boys outside her window again at 9pm.

It was supposed to be a school night. Haven't these boys no respect. The girls separate running either side from the window as he yelled

"I bind you Satan!". "Get out my life and my home!".

Give me back the joy you stole from me!".

"Give me back my peace!"

Paul saw peter rushing out to front and around the side and he followed. Quickly peter caught up to one the twins and pulled him of the car before he could closed the door. The tackled each other to ground. One being stronger and the other with height and anger. "Didn't I tell you to leave my sisters alone".
   peter asked Trenton in a rage of uncontrolled anger.
   He had him pinned down and his anger was in his fits.
   Peter stroked him just before Paul could get separate them.
   It was a strong horizontal strike dead on the side of a young, clean face. The mark was immediate and as Paul pull peter away.

Trent helped Trenton up and he spat blood.
Heather rushed out and spoke to them.

"Do not come back here". "I don't want you to see or talk to these girls!", "no more!".
   She was angry.
   The swelling started slowly on Trenton's lower left jaw.

She offered to help. She could smell a little alcohol on Trent's breath. They insist they wanted to go home.
   Already embarrassed and and out numbered the Malcolm don't stand a chance to tonight.

They sped off.
Heather came inside and asked the girls to switch rooms with peter and Justin.

Paul left close to 11pm.
He offered his help during the changeover making everyone comfortable.

Heather woke the next morning to a voicemail from the Malcolm's regarding last night's incident and it involved something about charges and lawsuit.

She had not said her morning prayer yet and the devil had a early visit.

She hummed. "Take me to king". "I don't have much to bring." (Tamela Mann.)

Chapter 20

The prayers

Heather ignored the message because how the Malcolm's got her number only gods knows.

But she would not let them bring her to place she was coming from. For sure crowd would have lined the street if she was living in pasttense. 'Forget the past. Don't not dwell at past". (Isaiah 43; 18)

People dwell in the past because they are afraid to forgive, forget and let go. Don't hold any past event against yourself. OUT GROW THEM.

But thank god for Jesus she had taken a second chance at living. Where All her burdens are light and stress should have avoided her door steps. (Psalm 55:22)

It's a raving reality to say trouble had open her door and let themselves in.
But if they did it must have been by mistake, wrong address. She pleaded the blood of Jesus again her situation. (Revelation 12:11)

The kids had just got up for school they are accustomed to this rough awakening.
"Better this". Peter thought the first morning after she started with the prayers.

He remembered when he had to clean her from her own vomit. Wait for the hangover to past so she could be herself.

She then had made bad choice of friends and what they did, she did. (1 Cor.15:33) This is why Peter now have some faith in God because he too has seen the change in her. (2 Cor. 5:17). From warlord to prayer warrior.

He said his own prayer.

"Lord let this Malcolm fight come to nothing".

"You know my cup was full".: Help me out of this situation with Ms. Jennings".

"Lord help me to get past the feelings". "Even though sometimes it's more than I can handle".

"Lord give my mom", "Paul as her husband he is a good man."

"Help my sisters lord let them see what mommy a talk bout".

"Let them see the world with there eyes and not hearts and their feelings".

"Lord it's rough but i am thankful that you woke me up".

"Look over Justin give him the power to be strong not just for himself but for people who are quiet and are labeled as stupid".

"Help not to believe what people say about him". "But help him to know you".

"Amen".

She knelt down and said a similar prayer as Peter's.

She blessed the Church and prayed for his work to manifest in it.

After her prayers she started breakfast. Some oatmeal porridge and a few slices of bread. And some mint tea. Still she praised God.

The twins were still afraid to come out their new room which is now closer to hers.

"You go first". Natasha said.

"No a you born first so you go first".

The girls finally came out impossibly at the same time.

When Heather she said.

"It look like it's a weekend today let me see what day it is today?".

They knew she didn't play and still they are bonded by peer pressure "to belong', 'to be recognized', 'to be cool.

A great number of people are smokers because their friend smoked. "Where is that friend now that you are an addict?".

They rushed to washroom the one they didn't even liked cleaning unless some strong tantrums was thrown by Heather.

"Not the two of you at once!".

"Natasha come here?". She said.

"Did you pray last night before bed?

She asked her.

Natasha was thinking up an answer.

"And you can't lie to God Natasha and can't lie to yourself either".

"No mommy".

She said nervously.

"That's not good". She said.

"Now say your prayers".

"Kneel down and close your eyes".
"Begin".

"Lord please watch over this house and everyone in it".

"Lord please help us to behave well".

"Help us to be bright". "And successful".

"Help us to be able to have dinner", "love and peace and a happy life".

"Amen".

"What's wrong with your that prayer?".

Heather asked her.

"I don't know". Natasha said.

"That's a selfish prayer". Heather pointed out.

"You keep asking for things". "And I never heard you once thanked him. Or praise him in your prayers".

"Lord I lift up your name".

"Lord I worship you".

"Thank you lord".

"Bless your name lord". Heather gave her some examples.

"Bring your school book and let me what you did yesterday?".

"Bring both books and bag".

Heather demanded.

"And remember I have your teachers numbers".

She brought them and after went through a few book. Matching them with the copy of the timetable the form teacher gave her.

Natanya was trying to sneak pass and the baton was exchanged.

"Your time to go bathed now".

Heather said to Natasha.

While putting Natanya through the same routine.

She had just corrected the selfish prayer she had said. Just as her sister did.

When Paul called.

She excused Natanya.

"Hello woman of God". "Good morning"? Paul greeted her.

"Hello Paul". She answered.

"Good morning to you too".

"Look I just made some Ackee and salted fish with Johnny cakes and hot chocolate".

"I know it's kind of early to offer but if you want to have some I can stop by before work".

"That would be nice I won't have to eat my own cooking for a change". She said smiling.

Paul had seen that there was not enough to make a health breakfast for each person at Heather's house from previous night. He planned to surprise them with breakfast.

"Paul"

She continued.

"May God bless so in so many ways that you won't have room enough to store it".

"I think he already did that".

"Making you accept me as friend", "is blessing enough I don't have room to receive this blessing".

Paul brought the food over and they had a nice little breakfast and this time. She asked Paul to pray.

"Lord I call on a name bigger than life itself". "Because you are life".

"I thank you lord for Heather and her family to join me in partaking of this meal".

"Lord you know a house is not a home if and when you live alone".

"Lord everyone has his troubles, some more than others". But lord I never pray for the trouble to go away but for the strength to go through them".

"Because lord experience". "Until it's felt by you". "You can't relate to it". "Share it and be able to inspire someone by it".

"Thank you lord", "bless Heather and her family and may your will be done throughout our day".

Amen.

Later that day after work Paul accompanied Heather to police station. To give an account of what happened last night and prior nights.

Officer Riley took their complaint and listened to the part threat part lawsuit voice-mail that Heather played from Mr. Malcolm.

He assured her not worry as they are previous reports made against the Malcolm boy's.

"They allow these boys to roam wild because they can pay for them not to be put away".

The officer said to himself as Heather and Paul walked out of the station.

"But I am here and those boys are not far from turning 18". "I will be here". He said looking at the holding cell.

On the way back home Paul offered Heather to go for ice cream.

"Guess who was at the Ice-cream shop?"

Chapter 21

No Match

The Ice-cream shop was a little crowded. It was a hot Jamaican summer and everyone wanted to cool down and refresh themselves.

So did David, the Pastor, his wife First Lady Amanda a nice, calm and classy first lady and another church sister. Her name slipped Heather at that moment. But for sure she remembered when she got baptized. She was from a good background, a middle class family.

Yea she got her name now 'Debra'. Le- chin. But she is not Chinese. A mix of Jamaican and Syrian. She was adopted raised and branded with the last name. She was sweet looking. An innocent nature good haired girl. She spoke well. Her posture too was correct. Never a hint of over play just real class from the old school Jamaican times with a modern twist. Neither of her parents were alive.

Her dad was killed in his home land in a war. Her mother during child's birth to her brother Daniel. Who was now 14. They were staying with pastor for a part of the summer. Debra was turning 30 in a month's time. She sure was pretty.

She and Paul said h i to each other and exchange a small smile. The action was mirrored between herself and Heather and finally the First Lady

She seemed fitting with David persona or one could see them getting to know each other lord permitting. She was pastor's niece. The mental match society would had them in mind easily she thought. No judgment handed down but perfect for perfect like mankind see it. (2 Corinthians 7:1)

Who decided what a man are a woman should look like?. The world have already put a look for perfect and everyone wanted to be perfect they hair the eye surgery implants

The bible said in (Genesis 1:27) we are made in his likeness.

Our body is the temple of the Lord.

(1st Corinthians 6,19 - 20)
and (Peter 3. 3-4)

As if Heather had not had her day's delima and wanted to eat an Icecream cone could have probably been the highlight of her day.

"Hello Evangelist Johnson".
The pastor said.

"Hello pastor".
She announced with her usual smile and upbeat personality. You can never know Heather was having a bad day unless you lived with her and gave her trouble.

She had been a usher before just in the first year of her ministry she had seat a number of persons, with that great smile.

For some their seats vacant forever, some still sat where she one placed them in the Church.

After Paul had order the two cones. Her favorite was pistachio. He remembered from their first conversation they had.

"Wow how did he know what you wanted you never told him". David gave out acting shooked.

He tried to show up how close he assumed they were.

The pastor looked at him. Because for sure the landlady who was connected to the Pastor. By virtue of being his third child's mother from his wild days. Had already filled him in on the Malcolm fight, the punch, and the room change.

How late Paul left, when he brought food etc. TvJ has no information Journal as well kept as how landlady Rita kept the community business. No news goes undistributed.

Though their 19 year old daughter Jenail was overseas and the relationship between the two parents had subsided. Rita still felt as if she is owed some respect for moments they once shared. She was also not a saved believer and is one of the town's biggest judge of character.

The thing is the pastor listened to her.

"So this is Paul?". "You are more famous that our Olympians".

The pastor joked with him.

The pastor was a tall man of mid built with broad shoulders and a strong frame. Journeying towards the age of 62. He was a fire ball for words of God. But in some cases his decisions may not be properly thought out. Called it a case of righteous ego and old rules in a new city.

No one is knocking the pastor faith because man as no place in that. It was his personality and human flaws that made him standout in the community.

"Hello Pastor".

Paul said Reaching out to shake his hand.

Paul encouraged and embraced the handshake. Giving him a confident and impressive handshake.

Not often does the pastor greet people who are not faith-driven or christ like in name and nature.

Those are the people he should meet and greet and bring to the lamb of God. (Roman 3:23)

"So Paul when are you getting baptized?".

The pastor wasted no time in Confronting him as they sat under the air conditioned Ice-cream parlour.

"It's not a matter of when I am here trying to take in as much as I can so I can make an informed decision".

"I do love the lord". He said.
"I have read his words and I prayed for understanding the way God intended it". So I don't operate on my own beliefs". "Once I surrender all to him they should be no looking back" Paul enlightened the darkness of those who prejudged him. Sending the pastor to scriptures.

"For a man to be truly born again". Pastor started.

(John 3. 1-16) Paul said.
"He has to be baptized in the name of the father son and holy spirit".

Paul went on ahead of him.

Declaring that he had really read the bible so it not match of bible and words.

"I am making small moves". Pastor peter started to lead the conversation, in such a way that pastor was thinking he can learn something from.

When the argument got warmed up and more personal David and Debra excused along with the pastor's wife. They took a walk along the path, where the morning glories bloomed and some opened in celestial red.

"I don't want to rush in and then fail". "I am not disobedient".

"We are not disobedient". Paul pulled Heather into the conversation.
"We being friend pastor just talking sharing a meal".
"Helping the kids to grow".
"I know you're going to say there are going to be feelings".

"Yes they will be".

Heather hopped in.

"But we or not living together pastor".

"He visit me and the kids".

"I cannot tell how to live your life Ms. Johnson".

"But parading with a man that you're not married to may lead to your demise".

"We have asked you to dismiss this friendship".

"No disrespect Paul.

"But it just don't look good from a church point of view".

"Pastor this man is friend and only God can judge me".

Heather said firmly.

She stared at him, her forehead and eyes were directed at him. Out of a bright star a teardrop ran from each eye as she looked at the pastor.

"I have nothing further to say you two".
The pastor said.

"Except he be baptized stop keeping his company".

"Walking and playing around town like church puppet".

"With a man that not even asked you to wed him".

The pastor spoke strongly.

"How dare you pastor". She announced.

"Don't be disrespectful".

Paul cautioned him.

"I am just being honest Evangelist Johnson".

Pastor added.

Paul pulled in from the relaxed position that he was in and finally spoke up.

"You truly don't know what friendship is do you Pastor?".

"It has nothing to do with marriage and babies and love".

"It start as like", "favors", "talking", "understanding", "communicating" "sharing", "eating and praying together".

"If this is what God wants then no man can put it under".

"We are just friends pastor".
Heather made another plea.

"Just stop this right now Evangelist your have been warned".: You can take it up with the head Bishop or whom You like".

"No one will back you and this play in park".

The pastor shaking his head getting up from the table.

"Excuse me".
He said he low tone.

Pastor was adamant about his decision. This was not the place or the time. Still there was a lot discussed.

The pastor was being too head strong and forcing a friendship to suffer. If they are to be better friend and make the bolder decisions they need the little moments. Like the walks to mall, the Ice-cream parlour without scrutiny. But not in this imperfect world. She has decisions to make and each might lead to a domino effect.

Pastor walked away and Debra waved back to Paul smiling.

Heather sat there still lost for words. and shocked at the pastor arrogance.

"Maybe I am causing you too much pain". Heather Paul said.

He remembered what Peter had said about her getting in trouble at church.

"Maybe we should spend less time together".

"What you think Heather?" He asked her as she sit and stare into the open space.

Chapter 22

Don't judge me

A nice change slowly made its way regarding the weather and the sun had slid behind the evening clouds. Casting a nice shade over the cool evening breeze coming from the sea.

As Paul and Heather walked home.
She was taken aback about what pastor had said.

"Why would he make those remarks?". She asked Paul.

"It just shows he was fed a lot of information". "He acted like there was more to what we were saying".

Paul reasoned with her on the same logics.

"Do you know if your neighbour or anyone is close with the pastor and maybe feeding him with some information?".

"I don't know and you know I am not for gossip". She answered sharply.

"That's true let's just rest it a bit?"
He said.

"We are not going to stop being friends!".

Heather added.

"Maybe for any other reasons by not because of what pastor said".

"It's just that I think he thinks that I am the issue."

Paul interjected.

'This not the right way to approach this and I think pastor is taking matters in his own hands'.

'And why he is being so rude about it'.

She asked herself.

She can't remember doing anything that should offend the Pastor.

"Remember you start working Monday"

Paul reminded her.

"So put all this behind you and keep praying".

He said.

"Life is never easy if it is". Then you may have to worry about the safety and stability of your future"

Paul added.

"It's like fighting a different war everyday". "One that you can't win".

"Your winning".

He reminded her.

"Every day you're awake you have won".

"You may not know how you are going to get through the day but God knows".

"Give yourself sometime he will help you figure it out".

Paul continued she saw excellent communication skills, a friend and guide

"The race is not for swift nor is the battle for the strong".

"But it's for those who can hold on to the end".

"I am not giving up on our friendship".

He told her.

'If you want to give up it's your call".

"But I will give you sometime to sort things out"." With yourself or maybe the Church".

"If you think I need time then that's OK with me".

"Or you are the one who needs time?".

She asked him.

She was about to remind him of the last drama but she didn't.
Soft answers turns away wrath.
But grievous words stirs up anger.
(Proverb 15:1)

She don't want to be seen as a nog. (Proverbs 21:19)
Once you forgive someone of something you should never repeat the story, remembered you did this and that. It means you have not passed it.

It was a case that Paul was feeling overwhelmed by the pressures of the Church and the community people.
Their eyes were watching and their lips were moving. (Matthew 6:12)

'Do you like changes Paul?. (John 5:8)
She asked him just as an open question.

"I don't really but any good change I am for it".

"All that is around me temptations", bad decisions making and problems!". (Corinthians 10:13)

She expressed he frustration in a way that he had never seen her did.

He felt her pain, even more intense because he has been there living almost every moment of it with her.

He was thinking. 'It's too late to give up now'.

They have come a far way and if this was real, life then it takes real action.

They will still have very much further to go.
If they want what they are building to work.

"We have to stand to criticism the judgements and even the failures".

"They mocked and jarred Jesus they spot on him".

"Heather we can make this work our friendship can survive and grow further".

"I can't promise you any big thing but I can promise stability in a friend.

"Nothing fast".
She said looking at him.

"No complications". "No stress"

She look up to him, she admired his strength, his willingness to fight because life was, is, and will be filled with fights.

She wasn't a pushover either. Someone like that will inspire her. Because women like when there male counterpart are interesting in their growth.

"Let's forget about this for a minute".
She said.

They were close to her house.

"I am not coming in" He teased her.

"Don't let me have to pull in".

She laughed.

"And the ice cream you bought for kids is going to melt".

He stand holding on to the gate post and gave her his natural sense of humor and she was enjoying it.

"If you don't come in I will call the children to come and get you".

He was laughing and she smiled.

The same smile he had seen. That made her his choice for a friend.

Truly he wanted to get to know her better. She was looking for the same.

To share ideas, talk and build a bond.

Relationship should not always be about keeping the bedroom door closed. That should just be apart of the magical show. But not the entire show. A touchy topic still but knowledge should be the key in all doings.

God is interested in the affairs of your heart. The right and wrongs. The morals and inner being.

"Tell me about some things the secretary at your work did?"

Heather asked paul so she can get a picture of what will be expected of her after the interview that was set for Monday as well. If she passed it she in for the summer or even more. The favor came because the boss trust Paul and valid him as a dependable and well organized and productive staff.

"Well they are three secretaries. Each assigned to her boss and his clients. She sat there on the verandah while he explain what her job would be like.

He was so patient, Calm and sometimes a comic.

The Kids were happy. Life was looking up for the better.

"I think a little more outdoor will be good for Justin'.

He said to her.

"That could work".

She responded.

"Yes man teach him about plants and animals he learns fast".

"He would like that" she concluded.

Peter had made up his mind to go see Ms. Jennings for a hour or two.

He offered her to come if she promised to meet at half way tree and they will just talk at Devon house or maybe a nearby mall.

She agreed and he planned to get Paul to help him make his disguise work so he could go without being drilled.

Already that very galaxy note 3 cost him a slap from his mother. He lied about how he got it. It wasn't until he showed her the receipt that he purchased it. Only then is he was allowed to use it.

"Paul do you like football?".

Peter asked him.

"Yes man that's my game".

"Ok so maybe next training you come warm up with us". Peter added neatly while waiting for his mother's response.

If she was not excited about the job enough it won't work.

"You have football training today?".
"Well it's like it's --yes mom!".

He answered surprised that it may actually work.

"Can I go please".

He said playing and touching her hair.

He had just used Paul as a card in his getaway plan.

"Please be in here before 10pm".

He hugged her.

"Paul isn't Ms. Heather a nice woman?".

He Pointed to her like an auctioneer showing off his best piece of merchandise.

"She is a wonderful woman". Paul said looking her in the eyes and made her blush.

It was close to 10 pm when Heather phone rang. It was the police.

Chapter 23

Who feels it knows it

"What happened officer?" She asked in a nervous tone.

"It's not that serious ma'am". "Sorry if I woke you". She could hear cars going by in the background.

"We have a Peter here stating he is your son". "He is drunk so I have his cell phone here".

"He was in a car we pulled over with the driver who was driving drunk".

"Lord have mercy".
She said

"Are they ok?". She said sitting up from her nap.
Her heart was a wreck when he said it was the the police. Now it's a little better.
But somehow she felt like God was watching over him
(Hebrew 6:10)

"Officer can you keep him in the lock up over night?".

"Just to teach him a lesson".

She asked kindly

"No Ma'am he did not do anything wrong and he seems to be a juvenile". The friendly officer responded.

For once he sounded well tuned to be an officer and he was not dictating and arguing with her. He was being professional and courteous with respect to the law and his duties. She sure valued and respected way he handled this matter.

"I was just joking she said but I don't have a ride to come get him".

She added.

"He seemed to be drunk". The officer said.
(Ephesian 5; 18)

"Where exactly are you". She asked.

"In the new Kingston area".
The officer told her.

'He was supposed to be at school just off windward road at football training officer that's what he told me'. The officer could hear the anger in her tone.
(Proverbs 26:26)

"We can take him home but after we process this lady driver charges".

"Thank you officer".
"Please be careful".

She begged him.

She was not afraid to let him stay overnight at the lock up. To teach him a lesson. Because he lied to her and use this time to get drunk and was in a car with a drunk driver.
Why would an educated person drive drunk anyway she asked herself knowing it had to be that teacher he was seeing and lying about it.

If it's her she hope the school board will know about it and they will act accordingly.

Because peter might not have lived if something more serious had happened.

"What do this women want with Peter?".
She was now on the phone with Paul who had just about to nap himself.

"Peter acts mature and these ladies are about energy and youth these days".
He added.

"I am not saying it's right it's just the concept and beliefs I am identifying".

She find him very intellectual and he is her best person to talk to about anything.
Paul had left after he taught her how to tie a simple not. He was very encouraging and demonstrative. She liked being around him.

"Do want us to go get him?". Paul offered.

"No the officer is going to take him home".

"Oh ok". Paul answered.

"There is always something in my way always something brewing". She said.

"Because the lord will only let what you manage affect you".

Paul was trying to comfort her.

"Sometimes he give us signs of what is about happen". "If we don't take heed or tighten up". "In this case peter need to check himself". "She is not doing him any good if she offered alcohol".

"Even if he had the alcohol she should have stopped him".
Heather said.

"Well I am not sure if was she exactly".

'I am waiting for the officer to bring him home".

"Do want me to come back and wait with you until he come?". Paul asked her.

"You left about an hour ago"?.

"I didn't ask you when I left I am asking if you need my support".

He said. Being as firm as he as always been.
when it came to serious issues regarding her and her family.

Tracey was texting and he is not responding to her. She is mad because she won't get her little bi-weekly money.
(Romans 1:29)

He couldn't care to help out the kids but her, no way. She should have had better sense than to do what she did. Neither did he want to have a side affair with her.
And try to convince Heather that he was a man of substance.

He figured this was the reason based on one of her text that said. "We can work out a compromise".

He knew her too much and the games she played.

"I am on my way" Paul said.
Before Heather could have given him an answer.

She think and she could not match a single responsible man like this.

"Ok the grill is open".

She was thinking she would be ok with meeting his two Boys. If he was this kind of man his sons must be little gems.
'No he did mention that they were rude'.

Her mind was all over the place skipping thoughts and coming right back to Paul.

And then she was hoping that Peter was doing okay. But yeah he's going to be okay. Because Paul is on his way.

God is good he will send you a savior when you need one because he works in mysterious ways.

There is no way she would have pulled through all the is without Paul. And God being her refuge and strength.

When Paul arrived she had changed back into a nice house dress. Very conservative but classy. She offered him tea. And they drank and chat.

I am going talk to pastor one more time this Sunday and if he still behave like he did she said I'm going to find another church.

"I am with you".

He said.
"And I am coming to church on Sunday".
He said.
"I am not there for pastor or what they are thinking or saying I am there for me".

"I Hope You are there for you and then we can be there for each other so god be there for us". "If God is for us who can be against us". (Romans 8:31)

"I don't want to be fifty and still looking life". He stated.

"I want a good life with lots of fun and hard work". "I am not afraid of hard work.

He stated and she knew that was the truth.

The police car pulled up with peter and the landlord was out on her veranda taking note of what's going on. Heather and Paul went out to meet the officer as he escorted Peter inside. They helped him to the door.

Paul took Peter to his room.

The girls took a peek out once they heard peter mumbling and laughing in his drunken stupor.

"Mi sorry for him and mommy Natanya said. "Poor drinking Peter".

Natasha said with a sad look on her face.

Heather was thinking he must have picked the drinking up from her. From her past life. She saying to herself that she may have ruined him. But God can fix anything. He his a miracle worker.

(2 Sam 22:30)

Peter was having flashbacks about how his night went. But it was like the room was spinning. And he saw two of everything whenever he opened his eyes.

He remembered being picked up at half way tree and she offered the drink because she said she was driving. They got to Devon House and the spot to chill was very nice and secluded. He had a joint he had saved and they smoked it.

Two deadly substances in an undeveloped brain lead to him acting out adult role in a intimate nature.

Now he is trying to recall if he was safe about it. But for now he just wanted to sleep. Otherwise he would be up listening to loud. Tasteless music. Heather was observing changes in him. How he had become carefree and loud and angry. It could be as result of his drinking and smoking. She had to stop him.

Paul had squeezed some lime in his eyes. "This will take out the drunkness". Paul said.

Heather had offered him some ginger tea. But it too hot for him to handle it.

Paul had idea of went on but he won't tell Heather the whole story let Peter do that if he wanted to.

But luckily for peter he was not seriously hurt.

Heather was in a feud when the officer told her how fast and careless the driver was operating the vehicle and she was on a high.

"She is much older". The officer said.

"It's obvious that they are being sexual". The officer point out. 'He is still under your care mother". "You can put an end to this".

'I could have called you to identify your sons body".

"Sexual" Heather repeated the to officer. As if it had just registered in her brain.

"Good night ma'am keep an eye on your son". "Here is his cell phone". The officer said.

"Thank you very much and good night officer".

Before she could walk away and close the grill. Peter cell phone rang. It was miss Jennings.

Heather answered the phone.

Chapter 24

Leave my child alone

"Hello".

Heather said. As she waited for the slurred voice at the other end. From all indication such as the blowing and the inability to hold a on going conversation. Total intoxication have already showed up on the police breath test.

"Hello I am Heather mother of Peter'.

"The 16 year old that you got drunk and took advantage of I know he played a role in this".

"I want ask you this as a person". It's obvious you are not a mother. "Because a mother would never do what you did".

"How careless, rootless and moraless can you be?"

She didn't answer.

Heather went on.

"Ms. Jennings this is my personal warning to you". "To leave my child alone and go and find your age group". "In fact go and find God". (Romans 6:23)

"Because for sure you're going to need him after the school board is done clearing out your pedifier desk".

"I am in love with Peter can I talk to him?"
Ms. Jennings added sounding like a pitiful teenager.

"No you can't talk to him and he is not in love with you". Heather said wondering how could this be. This must be the devil.

Paul came out of Peter's room and told Heather that he was coming along.

"I think he drank on a empty stomach".
He said.

Before Heather indicated she was on the phone.

"You can't stop what Peter and I have we love each other." Ms. Jennings declared.

"You must be really drunk".
Heather lashed out at her.
Because God will not let the devil win.

(James 4:7)

"I need to talk to Peter".

"Just give him his phone."
Ms. Jennings demand.

"I promise you if you hear Peter's voice again.

"It's whenever he visits you in prison and not even that I would allow."

"Do you have money for lawyer?. A outrage Ms. Jennings fire back at Heather.

"Do you know how many days I offered peter lunch money". "Even the phone you're using I bought him it". "You don't believe a woman should take care of her man".

"This is a new era". "Get in line".

"You're acting like you're standing at heaven's gate when the man you seek has not asked you for your hand in marriage". Ms. Jennings said without remorse.

"How dare you little devil of a woman". "What do you know about my life?". "You are so out place right now!". "But really can't blame you".

"Because you're a addict and drunkard". "I use to be you Ms. Jennings".
Though I use the Ms. term loosely". "Because you yet to act like a lady".

"As for your phone I will ask the police to return it".

"Just leave my child alone".

Heather hang up." Out of order!".

Heather said putting the phone on the dining room table.

Ms. Jennings don't see anything really wrong in this. She is willing to pay off the fine and plead guilty and use her medical Marijuana card to cover up her drunken behavior.
She knows how to play the system.
But with a strong contender like Heather it's hard to tell if she can bring her old routine to the battlefield.

Paul could tell that Heather was mad. He offered her a glass of water.

"Calm down Heather those are just words". "Anyone can say anything".

"But it's what you believe that hurt you".

Don't let her take you down that lonely dark road with her.

"We will fight together we will protect the children".

Paul was disappointed in Peter's behavior. He thought that for sure that Peter had ended the Ms. Jennings Saga.
He understands being a youth and the popularity that comes from dating a teacher.

But it's the morals and the brokenness that will follow. The empty hearts that will be left with emotional damage and possibly outrage or violence.

'Lord help this house Heather said thinking her troubles are way more than her with'. 'But she was actually doing fairly well'. 'This how the devil ties to steal her joy'. 'He can't unless she gives in to him'. 'He will stock up all the odds and make it seems like there is no way out'. 'But he knows himself he is a liar'. 'He need not be reminded'. 'But whenever Heather plead the blood he trembles and hide'.

'He can only face her if she let him'. 'But the god she serves is standing guard by her door steps at her windows and in and around her heart'.

'Lord help me bring these kids to you she began to pray lord I leave all in your hands because you are suitable for all situations sickness', 'addiction','mental health'. 'God you are god and if you can change me you can change anyone'. 'Lord help me not to be quick to anger and make premature decisions'. 'Give me wisdom and guide me'. 'Lord I thank you for my troubles I know I am still in school to learn of your miracles and to bring people to your kind of life'. 'Because these troubles today will be my testimony in the future'.

'I thank you for Paul and all the help he had offered lord you have truly blessed him'. 'Because his mind and heart is set upon you'. 'Help him lord to make the full transformation'. 'Help him'. 'To come to you'.

'Protect and guide our friendship and if you see it fit for us to go in the future together then may thy will be done.

Amen. Amen Paul added.

(1 peter 5-10)

The prayer touched Paul. She was so powerful and he could feel an energy that made his heart and soul feel so at ease.

(1Timothy 2:1-2)

He was so in agreement with that prayer for many reasons and for a particular reason as well. He admired her level of belief. She thanked god for her trials. She welcomed her trials. Oh glory be to God. She acknowledged that there will always be trials and she has welcomed them. Knowing that they won't last forever.

(John 16:33)

It was a Friday night and he would be off work until Monday. If the girls were well behaved. He was thinking that himself and Heather could have gone to a nice movie or something but it was what it was. He don't mind hanging around her place and help out where he can.

The Malcolm's were called in by the police and all the reports were laid out before the parents.

When officer Riley read out the contents some of which they won't even aware of they were startled.

"It's a Friday morning officer Riley I need to run my business" Mr. Malcolm said.
Trying to get him to overlook some of the allegations brought against his sons.

"I sponsor your police club". "Officer Riley we can work something out". Mr. Malcolm bargain.

"Forget the little starches on your sons face". "There is a lot here to give Ms. Johnson a good win".

"Also your sons went to her residence".

"I am sorry Mr. Malcolm if these boys were 18 today I would've arrested them myself".
"But this is what you can do make sure they are clean for the next 6 months".

"No more forcing on to girls", "paying their way into restricted clubs".

"And I heard they have a history of drinking and driving your cars".

"Yeah Mr. Malcolm straighten them out".

"Also Ms. Johnson the Evangelist lady". Make sure they leave her girls alone".
(Mark 10:14)

"You're looking at big charges and not even money will be able to save them then".

The Malcolm's looked at each other. Knowing as parents they did not do the greatest of job. It's never too late to teach your child morals respect and faith in god. For as long as they live and troubles rise they will hasten to the throne of grace.
(Proverbs 19: 14)

"I am going to go now Heather". Paul uttered trying to embrace her. She hugged him back and they stood there for a moment.

"It's ok you don't have to go if you don't want to".

"Plus it's raining".

"You can sleep on the couch".

Chapter 25

The birds and the Bees

"I can't promise I will stay over"

Paul Whispered.

Close enough she could feel him breathing.

"Maybe just until the rain hold up".

They refrain from the hug and sat on the couch across from each other.

With the small coffee table between them. She had just lit a nice vanilla scented candle. And place it between them and then she offered him a cup of tea. "Mint, "ginger or soursop leave?".

(Genesis 1:11)

She asked him.

"Soursop". He said.

She toyed with him.
"Nerve damage?".

He laughed.
"Maybe". He toyed back at her.

Trying to hide the big smile on his face.

"Thanks for everything". She said offering him the tea.

"Your welcome". "Thank you".
He said.

"You owe me nothing"
"All that I do is from my heart".

He was as sincere as a white dove in a darken sky.

(Joshua 24:14)

She could see that behind his charming smile he had a good soul.

"The officer said Peter is sexual active".

"I don't want him getting in trouble can you give him that talk?".

"You mean the birds and the bees?" Paul said.

"I am sure not ready for grandkids".

She added.

"And you know the situation here better than anyone else".

"Peter is a smart guy I will talk to him". Paul said.

"And you don't be too hard on him now".

He warned Heather in a slick kinda way.

"I am going give him one big lick for having me worried and getting me into a phone fight".

"The nerve of that teacher". Heather said. She sighed and shook her head.

"You also need a church sister that you can share things with".

Paul encouraged her.

"No I don't have luck with people like that". She added quickly.

"I understand but you need an outlet to get out some of your stress".

"Like a friend to talk to if not go for walks", "running," "exercise it make you feel better about yourself."

"Have some fun good fun".
He teased her.

"Go to the movies or something".

"But the kids". She said.

"Take them to park hang out with them watch a movie together". "Show them you love them". "And they will love you back".

"As parents we all love our kids". "Do we show them?".

"Instead of saying you're worthless and hear is the line I don't like". Paul added. Being the comic he was.

"Yuh worthless like yuh pupa".

"For sure we are already pointing the child to his/her future".

If a child is always condemned, belittled and downgraded that how they will react.

"Children adopted behaviors too".

She added.

"Sometimes you do your best and they end up on a side that you never expected them to on"

"Because they are rebelling something is not going right".

"Girls need fatherly love advice and guidance". "If they don't have that they will find elsewhere". She listened.

She like the way he reasoned Pure logics.

"Parents should spend more time with their children".

"instead of buying them toys. Jordans and expensive gadgets to make the happy".

"That temporary happiness".

"Yeah on the hussle". but
When a child hear I love you". "I am proud of you".

"When your daughter hear her mother say to her you're beautiful", "you're pretty", "your smart".

"You can be independent".

"You don't have to make the same mistakes that I made".

"They will love and respect their mother".

They will adore their dad if he gives shows them love.

Paul ended in a passionate tone.

"You know this is Jamaica and most men don't stand up to responsibilities?".

"Why is that?".

She asked him.

Maybe as a real man he can give her an insight on the ever popular trend.

"Because the four of them in the rooms there".

She pointed to kids rooms.

"About two years well I don't say thanks to a father".

"Who live in jamaica I see them and their new partner all looking good and well".

"Their other kids look ok.

"And these ones here nothin".

He can tell it has been a roller coaster ride for Heather and male species.

(1 Timothy 3:5)

He punched in nicely.

"And that will get you upset".
"But you should never take it out on the kids". "Or tell them bad things about the father/mother."

"Kids can see", "they will eventually asked their dad why?". "But don't fuel the fire".

He was so honest in his response.

To answer your first question".

"Some men will run away because they're too young to accept that kind of responsibility"

"Also some men will run away from the woman and her controlling", "conniving", "manipulative and money-grabbers".

"This leaves the kid(s) without father and a and a upset and miserable mother".

He concluded as she shook her head in agreement.

"It's hard but God won't let me do it alone".
Heather said.

"And then people will say that your bad mother when your kids disobey your rules". As if you have never trained or warned them."

She was reflecting on the numerous times she had Warned Peter.

Paul try to cheer her up as usual but practicality was method.

"Kids will do kids things we did them too".

"And people will always talk for example look at Oprah". "She had done all there is to humanly do and some people still talk bad about her".

"A bigger and better example Jesus". "He heal the blind," "raise the dead and feed the hungry". "And they didn't even just talk bad about him".

"They crucified him". (Matthew 27: 35)
"So there you have it". "People will always talk".
"But if they can but she tries" or he tries after all the bad they have to say". "I can take that". "Because to men we owe nothing".

"Glory to be god!".
She said.

It's like he is revealing her story.

"Half the time people are marveled by us". "They take their strength from you".
"Look how much she has been through and he /she never gave up". "I am not giving up either".

"Thinking despite the odd he/ she still looks good".

"All his/her kids are in school". Not everyone says bad things".

He ended.

He was just having a little chat with her and she felt like she couldn't pay for any professional for such uplifting session.

"So how about Tracey?".
She she asked him.

"Do you two still talk?".

"She text me a few times but I did text back".

He he answered.
With his head slightly lowered as if he didn't want to make a full eye contact with her.
He hated making her feel bad or have doubt in him. He really wanted to gain her trust and respect. For any good man to when a woman's trust he has to be honest. She has to know his boundaries and the reverse.

"So are you still interested in her".

Heather asked.

Because she wanted to know where his heart and mind were. She don't want to be in a broken down bus of a relationship down The road.

Just because she didn't ask the relevant questions at the beginning. She don't want to jump in full of expectations and when they are not met. She bus wobbles and screeches and come to miserable halt.

Surely she has been having flesh like emotions toward him. She can't stand to look in his dark brown eyes.

He can't stop gazing into hers and he pictured him coming home to her and all their kids.

And she was pregnant with the last one that they would spoiled because it would have to be a boy and they would name him. And then he snapped out of his daze.

"No I don't have feelings for her". "And if I did her behavior had made me regret be acquainted to her". "So I will keep my distance when it comes to her".

He looked in her eyes and his words sounded so sincere.

"And how can I trust you".

Heather asked him.

"Because I am here with you and if not I am home". "My phone isn't lock I don't need to lock it'. "I am grown", "I am open and I don't keep secrets".

He said and then smiled.

"Why are you asking me these questions?".

He blushed trying appear contained but his smile gave him away.

"Because your a nice friend" "not bad looking", "Well I am joking you're very handsome" kind",: willing to go to church".: Maybe I would".

He cuts her off.

"May i take you for dinner Monday evening after work?"

he asked her.

"I am sorry,

He replied for cutting her off

Allowing her to continue.

"I was going to offer to take you out". She said. Pushing his nose playfully.

He smiled and said

"ok it's a date.
Her face glowed in ambience of flicker candle light and the moment felt special to both parties.

They chatted and laughed. Shortly after peter came searching the pots and the fridge for food.

She got up and helped him to some food and reheated the cup of ginger tea.

"Peter what happened tonight?".

She asked him.

As he sat down and ate like he was being starved.

Paul knew what it a combination of good and bad. But Heather didn't want to confront the elephant in the room all by herself.

Peter was glad that Paul was there. So he wouldn't have go through this 'talk' with his mother alone.

"What If I take a stick and just start beating you Peter?".

She asked him.

"Mommy I would deserve it". He said.

Looking up at her with those same baby eyes.

She remembered when they had nothing and he would say he wasn't hungry to make everyone else eat. She knew he wasn't all bad but it's the company he kept.

"I did go to training and then rain set up and Coach dismiss us. "She called me and come and pick me up and we went to New Kingston".

"Then we went to Davon house".

He was trying to eat and talk same time the same time.

"We bought ice cream and then I drank some more drink" "who had the alcohol?". Heather investigated.

"It was her but I drank it she didn't force me".'

We were drinking and smoking.

"Where did you get the smoke from?".

Heather asked.

I had it from yesterday from one of my friends".

He was being honest and what happened next and then

"We and you kept saying we 'we'.
Then Heather said. "ok!' "ok!"

What happened after that Heather drilled him.

"Then the rain started to fall and then we she drove out".
"But she was like too drunk to drive and then the police pull us over"

"That's all I remember"

Then he started eating again. From his heavy eyes and rocking back and forth in the chair. It obvious he was still feeling the effects of drinking and smoking.

She was hoping Paul would jump in now and save he.
He did exactly that.

"Were you safe about what you guys did?.

Paul asked Peter.

Peter responded

"I'm not really sure I'm trying to remember if anything I can ask her?".
"You don't want to do that?".

Paul said getting up from the couch to join them at the table.

"I remember taking one you know (one) with me and I didn't come back with it so I am hoping and praying that we did use it".

"Hopefully you".

Heather said from the other side of the table.

in a little upset tone because this is what she would never want for him at this age and at this point in life when everything is a struggle to father a child.

Paul continued and said the same. "Hopefully you did the right thing and protected yourself."

Heather looked at Paul.

"When you're more wake things will be clearer".

"But it is inappropriate", "It is not proper or healthy to date somebody that's older than you".

"And especially to be having relations with them".
"This can lead to a number of problems in the future". Paul advised him.

The three sat there talking and then there was this knock at the door at. 11:15 pm.

Chapter 26

Unwelcomed visitor

Peter looked at the clock on the wall and was thinking who could this be now. Knocking at the door this hour of the night.

Paul slowly got up and motioned for them to keep quiet.

He tiptoed to the door and peep through the peep hole. He did not recognize the person at first.

Until he played in his mind the description that peter gave him a bout this petite lady Ms. Jennings. she looked way better than peter describe.

She was now on the doorsteps of her self acclaimed boyfriend.

She banged on the door a second time and the landlady Ms. Rita came out from the other side of the huge verandah.

Luckily Paul had fixed the lights recently or it would have been pitched dark.

"May I help you?".

The Landlady said even though it wasn't her door that was being called attention to.

"I am not here for you!.
Ms. Jennings laced at her.

(Romans 13:7)

Peter had already given her the low-down of the house dynamics. She knew that Ms. Rita was the nosey landlord who notice everything and everyone.

She was pairing under her tested glasses. with her face all screwed up. Filled different versions of her attitude. Looking at Miss Jennings whom have been way out of line in Rita's opinion.

"Hello you're on my property!". Ms. Rita remind her. "I can pay for three months rent".

A rude and vivacious Janet Jennings replied.

Stirring up the night's already heated pot.

(Ephasians 4:29)

Paul had allowed Heather. To take a look. She then asked Peter to confirm this was indeed Ms. Jennings.

"What is doing here peter!". Heather almost screamed at him.

"Mommy I don't know".
He responded.
Just as shocked as Heather was.

"Listen take her phone and whatever else you have for her and give her".

"Let this be the last time she come around her and the last time you see her".

"Who can't hear will feel".

Heather said.

Knowing that Peter didn't like to be embarrassed.

"Hurry up and let her stop her noise out there".

Peter reluctantly opened the with Heather and Paul keeping an eye on him at the window. They turned the lights off so no one would see them watching.

"Why did you come here?".

Peter asked her. He was trying to be a as calm as possible.

"Excuse peter let me put out this out of order garbage". "How did it blow and get on my verandah?". "I don't know". A very dramatic Rita blazed out.

This is exactly what she wanted a big brawl to wake up the community. And put Heather name out there again on lighthouse top. As our grands and great grands would have termed it.

(2 Kings 9:10)

"Who she calling garbage?" Ms. Jennings then became loud and boisterous.

The devil was stand in the mids and playing them against each other one hurtful word for a next.

Peter held Janet and pulled her towards the taxi that she had waiting for her.

"I just came to see if you are ok baby?" she said to peter touching his face. She was still tipsy. This is another big story the community mix up news.

'Her son dating older woman and she wanted to beat me'. Rita was already making her gossip headlines.

When Heather Joined the Church. Rita's friend Mavis was next in line to become evangelist.

God saw it fit to bless Heather who was doing all she could. like cleaning the Church on Saturday nights with her kids. Volunteering in different areas as long as she had the time.

She prayed ceasely for God to use her. She was then anointed and filled and God saw that her heart was good and took all her burdens away.

In Rita's mind Heather worked her way up to evangelism. By trafficking gossips and making strives against mavis.(So a man thinketh so is he.) When mavis was showing up her own incompetence. Showing up late for meetings. Acting in the position before it was handed down and also she was the editor for the community gossip team.

"You have to leave!". Peter said. While landlady Rita was getting louder.

"Talking to me like you want to fight me in my own yard". "Your are very rude".

The lights began to come on in a few houses.
Including her friend Mavis who lived two houses from her.

And here she comes now in her night robe. Coming to intensify the situation.

"Who want to fight you Rita?".
She was loud and bellowed out waking up more people.
She was like the towns big Mama.

Someone must have called pastor because his car came ten minutes after. The brawl had started.

But peter had managed to get Janet to leave even.
Though she created a love scene.

"Promise me You're coming over tomorrow?". She begged him.

While a few neighbours watched and laughed.

One youngster uttered." This must be Romeo and Juliet".

"I will". He said. Just to get her to go.

The driver was honking and she was pulling on peter to come with her.

"Look at me". Peter said.

"I am coming to see you tomorrow".

"Then take the phone back please!". She pleaded to him.

"Promise you won't leave me". She begged again while pulling peter in the car.

"I won't leave you"
peter responded.

Unaware of the words he had just used to her.
From age twenty she had been seeing a psychologist to overcome her past. She was doing well up until three months ago when an incident she read in the paper triggered her emotions and sent her back into a mental depression.

Heather was tempted to go out there but Paul told her no.

Being the time it was he didn't want to be seen leaving or around the house. Not that they are bidding anything but avoiding some undue gossip.

Peter finally got her in and close the car door. After she had hugged and kissed him so many times.

He sighed just before Heather rushed him she felt like slapping him so bad. But Paul pulled her away.

She felt so ashamed.

"What have I done wrong?".
She asked him as he tried to walk away.

"Don't leave" She command him.

"This is a big one peter". "She needs help can't you see that?". Or maybe you need help too".
She screamed at him.

She had very little tears left to cry now.
It's just her will to survive that is now keeping her afloat.

Paul sat her down.

He allowed peter to go to his room.

"Heather get yourself together".
He told her.

"What beating him is going to change".

"I have had enough from one extreme to the other".

"Now I am beginning to doubt myself". "Is only the grace of God is keeping the rest on me together".

She said sobbing.

She was using what is the reserve of her tears. She was hoping God had a better plan for her than she had for herself.

The way she saw things was just pack a little bag for herself and Justin. And forget about the others.

But she can't go through with this because she is a mother, a true mother with feelings and love for each of her children despite the troubles they may shower down on her. Also she was a child of the most high. The God of Moses. Daniel and Jacob. He will deliver her like Daniel in the lion's den.

He will come through for her like did in the days of Noah. He will restore her soul.

(Psalms 51:12)

A sense of calm came around her.
And since she saw pastors car through the window she knew he will come knocking.

She won't asked Paul to leave either.
After all she didn't felt the need in her spirit to do so.

God had marked her time, it's time for a change but the first step begins with her next move.

"You know pastor will be coming to investigate right?".

She asked Paul who was busy consoling her.

"Yea I am waiting to meet him".

Paul answered.

Chapter 27

Visitor #2

Before Paul could have paused and say his next sentence.
The was a knock at the door.

It was a powerful knock one that gave hint of control or as if the knocker had the right to do so.

This time Heather went to look and behold the pastor was standing on the verandah that was cleaned with red polish and dye. It gave off this shining reflection. But it did not ignite the sparkle in pastor's eyes because there was none.

She opened the door and he came in.

"Good night pastor". She said to him as he passed her.

"Night Heather". He said.

"What are you doing here?".
He went straight after Paul with this speech.

"I am keeping Heather and her family company".

The twins of course were constantly peeping to see who was there. They have already observed Peters saga through the window.

Natasha was snapping her finger as she knew it may be a battle of words, ego and self righteousness.

"Isn't it too late for company keeping Heather?".

The pastor asked her. With his eyes peeled.

"It's never too late pastor".

She said.

"Based on what I have been through company is good for me right now."

"I hope he is not sleeping over!". The pastor added.

"I am". Paul said.

"On the couch".

"Do you know that you're causing your own problems Heather?".

"How is that Pastor?". She asked him.

"Your inviting darkness into your life Evangelist Johnson".
"You're not following the rules, you are becoming reckless".

"Now I believe sister Rita when she said it was Mavis who should have gotten the position".

He was pointing his index finger like a father scolding a child.

"I saw good in you then. But you surprised me."
What happened this man don't understand that you can be in uneven yoke.

"Pastor for the last time we are friends and we are slowly getting to know each other. Heather tried to defend herself.
"Don't tell me that nonsense!"
Pastor yelled.

(Luke 18:9-14)

"Pastor the kids are sleeping!".

Paul quickly alerted him.

"Oh so you're telling me I cannot speak.

"No I am telling you cannot shout". Paul said calmly.

"Oh so you're the man of the house?".

Peter and the twins were listening inside their room. Secretly cheering on Paul.

"I am Heathers male friend of the house".

"I don't think that it is right for you as a respectable Pastor came up here at 12:14 PM". "Shouting to a lady and Evangelist of your church".

(Genesis 1:1-12)

"Wow you seemed to have me on your chest". Mr. Paul.

Pastor replied.
Trying cover up that he wrong by means of his approach and insinuation.

"I think we should talk about this tomorrow Pastor".
"It late the kids are asleep". "I am tired". "I am sure your tired too" Heather said.

"I am here because I heard the police was here". "Then some drunk lady who wanted to fight your landlady".

"I guess Rita has filled you in alright". Heather replied knowing it must have been her. Pastor remained silent.

"Ever since you brought company home your house has not been a home".

Pastor said.

"Are you saying that I am bad luck?". Paul asked.

"I didn't say your name paul"?.
"Well thank god everyone is alright". Pastor said.

"I will see you tomorrow evening at 5pm at the church Heather".
"It's very important God don't like ugly". He concluded as he saw himself to the door.

"Good night Paul".

"Good night pastor".

Pastor then closed the door and left.

It's was a tiring night and before you know it.

Heathers household was asleep. A walk through will be like a still mannequin challenge. That would reveal. Paul on the couch. Heather in her room with her door closed and one of the twins up reading while the other slept.

Peter too was up he was doing some English homework.
He knew they night's excitement was caused by him. Doing some school work at least made him feel better. He was hoping that his mother would look past it.

That all wasn't his fault. He was hoping to just put all the misery behind.

Saturday morning came racing in and the smell of hot chocolate greeted Heather as soon as she got out of bed.

She had overslept a little. Paul had asked the kids not to wake her.
He knew that she had had a rough night.

He went to his garden and got some fresh pop chow and then he made fried dumplings. Nice crispy and golden he added a bit of salted fish to the pop chow with lots of onions and big red tomatoes scallion and thyme. The smell was delicious and for those who have already joined the table. The taste was scrumptious.

(Genesis 1:29)

Heather was delighted.

She could have just kissed him. Well if she could.

"Thank you Paul?". She said as he set her place at the head of the table.

The girls were smiling.

"Romantic". Natasha whispered.

As he placed fresh flowers on the table.
Did you pray already Heather asked. Yes Justin answered.
He was igor to go back with Paul down to house and to go feed and pet the rabbits.

His favorites were the pigeons.
Already he taught Paul who is the father and the mother of which baby pigeon.

"Prayer can't be enough?". Heather said.

"Close your eyes". she said.

"Lord I feel a change coming along".

"I pray that it will be in your will that my heart and all hearts around will listen and be directed by you".

"Lord I thank for the struggles", cover my children under your blood".

"Watch over them. Keep them from danger". "Like you did last night".

"Thank you for bringing him home safe".

"I can't stop thanking you for Paul.
"My rock that you have provided me".

"Lord point him in your direction".
And may your will be done".

"Amen" she concluded. "Amen". The rest of the table sealed the prayer.

"The food taste so good". Peter said. Feeding his hangover.

"It's because it's a man cook it". Natanya said.

"Men are better cooks than ladies". She continue.

"Not really but they are some good male cooks and Paul is one them". Heather added smiling.

(Genesis 18:19)

For a long while it finally felt like a little family.

"Today I am going let you all meet my sons".

"Kyle and kushan". "They are close to your age girls".

"They like movies and music skating and football and outdoor activities".

"I am sure if we all spend the day together".

"We going to hope gardens?". Paul announced

"Really?". Justin asked

"Well if your mother says yes?".
Paul added nicely.

"I have a meeting with pastor at 5pm". Heather said.
Knowing that what ever comes of that meeting. Will be of God's will.

"We will be back by then".

Paul said to her and gave her that smile that made her can't say no.

"Mommy please?".

Natasha begged.

"OK ok"

"What time we leaving".

"Around 10am". Paul said.

They were having a wonderful time at Hope Gardens.

First time for the girls and Justin.

Peter can't say out loud who he had been there with and worst why.

Kyle and kushan were replicas of their dad.

Kyle was almost 13 and Kyle was 14. They bonded with Peter through a game of friendly football.

The joked around and played a little with the twins.

Justin liked that they treated him normal. Because that's how he saw himself.

He is doing better. The bully had not been in school for a while. He was on a free pass. But he is getting stronger and his self-esteem was improving.

"Your boys are not as bad as you said they were".

Heather confronted Paul playfully.

"They are new give them time". He smiled at her.

The girls still had their little texting games going on.

But the Malcolm boys are in trouble with their parents. So they are not pushing too much heat until the bond placed on them by their parents was lifted.

"School will be out in a couple of weeks bro"
Trenton reminded Trent.

"And there will be fresh meat man".

"Don't look so sad".

"I am thinking about Natasha". Trent said.

"OK then call her later then". "And stop killing my vibe".

"Now which car you like on this site?".

They were picking their cars for their 18th birthday.

The bond was that they can't leave the house except for family or school activities. They both attended a private college. To enroll in a local or overseas university the following year. The choice was theirs. They didn't have bad grades and even if they did the parents could make up the difference in cash or gifts.

Talk about the idle rich. And you would have mentioned them.

While at Hope Gardens Paul and Heather casually walked away.

To where the ducks were swimming in the pond. The flower that lined it were her favorite some gorgeous white and purple Orchid.

The ducks made a beautiful display of affection for each and splashed the water all over.

The moment was naturally magical and the soft cool evening breeze caressed her hair and lingered on Paul's face.

"Heather I can't hold my feelings anymore".

He said. Looking in her eyes.

"Heather I am having feelings for you"

Chapter 28

Butterflies in the stomach

Heathers eyes grow huge and her heart as never felt so much joy.

Butterflies hovered in her stomach and her knees had no bearings.

She wanted to just rush in his arms and kissed him gently. There and then she would have stayed in his strong muscular arms forever.

She replied to him. A little shy against his forwardness.

"I am having the same feelings too".

He held her hand as they walked a bit further.

"I don't want to rush things".

He told her. Reaching to the softest core of his voice.

"If I am going too fast please caution me".

"I will". She replied almost giving him baby talks.

Knowing that men can be more pushy than women when it comes to affairs of the heart. While females are more emotional regarding the subject.

He has been good so far. Well he has been excellent. A good cook, A father figure, responsible, understanding the whole nine yards.

She thought, compared to all the men frame she had been with in her past.

Since walking with the Lord things have changed for the better in some cases. At least she feels better about herself.

More confident that a change will come. And it won't be man made it will be ordained from heaven.

(Proverbs 14:23)

She knew being a child of God is not going to be easy no one said it would be. But by faith she knew it will be worth it.

She felt proud to hold his hand. This a man who would put his woman and her kids beside him in a picture and of course with a sturdy frame.

(Ephesians 5:21-32)

They kids were happy.
The girls were intrigued by Kushan and Kyle outdoor skills. They were teaching the girls boys scout ideas and basic self defence.

Justin liked walking around and discovering things by himself. A little nature boy. He is very content with this trip and the array of animals he saw.

Peter was hiding and texting his favorite stalker.

She had calm down quite a bit. Her text where finally making sense.

"Do you want me to come get you?"

"No not now".
"Family picnic". He messaged her.

"Also I think you need to go see your doctor again".

"I should be there at the family picnic". She added.

She tried to dogged the doctor conversation.

"Am I not family?".

"Not after your behaviour last night. Peter hinted at her nicely.

"I don't remember what happened last night". Her reply read.

"Really now?". Peter texted back.

Wondering if she is telling the truth.

His good heart wanted to help her. That maybe his problem. Trying to make everyone happy and sometimes leaving himself unaccounted for.

Heather and Paul continued their walk but kept a reasonable distance where they can keep eyes on the kids.

"I really do need a car or a family van".

Paul said looking around at the kids and how they all had to travel on the bus. Nothing is wrong with it he thought, but a car does make it life easier. He discussed this with Heather as they walked.

"We have to take things slow". Heather advised him.

"I know but it's been something I had planned since I bought the house".

"That's good that you own your own place". Heather said.

"That's a long last dream of mine". She said to him.

"Nothing is far fetched in life Heather?".

He told her with his wondrous smile that one could get lost in.

"You have to really want something bad enough to go after it". "And not because you have failed the last nine times"
"That doesn't mean that the tenth time is not your time to shine".

"But you have good faith".

He continued.

"With that and your belief in god the sky's your limit."

"And if we make it as a couple then I will be with you all the way".

"How can I not like you?".

Heather replied. With a uncontained smile or a blush, leaning into him as they walked.

The roses could never be more beautiful.
The yellow spliced with green coloured doctor birds and deep blued and mustard yellow Swallowtail butterflies seemed to be serenading them as they passed by.

"When are giving your life totally to god Paul?".
She asked him in a gentle genuine tone.

"If it means getting closer to you then let be as soon as possible".

"Because from the first day I look in your eyes". "I saw something unique like a bond".

"It's for that very reason I wish to hold your hand".
I know you may need a lot more time to think things through".

"I do understand".

"But I hope you do make the right choice because I want to be the one".
The one to take away your pain be there for you when you need to be strong".
I just want to transfer all this feelings onto you and make you happy as your man".
(Colossians 3:19)

She was just listening, she burst into a great big smile and then tears filled her eyes.

"Thanks for that she said you're so full of old world charms".

"You bring out this kind of hidden passion in me".

Paul told her standing with her face to face holding her hands.

And slowly there was a slight kiss on his cheek.

"I am so happy when you're around". Heather told him.

"I want you to be happy that's my plan". "You deserve happiness". Paul told her as they held a magical steer in each others eyes.

"We have to leave soon if you're going to make it to your meeting for 5pm". He said.

"And whatever happened in that meeting".

"Stand up for what is right like you always did".

He told her.

"I have always stand for the god I believe in and wait for his inspiration and acknowledgement". "Because he will direct my path". "He is my soul keeper my revenger". "My rock of ages and my fortress". Heather said in her preaching tone.

(Psalm 71 1:3)

At the church all the officials were in attendance. It may be a bigger meeting than what Heather was expecting. They sat and the opposite side of the table. Pastor looking more serious than the head bishop and deacons.

"Heather do you know why we are here today?".

"I don't know what you have in your minds but I know what God has put in purpose and by whatever means possible I will worship him and do his work".

"Good speech Heather". The pastor said but are you acting like the words you speak?".

"Are judging me pastor?. because I don't think that's your place."
"With all due respect to position hold". "That does not exempt you from being human".

"I think you're getting the point Heather"
"In life there are punishment for crimes committed".

"What sins have I committed?". She asked them. Bold and powerful as she had always been. A strong personality, she had a no nonsense approach to her ministry.

(Romans 12 1-2)

He then took out a list of rules suitable to his knowledge. He implied that she had violated those rules.

She sat there because her mind was already made up.

Chapter 29

What if God was like man?

On the list the pastor presented, the one that she didn't even have to read.

She knew when he saw Paul at her house that would have hit a nerve and God must have spoken to Paul that night and made him stay.

She knew it was on the list among the police visit, drunken son and his psychotic Girlfriend.

She knew her messed up personal life. She wasn't asking for him to keep a record of it.

"I don't have to read my personal life on paper".

She declared.

"It plays in my head daily".

"Like when the head of the church, who should have came and prayed for me and my family". "Came and judged us".

"When the head of the church take gossips and hear says from other church members and use it against a child of God."

(Jude 1:16)

"When the head of the stream is dirty the bottom will never be clean".

"We are not hear to argue Ms. Johnson!".

The pastor said in a sharp tone.

Showing how disgusted he was of her doings.

He will going to have to stone her to death. Because acted like the judge but he only have five jury members today. Usually it would had taken the full seven panel. But he didn't want t revealed his assistants.

"We are asking you to step down as Evangelist of this church!".

"I am not stepping down Pastor?".

Heather said firmly sending shock waves across the table and having the Pastor breaking out in sweat.

"No writing on any man made paper does not make me an Evangelist".

"An Evangelist is seen".

"An Evangelist is known".

"An Evangelist must be easily identified".

She continued as if the battle was hot and she has claimed the victory.

"Pastor you know why you are doing this to me!?".

Heather said strongly.

"It's because I didn't take up your offer in being more than friends in the past".

"This has nothing to do with the work of God.

The pastor said sounding upset.

"Pastor you weren't married then".

"'You weren't the type of man for me".

"The age difference and the character you display as a man".

"It's your way or no way at all!".

Heather was most calm but very direct.

"You have these members under your control".

"Saying Pastor say this".

"And Pastor say that".

"What about what God wants?".

"What about what other humans want?".

"You can't live everyone's life for them".

Heather let him have it. She was so strong and poised. He

Like Paul had encouraged Her.

The moment was built up of intense redemption for Heather. She felt her tears coming on and she held it back.

Because she won't allow the Pastor or anyone that rose up against her, to see her weakness. Because though she walked through the valley of the shadow of death. She will fear no evil.

(The 23rd Psalm)

The other officials were astonished.

"Is this true Pastor?".

"Did you in the past asked Ms. Johnson to be with you beyond friendship!?"

The Bishop stand and towered over him.

"It's not the way she make it seemed?"

The Pastor added defensively.

"We have to reconvene this meeting".

"Pastor you did not make mentioned of this?".

The head Bishop was doing all the talking.

The second bishop was quite and the Deacons and Church Mother, were a little in awe.

"Heather you're dismissed see you at church tomorrow the head Bishop told her".

"You will see me at church every Sunday God's willing".

Heather said declaring Victory.
(Deuteronomy 20:4)

"Have a good day".

Heather said closing her augment. She wasn't even too head strong that she had won but she was more sorry that Pastor had pushed her to this.

'It's the will of Lord'.

She tried to console herself.

She had just flip the script on the pastor who is not very happy. Because she had refused his advances in the past. Now he can't stand to see her parading with Paul. It hurts is ego so bad and tramples on his sensitive pride.
Then he brought out David to remedy the situation and David failed. He felt the needs to take matters into his own hands.

Heather is smarter than what meets the eyes.
She is not afraid to fight back. An eye for an eye and a tooth for a tooth.

(Deuteronomy 19:21)

"Pastor what the Evangelist said was that true?"

The head Bishop asked him.

He was stuttering and blinking and in between words you good almost hear him thinking.

"You're not going to lie now are you pastor's?"

"I may have made a past at her a couple years back".

He grumbled out.

Now the man with the most powerful voice sounded the cat has got his tongue.

"Oh so now the puzzle is all solved".

"It was just last night after you called me when was in bed".
"I was warm and safe with my wife?".
"Hmm telling me that Heather have a man at her house".

"I was thinking and I even said to Evelyn".

"Why pastor after Heather like pitbull after cat?." "and she said it was other way around. Now I see her revelation.

The bishop slammed the paper down on the table. He was a heavy set, tall grey bearded man.

They called him Tyre. Means he at a rubber out sole.

A wrestle back in his wild days and he still looked the part.

He look the pastor in the eyes and said.

"What if God was like man?"

"Do you know what would have happened here today?".

"What if when you believe in God.

"Did he not show us mercy if and when we sinned?".

"I am disappointed!". "Because of a grudge you tried to make her life miserable!".

"I don't want to judge you pastor!"

"But this example leaves me no choice".

"The paper work his going nowhere just like Heather said it belong in the garbage".

Heather hurried home singing 'How great is god our God, 'how great is his name'.

Another win for her.
Like Paul said to her.

"Every morning when you have woken up give thanks because you are winner".

Back at Paul's ex wife's house a friend of hers saw Heather and Paul and kids at Hope Gardens.

She reported this to her bestie.
But that's not even the worst thing.

Paul's ex wife now feels the need for some attention and she is about to call him.

As Heather walked through the door.

Chapter 30

Basic skills

When she walked in the phone just had just rang out.

He picked it up and saw who it was he put it back down. Heather watched him slightly.

At the moment he was teaching the girls how cook dumplings.

Well the boys had joined in too just for the sake of the girls. Which he had already anticipated.

The plan was to teach them and talk to them at the same time.

"You all should know how to knead the flour".

Paul said.

"What's first thing to do in the kitchen?".

"Lit the stove!".
Kyle shouted.

"No man".

"Kushan?"

Paul asked. Since he was never a kitchen man.

And seemed their mother has not been upgrading their cooking and household skills.

"Gather the ingredients". Kushan answered.

Little Justin was just roaming through, he heard and answered the question correctly.

without even a pause from running his truck made out of box and cotton wheels from tailor down the road.

"Wash your hands".
He shouted.

"Come here Justin".

Paul shouted with a smile.

Justin came back being a little shy.
Paul gave him a sweet. Those little paradise plums the one that came in jar with the white sugar on them.

"Now there is a good cook".

Paul teased them.

"OK so wash your hands and gather the things you need".

He went on with the cooking lessons.

It might have just been his easy charms or he shows interest or reward efforts and follow with each child. That all Heather could think. Because they all odore.

He didn't look bad in the Apron she was also observing.
But he was saying the same for for her nice floral outfit.

Still he has be rough with Peter and he just wanted the chance to get him alone.

Dinner was on its way on its way and let them watched it with instructions.

(Ephesians 6:4)

'Curry chicken foot', nicely seasoned with Cho-cho, some carrot and the bright Indian curry. Dumplings, yellow yam and bananas. With mix veg. The smell perfumed the house.

"You don't hear daddy say curry takes a while to cook".

"Don't turn the stove yet". Kyle said. He know a little more in that field.

"Parents should teach their children how to do everything in the book". Natanya read from an article in star.
"Cooking, "cleaning, "laundry the entire household work".

"Boys are not suppose to do housework. Kushan disagree with columnist.

Paul overheard and step in Kushan.

"It makes no difference if I boy are girl do any chore". "Well of course there some times that boys are not expected to do".

"Like?".
Kyle asked him. "Oh lord he whispered to himself".

"Like most things about ladies are private when comes to their body". "So men don't get involved unless the asked for help".

"Maybe when Heather have time. she can explain it better".

She looked up from her daily reading. She let it slid.

"But cooking is everyone's need". "It's tradition that must be passed on". "From generation to generation for Healthy living". "Financial independence" maybe even cultural reasons". Paul said as Heather listened to this perfect father figure.

"Kids who learn to cook value what they eat as adult".

So Paul and Heather is not alone if they cool soup on Saturdays and curry once a week and stew peas on Wednesday". Because as a child their mom and dad did this. A number of people still follow this tradition.

He showed empathy and sympathize to each of them.

Heather smiled when she heard him apologize to Natasha for sharing her dinner in the wrong plate last time.

"No its ok". Natasha said.
"I should have should told you".

Communication is the key to raising kids. Once they can talk to you and don't feel judged. They won't lie easily.

"He is so kind".

Natasha whispered to Natanya.

"I am going call him dad".

They giggled.

All this time Heather still had the unanswered call on her mind.
And his phone was ringing again.

He finally got Peter alone. And he started on the topic.

"Peter how long you going to play this cat and mouse game with this teacher lady?".

Paul reasoned with him.

"Paul to be honest I just feel sorry for her the way how she behave most times".

He answered him.

"She need more help than you can offer".

Paul informed him.

"Like first she said it was depression and then it's was some post traumatic stress disorder".

Peter tried to justify her situation.

"Peter those things are mental illness", "bipolar disorder and schizophrenia and all those are among the list".

"Being a friend is OK to her but she is going abuse your love". "Without even knowing it herself until she is fully functional".

"If she can't see what is wrong and why it is wrong". "She need help and God".

"I can't tell what to do young blood".

That's how he called him.

"But sooner or later you won't you won't see her the way you do now".

"Her family don't really pay her any attention just when they need stuffs".

"Sometimes she said she feel scared for no reason".

Peter opened up and started talking about her experiences she shared with him.

"She maybe having anxiety that happened to a lot of smokers and drinkers after a long hall of drug use". "Then they become psychotic if they don't get help".

He looked a Paul. Thinking what a worth of knowledge.

"So one day we just let her check out a mental place and see if they can help her". She got some meds but it's ups and down.

"OK the sound good". Paul told him.

"I Think too often this Mental illness is thing her too often overlook. As someone being mad or out of touch you know what I am saying right?".

He reasoned with Paul.

"She wasn't always like this". He said to Paul bearing just a sliver of his empathy concern and the humanitarian that he was.

(Hebrew 10:34-36)

"If you see someone is acting different or just not their usual self". "I think family or friends should try to get help for that person".

Peter Continued.

"Because they are not really themselves at the time".
"The mind is so powerful that If you tell yourself everyday you're going be doctor".
"And you work towards it with faith", strong prayer and battle the struggles of life.
The end result is that you have achieved it already mentally".

"Just avoid the falling in love and heartbreaks". "Whatever you do be safe always be safe!".

Paul warned him.

"So what good with you and Ms. Johnson?".

Peter asked him. Referring to his mom in a decoy way.

"We are ok?"
Paul replied smiling.

Knowing that Peter was on his team.

Heather had greeted them and checked the pots and give her two cents to their cooking class.
who is the head chef?".

She teased them.

"Oh lord let me see if I have anything for heartburns". "Because I don't know who tell these kids they can cook". She made them all laugh.
she pinched the up the girls.
And rubbed the boys head.

They felt happy because she was usually tense under stress.

With Paul being around seems to open a whole new world for each person.

Paul can see that Peter was now growing his beard.
A stage of taking on manliness.

He knows soon he has to take a different approach with Peter.
More like a friend than a father. Or both at the same time.
For sure he is going to need it. If he should compete with other youngsters his age who has a support system. Who have been loved and well brought up. If Peter and the other kids. He count them all as his. If they should be successful. (Paul was in deep thinking.) He knew the healing and loving of these kids need to begin with a stable home. With lots of love room for mistakes, corrections with respect and again a whole heap of love.

Though he never got all this himself as a child. He wants to break the cycle. He want to be the change he wants to see in the world. One child at a time.

"How does a parent teach a child(ren) how to be successful?". Let him know he can he as the will to be successful. God want this for you. It's the purpose for which we are made to live and exemplify him.

Have you ever seen a Christian gone crazy or out begging?. Not if God provides from them. Even the ungodly he shows mercies to. Children need examples to look up to.

Work on projects with them. show them why they failed but don't belittle them. For sure love and nurture and being but fair works every time he was telling Peter all this to motivate him.

They had a little play time before they washed up and had dinner.

They played a game of friendly dominoes ladies vs the men.
The adults, Peter, Paul and the boys were the pros. It made them bond and saw some other qualities in each other. As competitors, games teaches tolerance and fosters competitiveness. So they will feel confident to compete for a job against other applicants and the God they are being trained to love now, will give them the confidence through faith to claim that job in his name.
(Psalm 128: 3)

They had dinner and they all hang out in front of the television watching the passion of Christ. Teary eyed. They all felt everything he went through. They're too had their own cross to bare.

The kids wonder about, leaving Heather and Paul to hangout on verandah. Peter was playing some nice soul music moderate and soothing and occasionally someone song a note or something. The good old Boys to men and 112. Dre Hill. "Good music Peter". Paul Said.

"Don't encourage him".
Heather teased.

They knew she had left the meeting happy because she was playful and in a good mood.

"So what happened today?". Paul asked her.
"Oh boy". She explained.

"So why you never tell about the pastor approach".

He asked her.

"I didn't want to cause problems".
She answered.

"Well I can't blame him for trying".
Paul said looking across at her.

Her radiant smile just brightens her face and her mind felt free for a bit.

Until his phone went off again.

he answered.

"Paul I need your help with something". The both paused.
"Please?". the ex wife. Asked him.

"What is that now?". He questioned her.

"you have come by the house to see it"
"It's the sink"

"can't it wait until another time". He asked her.

"No I turn off the main because it's leaking bad and I can't make dinner".

"Can you come now please?".

Heather was hearing the conversation and of course he was not hiding it.

He said give me sometime.

He looked at Heather.
"It's ok go".

She said.

But he knew she want one hundred percent happy.

She looked at him as he refreshed himself to go.

He embraced her. She said "make sure before you open another door"," you close the one before".

She gave him a hug and left him wondering what she meant because his ex means history to him.

When he arrived at the ex place in Bayview Bull Bay. About a 20 minutes bus ride depending on traffic.

The Sassy ex Mrs. Phillips, was wearing something that suggested more than a broken water faucet.

(2 Timothy 3:13)

Chapter 31

Delilah

Paul walked up the stairs and slid pass her. She was expecting a hug or something more welcoming.

After all she have not seen him since the divorce which was finalized months ago it could be more he stopped keeping track.

A little tedious but it was worth it. Though she wasn't the most captivating woman he had ever dated. She was the one that he trusted the most because she appeared to be trustworthy

Being free from her was what he wanted.

She was the one who hurt him the deepest.

(Psalm 56:3)

She trampled over his manhood not understanding exactly what a man is supposed to be. Well a man with emotions and feelings and thoughts and a little softness and a big old ball of love. She thought he showed too much emotions for a man. When some of her own friends said they wish they had a man they could understand, one like Paul.

She was looking for the the new facade, the new kind of men, who degrade, disrespect dehumanize and maybe even put their hands on a woman. Well this was what she knew. She didn't even knew her own value. That she was his queen of Sheba.

Now she wants him back in the blanket. She wants to control his movements.

To let him fall in love with her again to be honest she's missing what she had a good man in all aspect.

She finally realized her worth as a woman and now she wanted to match that with the kind of man who will uphold, respect, value and honor her.
(1 Peter 3:7)

The last guy she dated could not amount to a hill of beans. She practically had to take care of him

Even though they share the same age range.

She claimed to be looking for better but again she didn't exactly knew what she wanted. Until she knew herself. Which only seem to now that she had downloaded her history scan and saw way back and even presently who had been there when it really counts.

If it had not been for the way he treated her. Then she would not know have known what she deserves.

She was not a bad person of course they're people in worse predicament weighing in only on personality morals and beliefs.

She looked at how handsome he was. He has been working out again.

His muscles are toned and the sparkling is brown eyes reveal themselves like when she first met him.

The manliness behind the little babyface and the kindness behind that smile. The touch that once came from those tender loving arms. She admired his statuesque body.

She cringed inside knowing that she had betrayed all this.

She could not wait for him then, now she wished she had waited. She wish she had not stepped out of line. She wished she had not committed the ultimate sin.

She wished she had not betrayed her own written vows.

As he walked by her he said "Good Evening".

He went straight to the kitchen to see about the sink.

Pretend that he didn't even see what she was wearing. Yes it was inappropriate well if he had been coming home to her. The seduction would not have been a problem. She watched like a lioness watches her prey.

(2 Corinthians 13:4)

But to be honest right now he couldn't careless about how she looked. Because he can't wait to get back home to go see Heather again.

He had left the boys with Heather because he wanted them to be themselves around her.

He had them for the weekends that his a visitation right.

He rather they come to him then he visits them because of said reasons being discussed; inappropriateness.

It was hoping that boys wouldn't give her too much trouble. But he trust them they're good kids. They are just torn between two different parenting styles values and different morals.

She followed him into the kitchen making herself noticeable.

But he wasn't interested. He found out that the faucet washer was a bit worn out. But then somebody at tampered with it.

He asked her about it.

"Did you cut the pipe tap so you can have me come over here?"

"No I did not!".

"Are you kidding me?".

she tried to talk in that American accent that she picked up during her travels.

"But someone broke this tap off". He told her reminding her of her malicious manipulative ways.

He then went on to explain his findings like a police officer at the correct end of the justice system.

"It would have been cracked in several places with no smooth e edges.

No answer came fort from her.
He knew that she was capable of things like this.
Like the time she faked a pregnancy to keep him from getting this promotion that would have take him to Montego Bay.

He was thinking he could have made much better of himself if he had not married and stayed with her for several years that brought into a not so bad ending.

God is good he concluded in thoughts. You can't have something until you have been trained to take care of it. Meeting Heather is like he has been delivered.

A Delilah he calls her.
The fact that they had nice, comfortable house the only thing they didn't have at the time was a car and he was working on that.

She didn't have to work all she had to do was take care of the house, the boys, and her husband.
Anything she wanted. He made sure she had. Contrary to all this.

She could not wait she wanted things to move faster, she wanted to play in the fast lane.

She wanted to have too much fun with so little time on her hands.

But in life they say when the going gets tough the tough gets going. Not only is PAUL called a toughy but he was also very resilient.

He heard the pouring of wine because he smelt it too.

she could not have answered his questions. Mainly because she knew exactly what she did. and she knew he knew when she was lying. Thirdly her mouth was filled with wine.

"Have a glass of wine with me".
She said to him leaning against him almost like it was their honeymoon night.

"For old times sake".

She pushed him.

He didn't answer her

He continued working on the faucet and securing his tools in the small tool kit it took with him.

She slowly moved up behind him touching his back slowly asking him if everything was okay and how was his life.

"How is your new Christian girlfriend?".

SHe asked him.
"Don't to touch me". He cautioned her.

She stopped for a bit and then she started again.

"All your muscles are getting so big".

She said running her hands from his upper shoulder down passed his huge biceps, Almost to his elbow.

He could tell that she had been drinking. That use to be there favorite wine. Moscato.

That was when he had loved her and would have done anything for her. They had similar dress codes. So did the boys. The perfect little family living in a 'middle class Society ranking' at the time until she turned the tables around. Now she's living in the 'middles Society.' people who said to be between. The lower and upper class people of society. He is part of the support through marriage and he has to take care of his boys

He loves them so much.

Someone once said money can't buy love and it sure do can't buy happiness either.

If you want to ask him about money and happiness he's going to tell you to go and ask a Donald Trump the richest man in the world and still has so many issues and not one ounce of happiness but so much pounds in tons of pretentiousness because Society build people the way it wants them to be. Filling them with expectation that are not always met and then it triggers off on the end result someone is/was or have been hurt and someone wants to get even and then they do anything necessary to get the attention.

That they were wronged and some seek their own form of Justice. Eg. Mass shoot, bombing and even suicide. Put the bible had warned us. About the last days.(2 Timothy 3)

"Stay away from me". He avoided her.

She retreated not before wiping a smudge of her lipsticks on his blue casual sweat shirt.

stopped touching me he pointed turning around to her.

She saw that he was serious and went back to the stool sat down and proceeded to drink her wine. Ephesians 5:

He checked the time it was close to 8pm
He wanted to call Heather but he didn't wanted interrupting.

I am done here he announced when she met him at door. Just putting her whole body on the way blocking him. He knew if he touched her too hard it's a police issue and that he would never do. Men who beat on women have a angry past a bad childhood like Big red on the playing field at Justin's school

If he touched her too soft she may misinterpreted it.

Now he is standing there trying to leave. But she won't let him.

"Can I at least have a hug before you go?"

Honey she begged him.

"Can I please"

"I am not into this foolishness with you".

He lashed out at her.

"We are not together and you know the reasons why".

He told her.

Let me be.

"All I want is a hug that's all".

"Don't call me for nothing". Ever again he warned her.

"You just need a hug?".

'OK hug me". He told her without emotions.

Because he don't want to even see her. She caused him too much pain.

He hugged him and she leaned into his shirt. Leaving her make up stain all of over the top of his shirt.

He finally got her off him by gently pushing her aside.

He sidestepped her and almost ran through the door.

Unaware of all the miseries she had created with just a few simple touch he went to Heathers place.

(Jude 16:19)

Chapter 32

Trust

Paul knocked and Heather opened the door. She knew it was him. He has been texting and chatting with her since he got on the bus.

When she opened the door, those bright lights he installed showed up the makeup on his shirt.

She was smiling, then it too deserted her face. In exchange for a frown. She didn't want to greet him.

"You said she forced you to hug her but you never said that you were all over each other!".

She said in her rash tone.

She came out instead of letting him in.

She observed him.

"Paul what happened over that house".

She stood there waiting for an answer.

He turned and she saw the lipstick stain on shirt just at the back close to the neck. Like where a kiss would have landed, if the shirt did not prevent it.

"Nothing Heather".

He replied

feeling upset about what the Ex had done.

"There is lipstick on the back of your shirt Paul".

He too was stunned.

He was getting upset.

Because he thought he did good by helping out his children mother and she repaid him like this, another problem.

"Heather it's not what it looks like".

"Paul I don't want to be blocking you if this is your lifestyle".

"If you like a lot of women".
She paused. Sighed and took a deep breath.

"It was Tracey the other day". Now it's your ex-wife".

"I don't want to compete Paul".
She told him.

"Each time I give you a break and something like this happens. You take a piece of my trust with you".

(Proverb 11:13)

"You're playing with Trust Paul the most important thing in a relationship".

Heather is indeed right trust is a vital ingredient in a relationship. It is built up over a number of experience and chances given to each partner to see what their wavelength is like. (How far the will go, how daring can they be.)

But that's just the practical side, for the theory of trust character is the best judge. If you are a decent character and you're fair and honest. Then trust will start to develop.

It can take years to merge the theory and practical trust evolution together. But once they are lock in then you have one big whole trust.

Heather may need more time to know and trust paul. Though thousands of little butterflies play around in her stomach for Paul. It won't feel the same if trust is like a twinkling Christmas light.

"How many chances do you need to prove yourself?".

(Jonah 2;1-3)

She asked him.

"Heather nothing happened".

He tried to assure her. He held her hand and she resist it. "Take a seat Heather". He told her.

He sat beside her.
He was talking calmly and she was above her usual tone. It was close to 10pm.

"Where you drinking Paul?". She asked him.

"No she was".

Paul added looking up at her with his innocent eyes.

She wanted to hope that all he was saying was the truth. But subconsciously she cannot ignore the evidence.

Also if he had dismissed Tracey.
Then he may need another outlet.
She was hoping not to judge him.

"Are all men the same?".

All men are not the same. Men are made from the environment they grew up in and experiences they have had.

Because in history man have been forced to suppressed their emotions. Men do and act instead of feeling and talking and cry. "Oh sorry men should not cry because it's a sign of weakness".

So boys who then grew into menn holds the pain inside and it overwhelms him and he acts selfless unable to express his pain in constitute ways he fights.

Sports is a good emotional outlet.

"I am just a another move in his game of con?".

"Is he a player?".

(Proverbs 28:26)
"Is he the same kind of man as those she had dated before?".

"Is she making the same mistakes because this what she is used to?".

The all these questions plague her like in the days of Pharaoh.

She can't understand why her mind was racing and only contained negative thoughts.

This was not a like her this was the old her trying to steal its way back in.
But she will not allow this she will let the Lord lead her.

As she took deep breaths and breathe in and out and let the situation be in its own moment.
She she listened to his words and she made sense of it.

She whispered a the prayer in their mind.

"Lord I ask you for your guidance."
Guide me into the truth", "into the light where everyone shall see me".

"Take away all my faults my selfishness", "my human flaws make me more into your likeness".

"Make me into the true reflection of you".

"Make me Lord into a sanctuary of your praise", "peace" and your love".

She closed in her mind
"Amen"

She was thinking like she did without christ.

Even she had just prayed her humanity won't let go.

"I am trying to believe you Paul but how did lipstick stain get on the back of your shirt".

"Where you two fooling around Paul?.

"No its how many years now why would I just go back to her like that?".

"Heather listened to me". He took her hand again.

She was doubting herself again.

"I promise you nothing happened".

"I told her I'm not coming back over there so she should not call me"

"She is the mother of your boys.

"She will find ways to call you".

"Paul I don't think I have enough strength for this I am weak".

"Don't talk like that Heather,"
"please!"

He comforted her. By taking her hand into his. And looked her deep in the eyes. Silence crept through house like a cat.
He continued to pour his heart.

"That's what the enemies like to hear".

"So they can prey on your weakness".

Certainly the landlord was on her guard trying to hear whatever she could

This information may not even take her very far.
Since pastor had been spoken to by the Head bishop. Then he has to go see the Reverend. He had been hardly heard from.

The secretary may have leaked that this would be the pastor second write up for insubordination, malicious, self righteousness and abuse of power.

It takes three strikes in the man made rule and you're out. But look at the number of chances God gives us every day and moments that we are wake and fail to give him praise. To God be the praise. The Church Secretary Joanne had hinted her church sister and best friend Beverly.

"Don't tell anyone now".

she rushed off to her day job.

But for sure Beverly is going to tell her best friend jacqueline and the list goes on. Light house top business and gossips spreads.

She was way in her mind to point where we felt that she was at life's with end like in Revelation. She was thinking if this was it. If this was her end with Paul she would practise her survival skills.

'And even the song books and bibles will be taken. And the words will be be no more. In her heart she would just keep on singing and his words (gospel)will never end.

"Heather just trust me".
He he beseeched to her.

"I don't need to be dishonest to you".

"If I am trying to make it right".

"Why would I start with a lie".

"If I can't lie to myself then it makes no sense I lie".

"Furthermore I can't lie before God if I should love and trust him as my Lord and personal savior"

"I have observed all these things from you and they have drawn me closer to you".

"I have asked you to be my friend but tonight in this sad state that you are in".

"In your meds of your distrust which is me."

"In your sates of your misguided beliefs".

"Only God knows that I'm telling the truth nothing happened".

She was finding his plea so genuine.

But there was still a little doubt

"Heather I texted you what happened".

"Why I am fighting to believe like this?" she asked herself.

Because if he was such a man god would have not him enter her life.

She was thinking she needed time.

"Paul the boys are asleep you can come get them tomorrow morning".

"I need to rest and pray".

She didn't want to hug him with the stains on his shirt though it was the only reason.

She shooked his hand and bid him good night.

She was so crushed that her human countenance felt empty. She kept telling herself

"God will see her through".

Before she fell asleep the last song she heard from Peter low playing music was Michael Bolton's "Please forgive me".

A spirit broken Paul knowing the truth is that he may be paying for the men that came before him mistakes.

He walked slowly home. And the darkness of that night was the most suffocating. He felt like he had lost his will breath.

He kneed before the love that was unchanging towards him.

And he said a prayer.

(John 14:1)

Chapter 33

The Sermon

Paul couldn't not sleep and he tossed and turned and took up his phone several times to call her.

She did the same. Her heart and mind where in conflict with each other. She lay lifeless almost to the point of tears. The gloom of night sure rested on her heart.

She ended up falling asleep with the phone in her hand.

The sun sure shone in sufficient light to wake her up

It was Sunday and it's Church day, the Lord's day.

Everyone has to go to Church Whether they want to or not.

It was important to her that everyone who visits or even stay one night under her roof.
If the following day was a Sunday then they have to go to church.

It was a contribution to the Lord for blessing her when she needed him most.

She also knew that her blessings were not yet fully accomplished and she had a role to play. She knew you just don't pray for blessings and they happened you have work your way to meet them.

It's like praying for a car without a driver's license.

She knows that for blessings to be fully manifest the prayer as go in line with a series of action to get the fullness of the blessing.

She knows the devil is always a liar and put all the obstacles in her way for her to fail.

He wanted her to curse God and die like he tempted Job.

He wanted to rob her of her soul. But she knew God far too well and she was not going to give up on him.
Because she knew that he would never give up on her.

She woke the boys up fed them breakfast and gave them some to take to their father's place. And for them all to get dressed and come to church.

Sunday morning is always busy in Heather house.
She tried to prepare breakfast and dinner in one go. So she can have more relaxed time when she came back home from church.

But now the girls are getting more interested in the kitchen that's a very good help for her thanks to Paul.
He found a way to get them to participate in kitchen activities.

"Such an amazing man".
She thought in her head.

'Such a Pity he can't get his act together when it comes to having a lot of women'. 'Or maybe this is just her flesh telling her this maybe it's the lust it's or it's jealousy one of those Afflictions. That the devil had put in place to make her stay away from Paul.

'Because on the other side something was telling her that Paul was the ideal man for her

Paul was her rescuer who came to rescue her from her dungeon of loneliness from torture of sleeping alone.

Crying herself to sleep sometimes at night thinking that she was less than a human and no one wanted to share her company. Paul could put an end to all that.

She had prayed to God to find the perfect person that will follow her on her journey to praise his name and gain soul for his kingdom.

Paul seems to be the one but there are so many things that were hindering her from trusting and believing that this is, this was the blessed man that God has sent for her.

They all pitched in and got everything ready for dinner.

At church they met with Paul and the boys.
They all looked smashing; the boys wore shirts and ties and Paul was wearing a suit. He was looking radiantly handsome. that the Church Sisters walked by and gazed at him. Heather too had always had a glow when she was in or out of Church that kept Paul eye glued to her.

"Who is he?". Sister Beverly asked Sister Joanne. He looks so handsome and strong. Joanne added.

"Let me go welcome him!".

Sister Janice said looking him up and down.

That's when Heather walked up to him after saying her mornings prayer.

"Hi paul I am glad you could make it today".

The Church was huge one the the largest in the community know for the many weddings it host and the nice reception area it had at the back. It was blessing to behold on the outside. Maybe not the same as God intended on the inside. But his mercies endureth forever.

"I promised you I would and I did like in everything I do I try to tell you the truth".

He said humbled and his eyes bore his honest soul.

"Don't go there right now Paul!".
She tried to caution him.

"Its nice to see you today welcome".

Janice said reaching her hand out to shake Paul's.

"It's nice to meet you too."

Paul answered

she paused waiting for him to give her his name.

"Oh sorry my name is Paul". He furnished with a smile.

One that made Janice flashed a very open and blush like smile.

"I am Janice it's a pleasure to meet you may I show you to your seat?".

For sure she was going to seat him beside her.

"I'm fine I'm here with Heather".
"I thank you for your kindness".

Janice then looked at her up and down which was not the most promising look in Church. But she knew she was no match for this warrior of God.

Janice has been single for five years. She is a very lovely woman, and she can't seem to find the reason why she's still single.

She has done everything right. She was educated, spoke well, had a good job, a car, even a nice condo.

She was calm, she was understanding but yet she was still single.

Janice's faults seemed to be; she was looking for something that glitters. The tall dark and handsome, exceptionally gorgeous male counterpart. They are few of those. And some don't come with good character and most of them are idols of themselves.

Maybe someone like David would fit her perception of husband. He was too was not interested. She was hoping Paul was free.

When she got with someone like this she becomes overbearing.
Controlling and the person feels as if they're in a trapped vault. And she has all the combinations. This scares men away.

She looked around at Paul and said.

"Let me know if you want anything".

"I sure will".

Paul answered her politely as they walked in Heather.

She showed them to their seats.

It was no moment sooner, the Pastor was up on the pulpit.

And he made mention of welcome to Evangelist Heather and her family. Then he made mention of Heather's friend Paul.

He asked Paul if he would like to say anything because this was apparently a second visit to the church.

For sure Paul would not declined an invitation like this
"Just say a few words to the church".
Pastor said handing him the microphone.

Pastor was hoping this will be a mockery on Paul's behalf.
But what is intended for evil. God will use it for good for those who love the lord.
(Genesis 50:20)

"Good morning Church".

"Special blessings to the ministers and officials of the great rock of god".

"Amen"?".

He said making sure he had their attention.

Now pastor wondered if he had set himself up.

"I thank you all for inviting me to worship with you".
"I know I am not even worthy to be in the presence of God"

Paul continued

"I thank. Evangelist Heather for making it a priority that I attend Church.

"For I am only a sinner and I need his Grace".

"I am open and honest enough to say that I am not perfect and I will never be".

"I am not pretentious", "greedy or envious".

"Like any man, I will wait my turn from the Lord.

"I hope the members of this church will pray my strength in God and not weigh me down.

"For I don't want to be discouraged or bear false witness against.

Pray for me and set examples so myself and my boys can rise up and see the true potential and the true love of God."

Prayed that I will be blessed and surrender my heart my soul", my everything to him. I have been a believer"."

I not yet baptised. Yet I have enough faith to believe that whomever god put together no man can separate.

Everyone looked at each other in all awe.
How eloquently spoke. A few ladies looked over at Heather.

Wishing they had not spoke negatively against her name.

They so wanted to get know more about this magic of a man call Paul.

His demeanor was so calm, poised and it was as if it took a certain grace of God with him.

Every word of God spoken by him had hit someone's conscience. Six people went to their knees and wept and prayed and screamed and yelled.

"for I have sinned and come short of your glory forgive me oh Lord and the show me mercy".

(Romans 3:23)

Pastor preached a sermon that tied himself up

He preached about lust and jealousy. The same afflictions he was struggling with.

He wanted to turn the table over to Paul. Show him up that he was in wrong place for wrong reason.

Yet was he not conscious of his own Gospel being spread around the Church of the letter he was supposed to be served at the end of this service.

Paul and Heather listen to the service very keenly.

At the end of Church Pastor was called into the chamber and received this letter. Stating all the infractions of the rules he had broken.

But this only gave him more power to go after Paul and Heather.

He knew he was already married but in his mind he did not find the perfect fit for him.
(Proverb 1:19)

He was thinking that he could have of uplifted Heather and take her from the valley to the mountains.

Showered her with is love and material things.
Use his power to build an Empire. He was acting like it was the days of Saul.
(1 Samuel 13:5-14)

For some unknown reason Heather is the apple of this pastor's eye. and he won't give up, even if it meant losing everything.

In fact he doesn't even know if he has love for Heather.

What he might have is infatuation or just the need to possess her as another asset his game of conquest.

After church Janice tried to talk to Paul for a bit.
Heather allowed it being civilized
While Janice was rocking, swaying and smiling like she was losing yourself in the middle of the conversation.

Heather stood there watching her like she can seemed to understand why Janice would really do this in front of her.

Trying to pick up Paul.
There's was a few single women in the church. But it doesn't have to be like this. Heather thought.

Paul finally got away and they walked home on their way home they talked a little but nothing serious.

At home an amazing dinner was served. sliced fried escovitch fish, a lovely rice and peas. A tasty carrot juice with beetroot.

"This tastes so good!".
Natasha said just to start a conversation around at the table.

Because since prayer no one spoke.
Everyone was getting the idea that Heather and Paul was having a break in transmission.

They wanted to bring them back together.

After dinner the kids saw that Heather and Paul were still not the way they used to be.

Peter called all the kids outside and then call Heather into his room he asked her to stay there for a bit he wants to show her something.

Then he went out and got Paul invited him into his room and then close the door from the outside.

leaving them both in his room with slow love songs playing like "Hurt You'. By Babyface and and Toni Braxton. "Only Broken hearted" By Brandy.

"Heather I am sorry but nothing happened". His tone was so well contained like he never spoked a dishonest word.

Paul sat on chair as she sat on Justin lower part of the bunk bed. They released that Peter had pull a fast one on them.

"Paul I am just trying to clear my head that's all".

"Heather I don't want you to stop believing in me". "God knows I never meant to hurt you".

"It hurts Paul I won't lie".
Heather replied looking in his eyes.

"The pain of seeing her colours on you and knowing that you once loved her"

"Heather please forgive me". "Well a least forgive her". "Because God knows I did not do anything".

"Heather Please can we start over again?".

"I mean even if you just want us to be friends".

She listened to him. She was hoping she had the right answer. Or was it the words she was looking for.

They had a good pause.

He stared in her bright eyes that brighten his world like the sun. He too was hoping that her answer would soothe his aching heart.
(Psalm 38:18)

Chapter 34

Bridge over troubled water

"Paul just give me at least three days".

"Just to make sure I am making the right choice".

"Heather I don't have three days".

"I want an answer now".

"I am not asking you to lose your salvation Heather!".

He was getting intense. He felt like he was sitting next to the equator and his heart felt like it's summer.

He thinks she has been holding back. He maybe he was right.

Because her heart was beating like a Congo drum. And she wasn't even sure if she was sitting or standing. Whenever they were in the same room.

"Heather don't do this to me?".
He Pleaded.

"It's me Paul"

"I am giving myself to you"

"Just as I am"

"All my flaws and faults".

(1 John 1:8-9)

"Heather I Am giving you everything"

"Usually I would be patient but I feel the need to let you know how I feel".

"I hope I am not rushing you Heather". "But right now you have my heart."

He floored her with that speech. And made her heart wept quietly. In all her years she have never heard something so romantic and passionate from a man.

"You're making me lose concentration when you talk like that".

She barely got out of her mouth. Almost shaken.

"It takes time to build trust paul let's take our time".

(Ephesians 5:15-17)

He bearing her heart at this time.

"Heather am not asking you about time".

"I am asking for your forgiveness".

"I am working on that". She answered with some remorse.

It can be said that Heather is being too hard. Sometimes this is a good way to see if someone is truly interested in you. In most cases the players would ran off to the next victim. Not saying it can't happen after a long waiting cycle. But you would have invested enough time and energy to get into the make of this person and they likewise in you. This relationship is more likely to survive.

#Point (Author smiled)

The more one invest in a relationship the more interested they are.

Investment is not money, expensive gifts or bedroom acrobatics.

It's time and talking and solving problems together.

It's support. Waking up at 4am to him or her breakfast or lunch to because they start at 6am.

Giving him or her a special treat day massage. Cuddles. Tell me your problems hour. Little playtime.

Go out together. Don't limit yourself to age and finances.

A walk in the park can do it. Go running together. If single find a friend who wants to do the things you like. Humans are sociable beings we must have moments of company.

Heather continued to explain to Paul the reason for her stance.

"This is how forgiveness works".

She told him.

"When the mind has too much evidence to play around with." "It takes longer to forget".

"The saying that goes".
"What eyes don't see heart don't leap", "is the best Proverb to describe the situation".

"Because I have seen the evidence I can't forget in one go".

He leaned back in the chair, because she did make sense.

He can't fight her on that one.
If he is going to win he has to reach done in his heart and pay dear.

Give her some time and let her grow to miss him. 'Absence makes the heart grow fonder. But how fonder and how much absence when they work together tomorrow.

He can't do that they will men at work ready to through lyrics at her.

Paul continued.

"I won't bring up it again Heather".

He said touching her face pulling her head up so she could look at him.

"I will give you time".

"Thank you".
she said.

"Thanks for understanding".

"You're sweetest man I have ever met".
she told him.

"Well except for Jesus".
She smiled.

He smiled back.

"I can't compete with your maker".

He teased back at her.

They kept quiet for a while and this song played "End of the road Boyz to men".

They basked in the moment soaking up about half the songs melody and he song a note.

"Oh you can sing?".

She teased him.

He was shy about it. "Just a little". He said playing around with the note.

"Maybe one day when we are close enough I will sing for you".

He said looking at his watch.

"Tomorrow we starting 7am".

"So I have to send off the boys back to you know who".

He said looking at her like they are already married.

"Oh I going to miss them".

She said.

"They are so well behaved".

"Like their father"

He dropped that in. Hinting that he is a good man.

"Well peter lock us up like a prison warden".

'Peter likes peace".

she smiled.
"He don't like when people are mad at each other".

"He don't like to mad at".

"And he don't stay mad at anyone".

"But he has some anger".

"Each person has their good and bad". "We can't all be the same".
He added.

"All need to be is like christ". She told him.

She called Peter to come and opened the door.

He came running from outside where he and kids were playing Hide and Seek.

Justin was the master hider. No one can find him so easily. And when he was the seeker. He sure found them fast.

Peter opened door pretending he didn't know it was locked.
He saw smiles on their faces.

So mission accomplished.

Paul went out and got the boys to clean up themselves change clothes and look fresh.

He taught them how to take care of their clothes.

What is good. What is for play and what is for going out. Heather admired how they followed his rules.

He sat them down and talked with them on the couch. Peter was there so he just listened.

"No matter what happen between me and your mother".
'I love you boys".

They look at him shyly with the heads held down.

"Hold your heads up".
He said look me in the eyes.

"Don't ever hold your head down sons"
"That goes for you as well Peter".

"When someone talks to you from any class", "position or creed you hold their stare".

"The moment you look away or look down". "You have given them doubtful side". "You have given them the upper hand". "You have lost confidence".

The girls came in looking for more play but the met the counseling session instead.

Girls take a seat Heather said sizing them up with her eyes.

Paul continued.

"Your job as kids is learn all you can from us". "So you can take it and add to it and make a better life for yourselves".

"You have to fight it".
"Don't waste time in school".

"Study ask for help if you don't know". "Be honest with yourself and what you want to be".

He was talking calmly but firmly and friendly.

"Now let see those homeworks".
He checked the boys books.

Heather watched him. A man of order. He wanted his boys to succeed. He is standing behind them. Like a bridge over troubled waters.
(Psalm 127: 3-5)

"Go tell miss Heather goodbye". He told them.

The ran over to Heather. Of course they liked her she read all of them a nice bedtime story while there dad was away. She made them frozen pops. (Kool aid place in the ice tray and freeze).

They hugged her and kissed her on her cheeks. Each on either side.

"Hey who said you can kiss her?".

Paul Joked.

Kyle said.

"You're very pretty and kind thank you for letting us stay with you".

He had the charms of his father and soul of an ancient priest.

"Thanks miss Heather Kushan"
followed. He was more of a doer than teller.

"You boys be good and show respect to everyone like you did to me ok?".

"Don't be caught up with friends and get into trouble you can be anything you want to be".

"What you want to be kushan?".
"I want to be an engineer.

Kyle?" "I want to be a writer. That's good maybe one day you will write a story about my life". "And kushan can build cars that fly"

"I will write stories about all our lives". Kyle smiled.

He smiled and hugged her again. "They are so warm".

She said to Paul.

"Both of you are princes". She she teased them.

"Here is something for your ride home?".

She gave them coconut drops that she had made and hide from the girls and Peter.
Because there would be none left.

"Mommy"

Natasha shouted as all her kids joined the line up including Paul.

She couldn't help but laughed and handout the drops.

When she came to Paul she gave him a hug.

"I will call you'. He said.

"Because I have tell you about work OK". He wanted to make sure she answered.

She walked him to verandah.

Her evening summer dress flowed elegantly and she was wasn't even dressed up.

The sunshine made look so angelic and when she smiled she takes his breath away.

"You're sure are a sweet lady Heather in all dimensions". He smiled with handsome charming self. Not even knowing that when he walked away there goes her rainbow and it may be a cloudy day.

Until he called.

"Hi how are you?". He asked her.

"I am fine thinking about work?"

He asked her

"No you". She said.

"What did I do this time?". He said like a kid.

"Nothing". She laughed.

She cuddled into the pillows.
And he into his sheets.

"Did the boys get home safely?". She asked him.

"Yes they called and they said to make more drops because they are saving to buy from you".

"So at work there are a lot of guys who will talk you up". so just be cool". "It's not like they are rude are anything. But it's not like a choir practice either".
They just like to show off.

"I told them you're my friend so that will take some talks off your pretty face". He laughed.

"But there's one boss. "MR MCKEAN". "If you ever work for him beware ok?".

"He is very pushy and likes to think he own people".
"So pray him away".

"Paul God will put all who need to aside in their place".

"Because I trust God down to ground that I walk on. It shall not be moved.
(Psalm 23)

She replied.

"Very good so see at the bus stop at 6am".

"6 am sharp'.

"OK good night pretty lady".

"OK night paul".

"Go ahead hang up". He said

"No you hang up!".
She said.

Chapter 35

"Where do we go from here".?

"Haha".

"He laughed Heather are you going hang up?".

He said jokingly.

"Paul are you going to hang up".

She asked him more jokingly.

They chatted a bit more.

"As a team we can do so much thing together.

"It finally seem like my life is going somewhere".

Heather added.

"Now hopefully we can take down one dream at a time".

Heather was feeling good about the earlier discussion with paul.
She has lifted her band on him. He also was hoping that she survived work at the wharf.

She don't know those boys the will mouth people all day. But it's mutual fun until someone gets upset.

The first day of work saw Heather in a gorgeous skirt suit. Close and neatly fitted. She smelled heavenly.
She had layer everything out so her kids could be ready for school at 7:45am.
At the time she will be 45mins into her 8 hour shift.

She wasn't even worried about the interview because God's got her.

She knew that to pass an interview she had to pretend that the manager don't know anything about the subject.

And she would be treated like the first person of contact to provide such information.

She knew that when she was asked. A question like. "Tell me about yourself?".
That the interviewer don't want her to give about adjectives that I described her. Like I am honest, hardworking and knowledge.

The interviewer is looking for something along the lines of.

I am self motivated and see a given project to its completion. I take instructions well and from all levels. I am strong at team work and I like to lend a helping hand when called upon. I take my Christian values everywhere I go but I am flexible and can work with a diverse group of people.

This answer provide so much information in that little speech and have answered the interviewer's question.

The main reason people fail interviews is because they do not answer what they are asked.

They really know the job and can do it but they can't express themselves. It's ok to read up on a company and know what you're getting into Heather had done just that and she was ready.

Paul look even younger in a nice dress shirt and nice dockers pants clean neat black shoes. Nice and clean shaved, hair nicely combed.

Smelling like a tourist. He took great pride in himself and his appearance. So did Heather together they looked great. They Could pass for a married couple.

"Good morning".

He said just close enough to her hears. "You almost scared me!".

She said because she did walk by and did even see him.

"I know you're protected by God you don't get scared easily".

She smiled.

"Okay stop charming me" she smiled because she was so happy to see him and her night was a bit restless once he got off the phone.

"Looking nice".
He complimented her

"Thanks you"

"You so dress up where you working today?".

She replayed as they retreat from their warm embrace.

"Oh I am going for this little interview for warehouse manager position".

He told her.

"Oh Paul that's nice". She gently hugged him.

"So why didn't you tell me.

She asked him.

"Sometimes your own mouth can be block your blessings". He told her.

"Not that I wouldn't have told you". "But I just wanted to see at least if I got it first".

"What if I told everyone about it. Then I didn't even get it?".

"I understand where you're coming from".

"Sometimes I do the same".
"The tongue can be deadly"

She agreed.

(1 Peter 3:10)

'Sometimes you don't have tell everyone your business"." A trusted friend family member".

"But not the whole town".

She continued.

Because he was a good listener. Men who listens a lot, learn more about the women they wish to marry and the same can be said for the reverse.

"Not everyone want to hear the best about you".

"Then you wonder why it didn't work".
"Because you told everyone and your enemy got the message". "Now they can block your progress."

They talked between each other they agree on most things. She gave him some insights on interviewing skills and techniques.

Then the bus came.
He let the ladies go in first.

He would have stood if she didn't not save him a seat beside him.

"What is that you're writing?'. He looked over at her book?".

"A sermon I am working on for next week I am preaching at women's conference".

Here take a look she handed him the book.

He read through it.

"you can do it now he pushed her it's so good come on now!".

. "It don't have to be word for word just let it be from the heart".

"Ok let us pray".
She said.

They bowed their heads and prayed and she got her path cleared with God.

"To bless the passengers on the bus and released those who struggle with bandage who wrapped up by their own tongue".

She started of slowly as Paul hummed amazing grace in the background.

"You can't seem to stop lying". Tell the truth!".

She she blasted her voice was so loud she needed no microphone.

Paul was use to this that's how he met her. He cheered her on the bus cheered her on.

"No need to tell the neighbour what you had for dinner".

"How you slept in your bed".

"Which child of yours is bad".

"Which one is slow".

"No that's too much information".

"Now your neighbour will be judging you and your child".

"Here come her dumb son now". "Oh is the bad one this'.

"People will put their mouth in your life!".

"Keep quiet!"

"Asking your child all kind of nonsense".

"Making him or her feel and act stupid".

"Now you want them to stop and you started it".

"Keep your own secrets, your family dirt".

"Nobody asking you to lie".

"Ain't nobody asking you tell false stories about yourself because you want to compete".

"Because you want look bigger and better".

"Stop buying thing out of your budgets".

"Things you cannot afford'.

"Save for a rainy day".

"Stop showing hatred and show forgiveness."

"Don't be caught up in people's hearsay and gossip".

"See and play blind hear and play deaf".

(Proverb 21:23)

She was touching on some people corns because she was speaking to their core.

"Repent!". She cried.

She went off into spirit and she chased away demons.

The passengers could feel the atmosphere changing. She was good and firm and she was no play play Christian.

She called out his name. "JESUS!!" And broke every chain that bound them the passengers.

She came hack to her seat and Paul raised the hymnal

"Trust in the lord with all of thine heart and lean not to thy own understanding".

His voice so soothing the perfect ending to a powerful sermon.

She prayed for his interview to go well. She even asked the bus to pray.

"She is hearing from God".

One lady just shouted out and started weeping.

Her truth was among those said.

Having a huge credit card bill because she was competing with her neighbour.

Others started to weep too and she went the through and prayed for them.

She invited them to Church.
For God is calling them for his ministry.

If this lady can buy things on credit she can bring people home to christ.

She has good faith.

The spirit lead her.
And she followed.

They came to a close, a preacher and a singer.

The bus went on the driver too felt blessed.

People gave her money hugs and she blessed them.

They got to work and the boss assigned to their secretaries. Two bosses wanted to be assigned to her. One because she was new and two because she has a glowing recommendation.

When she met Mr. MCKEAN she knew it was him. But also he notice she was different. Her approach her mannerism. He saw that she was a lady not someone he could make office jokes with. And then touched and buy lunch and this may explain why last three secretaries went home on maternity leave.

But she was pleasant and the clients seemed to like her.

Paul was a little nervous for her and she for him.

But they had God by their sides.

"Hello".
Paul text her.

"will you join me for lunch just under the big mango tree?".

"I bought something you like and l have sometimes to tell you".

"I can't wait".

She texted back smiling.

Chapter 36

'How to make it work

Mr. McKean had already tried different approach to get her to submit to his kind of office management but Heather did not fall for not even one of them.

He was also her head interviewer and he gave her two hours in what they call 'the hot seat' to see if she could serve the Jamaican import and export customers on a front line basis.

She did exceptionally well and now he wants her to answer more questions.

"So you don't drink or go to parties what you do for fun Ms. Johnson?".

He asked her.

"I attend Church event and mingle with my fellow Church people".

"So If we are having a staff party here you won't attend".

"Most definitely I will but I won't go over the limit because of my faith". "I will try and make myself as flexible as possible but my faith is my covenant".

"OK I understand".

He said.

"I am please to tell you got the job!".
Congratulations.

He stood up to shake her hand. she knows that when someone is greeting you. You should stand and meet the greetings.

Her clothing was perfect because was not revealing too much or covering herself up. Just moderate and light jewelry.
She don't want to come off as flashy or conceited.

She was more anxious to go meet Paul. She was grateful to God for the opportunity.

She read through the policies and procedures and she was happy with the pay rate. And there was room for upward mobility.

Paul was ganged in an interview by the same heads of management.

He did exceptionally well. He only stumbled on the question. Whether or not he could cover some night shifts.

"I can try and filled as many as those as I can but I don't have a ride at the moment I am working on that". He answered.

That was a good answer it showed interest, willingness and commitment.
It showed he had fighting spirit and will rise to any occasion if and when he has been called upon.

At the Church pastor got word that Heather was working at the wharf. He immediately called Mr. MCKEAN a longtime associate of his.

"This call is about Heather Johnson".

"Sorry for my forwardness".

He said realizing he had not called Mr. MCKEAN in a while.

To be upfront only when he needs a favor.

"What can I do for you?"

Mr. MCKEAN asked him.

With his loud thunderous voice.

"I don't think it's a good idea having Ms. Johnson on your staff".

He quickly added.

"Why is that?". Mr. MCKEAN inquired.

"She is not fit for that type of industry".

The pastor said trying to paint a picture as if she was antisocial, uptight and a goody goody two shoe.

'I have interviewed her", "tested her and she is more than fit". "The clients love her".

"I guess you had interest in her?".

Mr MCKEAN dropped the bomb on him.

Well she's on my payroll now".
He kind of showed off.

"She is a great lady pastor". he advised the pastor". "I am getting to respect her and it's only her first day.

He sipped on his big cup of black coffee as the steam escaped on his face.

MR. MCKEAN was a tall man of great built. Light skinned and weighed closes to 280 lbs. He was not fat just stout. Neither was he at all that bad. He was just not comfortable with love anymore.

Because he had being wronged before. He too somewhat like Paul had a wife and business was fine. He couldn't find enough time for her though. And the Gardener had time.

He sure reaped what he sowed when Mr. MCKEAN'S wife could not take their third child home to their place of residence.

Simply because he was not the father.

A big nasty divorce followed and she cashed in. Because the kids were young. And the gardener went with her.

Now they live in Redhills. A nice place, payed for and all that good stuff. But again you reap what you sow. The gardener was now cheating on her.

People react to situations differently instead becoming a womanizer. MR. MCKEAN could have simple give himself enough time to get over his misfortune. Do some therapy or seek God as his refuge.

Now he too has a string of ladies and a few kids that he has to take care of under the title sugar daddy.

But how long will he hold this title or how many more girls does he need before he can heal from his emptiness?.

The emotions he is afraid to express is killing him inside. The hurt, it has consumed him.

He sees Heather as the type of wife he would have wanted. No he cannot try to be with her.

It won't work and he has found a high level of respect for her.

"Pastor I don't think it's your right to interfere with Heather's job".

"Based on her personal information sheet she has kids to feed".

"She has chosen not to sit and wait for handouts.

"She has taken her responsibilities seriously".

"A woman or man like that deserves a job pastor I know you would agree".

"She will not be dismissed even only If she wants to."

Pastor again hushed his voice.

"OK McKean point taken".

Pastor closed and hang up.

(Ephesians 6:11-12)

Lunch time came around and Paul met up with Heather. By the beam on each of their faces. It was hard to tell If they were happy to see each other or they had both got the job.

She shouted out first.

"I got it!". "I got the job!"

She raced into his arms. He held her with his strong muscles and swept her off the ground.

Their smiles were contagious.

"I knew you got it please tell me you did?" She said.

"I got it!".

He yelled.

"Let's give god thanks".
She encouraged him.

As they prayed together.

After prayer her showed her what he bought for lunch.

It was a nice tuna sandwich with whole wheat bread. A nice garden salad on the side.

He sat the area up like a small picnic.

"I have something for you". He said.

He knelt down on one knee.

"I know we are still trying to get to know each other".
Already I adore you."

He said.
His voice was like an archestra of pure soulful music to her ears.

"Your have sparked so much fire in me and I can't wait to do this officially".

"But would you accept this friendship ring?".

"As a token of my friendship and desire to make you the only woman I think of?.".

"Until you allow me the right to a more formal proposal?".
(1 Corinthians 13:4-5)

When he was finished she was in tears her heart had moved from Galaxies to glaciers.

"Yes! yes!" she cried out.

As he put the single band on her finger. Made from a set.

"Paul this look costly!".

She said still crying.

"Your expensive, more precious than rubies". "You're rear". "And to keep you is my goal". He replied.
(Proverbs 3:15)

As he hugged her. Her tears came and he wiped each drop away.

"I promise you next time it will be the real thing".

His eyes were sincere and his words painted the picture she had been hoping far.

And yet he was patient, humbled and she can't seem to stop crying.

He kissed her cheek.

Chapter 37

The four Seasons

For everything there is a season, for every time it's moment for every moment it's memory for every memory it's love. joy, laughter and even pain. For these moments have made you who are. Don't ever forget them. But don't dwell on them. The will pull at you but don't look back. Like Lot's wife.

(Genesis 19:15-26; Luke 17:29-33).

Because your one day more experienced than you were yesterday. Make each day counts either your earning some honest cash or you're learning something new (Ephesians 5:16).

Don't limit yourself, crawl, walk run hump out of the box. And explore be wise and seek things that peak your interest. Look for friends with values and not friends you need. Because she drives she is your friend. But you can't stand her attitude and she don't pay back her debts.
(Matthew 23:13)

Let me stop there before I tell on somebody.
Heather wrote in her book as she edited her sermon for the women's conference.

Heather has never been proposed and serenade in any form of way. Some people will want to take the bad memories of the hard life they have had and just open the window of their mind and tossed them out".

But she knew this was apart of her journey. She was in training.

Sometimes you can't get to your true potential until your back is slapped against the wall. When you have no one to hold onto and your so call friends let you down.

That's when you know your own strength because God is with you.

That little voice you hear in your head that says:

"Don't give up".

"Take the chance".

That's your lord and guide. You don't have to be a Christian hear him. You just have to have faith enough to believe in him.

Today Heather believes even more than she had ever believed in her life.

"Heather"? Paul said raising her head up off his shoulder.

"You have to eat". As he fed her with the sandwich.

She was an emotional wreck because he had wormed his way into her heart and now she was love struck.

She just don't want to run to alter either. She don't want an unfit wedding.

For sure she has had her winters- when her heart wanted to curl up and die. When depression, anxiety and loneliness took her for a stroll.

How many people has her heart for an emotional joy ride.

And yet it to just one man (God) to come into her heart and first showed her heavenly love.

Opening up her life to summer days and now Paul had came along and put the light of day in her summer. Know all she know are sunshine days. Just moments ago he wiped her tears away.

Her autumn has come it's time for renewal regrowth. The sprouting of new roots.

But the devil is not done yet.

While she began to eat her lunch accompanied by Paul who is more like the caretaker than the husband to be.

Her phone rang out it was the pastor. They both looked at it. On the bench that was provided for the workers break.

She didn't want to answer it.

Paul said.

"I will answer it".

"I don't want any trouble!".

Heather insisted. But she was too late Paul had already grabbed the phone.

"Hello Pastor".

He answered.

"Why you took Heather to that dumb to work?".

"eh"?.

"Is that the ambition you have for her?".

He blasted Paul because he was mad that Paul picked up the call in the first place.

"It's better than having no ambition for her".

Paul nailed him to his self righteous cross.

"Can I speak with Heather?".

Pastor demanded.

"She is having lunch Pastor.

"Sorry we are having lunch."

He could see pastor face how it's bent out its usual shining and fake smile that he hide behind and manipulate people so as to get what he wants.

"Pastor I will have her call you back"

"Is it's important?".

Paul asked him.

"No that's fine'.

The pastor hang and was in a angry and bitter mood.

He can't seem to find any colours in the wind that will stop Heather's progress. Because she has had her testing and she was climbing at God's speed.

She never missed his calls because she was always listening.

"You're such a fighter Paul!".

She Said to him.

She wanted to say she was proud but she didn't want to boost him.

"I won't just roll over and die Heather".

"This man is trying to make you weak!".

"He wants you to submit to him!".

"Who do he think he is?".

Paul asked openly.

"Paul he is just one of the Devils play toy".

"In time God will set him straight".

Heather said.

Paul was not having it.

"Every turn you turn is this pastor!".

She could tell that Paul was getting upset.

She held his hands gently.

"Paul in time it will work itself out". She tried to soft talk him.

"Do you think god don't know the path will be filled with troubles?".

"The moment you start to do right all the bad just blow up like a tornado".

She continues. A little more alert and with meaning.

"You just have to know how to control them".

"You take the more serious problems first". "That is making sure you're right with God". Then he will take care of rest".

"Though I walk through the valley of the shadow of death I will fear no evil for God is with me".

She asked Paul to repeat it and he did.

Already he was feeling better or was it the touch she gave him?.

He felt more comfortable for if she is content he is content. It's like the Ruth and Naomi.

"I think I need to talk to him?"

Paul said in his upset tone.

"Because if he doesn't get the right warnings he won't know when to stop!"

'Heather this not just about the way I feel about you".

"It has to do with all those other women that may have been under the same oppression from pastor".

"Yes he runs a nice Church but he is not a nice guy".

"Give him time".

Heather said.

Paul looked at her.
But something in her eyes told her that Paul would not listen.

They resumed work.

And the cheers came on from the guys.

They whistle and made a mock bridal party and jeered paul.

'Here comes the bride'

The factory workers sing. Teasing his outdoor picnic lunch.

That was their way of welcoming him as their new manager.

After work they boarded the bus together. She fell asleep on his shoulder.
He stroke her gently and watched her as she slept.

He walked her home and told he was going to fresh up and came back.

Another fifteen minutes later he was at the Church face to face with the pastor.

Chapter 38

A conflict of interest

"Good Evening Pastor".

Paul approached him.

He was busy putting some tithes and offering envelope in and along the pews.
(Luke 6:38)

The benches were elaborately shined and his demeanor the moment he saw Paul fell like a jelly coconut form the tallest tree.

"Good Evening how can I help you?".

The pastor said in a condescending tone.

"Yes you can".

Paul answered.

"You can start by leaving Heather alone!".

"What's your deal with her". "where she works who she sees and even what happens at her house?".

"So you come fight me!?".

The pastor declared on basis of assumption.

"I wish I could have said yes to that".

"Being a non Christian as your classification suggests"."

"But the good person that I am and the respect that should be shown to man of your age"

Paul paused. He looked at his fist and then looked at the pastor.

He continued.

"Which categorical you to don't fit the bill of someone who earned my respect".

He spoke like this because all this time pastor had undermined him.

Little did he know that Paul may not hold a degree but he reads a lot.

Paul continued to put him in his dark cage that he belonged

"But my good soul will not allow me to lay a hand on you".

Pastor tired to interrupted like he had always done with everyone else. Covering the topic and seeing only his views. But Paul was no soft soap.

"I am still speaking!".

Paul said loud enough to send a voice of control to the pastor.
Who once thought he was only the one who could raise his voice.

"You're not worth my fist pastor".

"You should be ashamed for calling yourself a man of God".

Paul crushed his spirit and reduce him to pure dust.

"And now you're judging me?".

The pastor said trying to gain footing in the heated furnace he created for himself.

"We have interest in the same woman Paul". "Be a man about it".

"I have had eyes on Heather since she entered this Church". "I tried all I could and still I can't get with her in a comfortable way".

Pastor said using his sad tone.

"The sign is clear you're not the man for her".

Paul laced him again. with his powerful killer words.

"I think a man of your calabra. Should take what the Lord has provided for you".

They were walking toward each other.
Pastor face flushed with anguish.
Paul eyes said determination and he won't let Heather name go dishonored.

"You just have to admit that you lost this one Pastor".

Paul said just flexing his muscles in a calm body stretch. As they met face to face in the middle. Paul was talking hard like he was about to set off a warfare.

"Why don't you stick to the wife you marry"

(Titus 1:6)

"And stop creating havoc in other people's lives?".

Paul asked him.

His words were harsh and bitter.

"My wife and I have not slept in the same bed for almost three months now".

The pastor replied still holding his satire tone.

"Too bad go home and fix it".
Paul said

(Matthew 22:19)

"Because if you call Heather again or give her any hard time whatsoever".

"I won't be talking pastor".
.
Paul stared him in the eyes and made sure his words sank in.

"I can have you arrested for threatening me!".

The pastor lashed out.

"That's not a threat did I say what I was going to do to you?".

Paul asked him.

He did not answer.

"A threat is when I say I am going to do A or B to you".

"You should know that aren't you the high priest".

"I may not be baptised or have the biblical theoretical background that you have pastor".

"But I am one hundred percent sure that in the eyes of God I am far more a better man than you would ever dream to be!".

The pastor was stunned. Could of wet his pants too. If it wasn't for shame and Paul telling him the truth to face made him want to just forget his position and start a fight.

"If you ever let Heather feel anyway or form", less than that delicate Orchid that's she is".

"You will answer to me".

"Yes".
Paul said and shaking his head.

He wanted this to soak in.
Like bread dipped in hot black tea.

"And you will have to Answer to God who is the highest judge".

"Shame on you Pastor!".

"And If you need more to think about".

"Let her show you her ring".

"I won't say nothing else have a great day pastor".

Pastor and his wife has not been in the same bed for performance reason. The age has nothing to do with it.

He usually take care of his responsibility. But lately he has been may be due to his spike in other activities that may not include his wife.

He was feeling youthful again. And for a person's point of view he was acting way out of line both on a human and spiritual scale.

As for his wife she was not bearing her weight in the relationship. As lovely as she looked, well on Sundays when she is all dressed up that is.

But on a random day or evening rather she is in a maxi night gown. With her head tied up. Looking like a Eskimo and the weather forecast predicted snow.

This cause the pastor to lose interest in the bedroom getaway.

Now he seems to be getting out of hand. Yet she can't seem to identify the problem.

Some spice is needed on her part. Age is nothing but a number. Eat healthy Exercise and keep a healthy stress free mind. End result? A happy relationship.

Now she wants to spend money on therapist or marriage specialist. When she is not doling up herself and make herself marketable to her husband.

She needed to be more spontaneous and jump out of the box like the last chapter suggests and make him. Want to stay home because he won't know what's coming next with all the surprises she can pull off around the house to keep this bird caged.

Religion doesn't limit one's relationship activities once your wed. It's considered private what one do in his or her bedroom. But a little safe fun can't hurt a healthy relationship that is supported by both partner.

Heather was still pondering where Paul was.

The girls saw the ring.

"Big things a happen for you though mommy!".

Natanya shout out. After their usual giggles and whispers.

Of course her glow and constant singing and humming alerted them to her new mood and bling.

"Mommy a diamond?".

Natanya asked her.

It's a friendship ring". Heather responded.

"I am not sure".

she said as the girls look at it.

It's beautiful mommy they said as they took turns hugging and congratulating her.

"I wanna be more than friends".

Peter song out pretending it was just a verse from a song.

Paul was just about to leave the Church when the office door burst open.

and it was Janice coming from the pastor office.

"I was waiting for you pastor".

She said.
Fixing up her blouse.

(Matthew 3:32)

Chapter 39

Break-Even

"Janice wait in the office I said".
The pastor instructed her.

But she saw Paul and she had a liking for him the from the first time they met.

"Oh why didn't you tell me that you had this handsome gentleman as a guest".

She said fixing herself back to a neat sharp look.

Again the attention for the Pastor had dropped and Paul was her new focus.

Paul knew exactly what was going on.

"Hi Paul" she said smilingly.

She almost ran up to him.

"Hi'.

He said in a calm tone.

Just enough to let her know. He wasn't into her advancement.

She retreated.
And stood where she had reached.

She saw is countenance was not appealing to her liking.

"Just remember".

"what I said pastor'.

Paul said as he was about to open the door to leave.

"You're still here?".

The pastor lashed out showing authority because he saw Janice.

She saw him as this mighty big man.

"Yes I am still here and I see what your have been upto".

"But I hope you tell Janice that she is not the only one you're after".

"And that maybe she will hit your refusal list soon".

"What is he talking about?".

Janice yelled.
Pretending she didn't have a clue.

"You missed a button Janice".

Paul pointed out.

"I hope that's all you're missing"
He gave an half smile. Before saying.

"Let me leave you two to what you do best".

He went out the door and pastor came rushing behind him.

"This is not what it look like".

"Paul".

The pastor called out to him like they are best of friends.

"Please I will leave Heather alone if you promise not to say anything"

"Please Paul your a good man".

"No am not I am a sinner", "who works at a dump". "Who can't get to know a Church lady because I am not worthy".

Paul gave him a dose of his own venom.

"You tried to show me up at Church by asking me to speak but God was with me".

"I don't want a deal from you go and 'Repent'".

"For its only a matter of time before your fantasy world comes crashing in on you"

"Paul I will leave her alone just please don't mention this to anyone".

Paul wanted to just (lol) laugh out loud but.

But he was looking as pastor pleading a (OMG) Oh My God moment.

"I don't have to say a word". Just take a look where you're doing all this misery". "In the house of God".

"What's done in the dark will come to light Pastor".

'Wake up you're in darkness Paul cautioned him".

"Paul I know I can trust you".

The pastor tried to manipulate paul.

"No you can't because first person I meet going down the road I am telling them".

"And I hope they have lots friends so they can tell them too".

Paul tore his manipulation card to pieces.

Pastor was looking hopeless like he had lost everything.

"This is a good time to write a lust and fornication sermon mmm pastor".

Paul jeered him.

"However I have to leave because Heather and the kids are waiting for me to come and sit at the head of the dinner table".

He nailed him again.

Pastor looked down. His words barely came out.

"Paul please don't say anything".

"I promise I will not bother her".

"And I won't listen when her landlord bring up stuff about her".

Talked about omg moments. Pastor had just confessed that landlady Rita was in fact his informant.

Now Paul had a full reason to to confront her as well or maybe she will want to give Heather notice. He held the thought.

"Pastor you're wrapped up in so much confusion that you don't even know yourself".

(1 Timothy 4:12)

"I don't even have to tell anyone about your business".

"Because soon by your own tongue it will be selling on the shelves like hot bread".

"You are a false prophet!". Paul lashed out.

And pastor was so enraged that he struck a blow at paul.

Paul moved out of the way.
And the Pastor weight tapped on one side and he fell.

Hitting the floor, hard.

Janice heard the tumbling sound and ran outside.

Only to see pastor on the ground and Paul standing over him.

"What happened?".

She yelled as she raced over to help the pastor.

Paul reached out his hand to help him up.

The pastor created the most dramatic seen.

"Get away from me!".

"He pushed me!".
He pointed at Paul.

"He punched me!".

The pastor yelled.

Now he is passing on the blame to Paul putting him in the hot seat.

"I didn't touch you man!".

"You're liar".

Paul defended himself.

"You came to my Church and you beat me!".

"All because I said you can't date Heather!".

The pastor said stumbling to his feet with the help of Janice.

"You're a devil!".

The pastor yelled at him.

Hoping he would get mad enough and punch him for real so Janice could bear witness.

"I am going to have him arrested".

Pastor yelled and threw tantrums and balls of fire like he does when he goes on the pulpit.

"I am calling the police Janice you stay there so you can say what you saw".

He commanded her.

"Pastor I am not afraid of the police I did not touch you".

"You swung at me and you fell".

Paul said calmly hoping the pastor would come to his senses.

The pastor called the police.
And then of course, Heather.

"Why did you send your boyfriend up here to come and beat me up heather?"

"What did I ever do to you?"

"He struck me to the ground".
The pastor sad sounding so poor in spirit on the phone.

"Luckily Janice was here to help me up".

Heather heart skipped beats and beads of sweat formed on her forehead.

"Pastor I don't believe this?".

"Oh so you too are calling me a liar like your future husband did".

"You took his ring didn't you?".

He forgot Janice was there and she was showing jealousy over Heather.

"You wanted nothing to do with me but you took his ring!".

Janice began to walk off.

"Janice hold on"

Pastor shouted.

'What's Janice doing there?".

Heather asked.

Trying to make sense of this whole situation.

"I will call you back".
Pastor said.

In the meantime Paul was calling heather.

He finally got through.

"Heather it's a lie!".

Paul cautioned her.

"What have done Paul?".

"I told you leave it to god".

"Paul if you touched that man you're wrong and I won't be dragged into it!".

Heather screamed.
Because she was really trying to avoid trouble.

"Heather I did not touch him?".

Paul said calmly.

"I am coming over there right now!".

Heather said.

The pastor was trying to keep Janice at bay now.

She thought she was the only one he cared about.

Like he told her.

"You're more beautiful than all the girls who come to this Church your Pastor's little pet".

Now she was not so sure and she was heading over to his house to unveil his deeds and the coach bag he bought her on the Church budget.

She sped off in her car.

What's in the darkness must comes to light.

(Luke 8:17)

No Matter how good people are at faking the truth just take a little more time than anything else.

But when it comes out it's a snowball effect. It keeps rolling from one person you have lied to and then to the next. Making a train of distrust, doubt and ultimately dismissal.

You have lost a good friend, a husband, a family member or a even a parent.

Bewise if something is not working out. Look at the options to get out of it.

"Then get out".

Don't hide and make yourself happy. Because if one has to go outside to fulfill a inside need. Then they are living in the wrong household and with the wrong person, partner or whatever it maybe.

To survive you need total happiness, for sure it will rain sometimes. That's when you will need someone to help you hold up your umbrella.

The police and Heather arrived at the sametime.

Paul just sat inside the church yard. After he has prayed that God would expose the pastor for who he really his.

Still he prayed for mercy on the pastors soul.

(Micah 7:18)

Then Janice returned with the Pastor's wife in her car.

Chapter 40

Dirty little secrets

Officer Riley and a new recruit were doing the investigation.

"Pastor you said Mr. Phillips assaulted you?".

"Yes he did because I caught him and that lady Janice kissing".

"And I said no not on my compound".

"He attacked me and beat me to the ground".

"Look I can barely move this arm".

Pastor showed his bruises from the fall.

"Did you witness this?".

The officer asked Janice

"No I was inside and they both were out here right over there". she pointed.

Heather tried to hear Paul's story. They were separated by the officers in a bid to get the individual stories and fish out the liar.

"Paul I told to leave it alone".

She said talking calmly to him.

"Heather I talked but I never touched him".

"This what he wants to get rid of you and it seems you're walking right into his traps".

"I came out of the Church and saw the pastor on the ground officer but I never saw this man do a thing to him".

Janice spoke the truth.

While eyeing Paul hoping this may gain her some attention from him.

Anything else you wanted to add?".

The young officer said as he make notes of what she was saying.

"I have been seeing the pastor the last three months", "behind his Wife back and he bought me gifts". "Today I found out he has been seeing other ladies in the Church".

She said in a remorseful tone.

"What?".

The Young officer asked as if he never heard such a thing.

"The pastor?".
(1 John 4:1)

"No man this want doctor phil".

Young officer Chase said scratching his head.

As the Pastor's wife stood there with the tears decorating her face. She knew something was wrong but not this wrong.

"I was going over the Church purchases and found out that he bought three coach bags and I only got one".

Janice added to her report.

The pastor was then asked to give his report but by then people were gathering in the front of the Church yard.

Being it was not so much a residential neighbourhood. People love to engage in other people's gossips.

This was not healthy.
Because it only make things more complicated even for the law enforcement team. It is distracting and can lead to more harm than good.

That's how most people become victims of police brutality and stray bullets. Half the people who get hurt have no relation to the incident being investigated.

But as our Jamaican culture puts it.
"Cockroach nuh business inna fowl fight"
The aim is to stay away if it's that serious it will make the news.
No need to go join the we want justice cry. Unless you're one of the moms who collects the blood money from your wrongdoing son. Or the girlfriend or sister who washes the blood stained clothes of the man who robs and kills to maintain you.

Don't you ever think his time will come?".
Then you're going block the roads to get attention because he had never done a bad thing in his life.

There is a saying the up holder is worse than the doer.

Walk away from situation like these.

"Let's take this inside".
Officer Riley said.

"Because I think you want your privacy right pastor?".

For sure pastor didn't want to have his dirty little secrets aired in public.

Paul the accused and Heather were on side of the room.

The pastor and his wife and Janice were at the other side.

Officer Riley sat in the middle where there was a huge chair luxurious in its design. It was Pastor's chair.

"I am not god". Officer Riley said

"But I want to hear your stories sniff through them and see if I can arrive at the truth".

"For there is someone lying here today and there is going to be hell to pay".

"Because I have criminals to catch and here the place that should pray for and stare our nation is fighting".

"He is not a Christian".

The pastor throw out showing up Paul as the troublemaker.

"Be quiet Pastor". The officer warned him.

"Now did you are did not date Ms. Janice here?"

Officer Riley pointed to Janice.

The pastor was trembling. His wife was right beside him. His heart pounding and his breath could stop any moment now.

"Answer the question".

The young officer commanded him

"We are friends in christ". "That's all".

The pastor mumbled.

"Take the stand Ms. Janice and tell us what's your relationship with the defendant.

"He said he is my big daddy". He Co-pay for my car and bought me other gifts'.

"Last summer we went to Florida together and went on a five day boat cruise".

She took the credit card receipt from her bag the young officer collected them and handed them over to the Officer Riley who was judging the proceedings.

"Objection!".

"That's a lie".
"We both paid our fare separately".

The pastor shouted out.

"Overruled!".
Noted the presiding Officer.

"Let the record show that pastor had lied this is your first count pastor".

"The receipt show your signature matching the one here in this bible".

"Is this your bible pastor the office asked him?".

He held his head down.
His upset wife nudged him.

"The officer is talking to you".

"Yes it is"

He answered.

"Paul did you hit this man or not?".
Officer Riley continued.

"No I did not".

"He swung at me lost his balance and fell".

Paul answered confidently.

"That's a lie!".

Pastor yelled.

"Can I ask a few questions?".

Paul said.

"Yes sure come to the center". The officer invited him.

"Pastor which hand did I struck you with?".

"Your right hand".

"The one with the ring on it".
Pastor said pointing to paul arm.

Paul almost laughed.

"Let the record show that I am left handed".
Paul said.

"I would never hit with my right arm. I can but it's not enough to struck a man to the ground".

"When you fell did I offer to help you up?".

"You only did that because you heard Janice coming".

"Thought you said Paul and Janice were together let me quote ".

Officer Riley said.

"You said they were kissing"

"That's a lie".

Janice added.

"I am not sure the fall may have affected my memory."

Pastor said angrily.

"Why would I help the enemy up?".

Paul put in nicely.

Heather watched him as he defended himself. He was very diplomatic and the truth speak out through his calmness.

"Heather how many times have this man called you?".

Paul asked.

Opening another can of worms to bury the pastor six foot deep.

"At least once a day".
Heather said.

"What do you think his intentions are?".

"To start more than a friendship".

Heather added.

"Did you ever told him no?".

"Yes several times".

"Did you ever called Heather's job and asked her boss to let her go pastor?".

Paul asked him.

MR. MCKEAN had related this to Paul and told him to be careful.

"Can the court see your cell phone pastor".

"No!".

"That's private!".
He announced.

"Show your phone".

His wife demanded as tears backed up in her eyes like a riverbank about to overflow it's banks.

He barely struggled to get his phone from his inside vest pocket.

"I see you kept it safe pastor".

Paul said.

The young officer collected it and handed it to the preceding officer.

Paul walked back and forth like a lawyer who has being on the winning end of every case.

He knew this was going to be strike two for the pastor.

"So We are checking you calls to heather and McKean at the wharf?".

"Is that correct pastor?".

Paul raised his voice so that the pastor knows he's a liar.

"Perfect matched".
Officer Riley concluded.

":So did call Mr. MCKEAN and asked him to fire Heather".

Heather looked across at him with pure disgust.

"Yes I did!".

The pastor said getting irritated

"I called to have her fired because I want to be the one to take care of her".

"I love her"

He said as his wife smack him in the head and task the wedding ring in his face.

(Galatians 5: 15-26)
"Disgusting!".

She shouted at him and walked out slamming the door so hard. The vase on the welcome table fell and smashed to pieces.

"Did Paul hit you Pastor?".

The presiding Officer asked.

"No he did not or I just can't remember".

The pastor said feeling ashamed.

(Psalm 52:3)

"Well let the record show that the first answer was "no".

"Pastor have you done, like multiple choice questions".

"You know if you shade two answers the computer automatically picks the first answer as the right one".

"So now pastor your liar!".
(Proverb 10:9)

"You will be charged for mischief".

"I don't know what your Church will do with you".

Officer Riley concluded.

"I am not God but if I were God. You wouldn't be pastor of any church".

"Lets wrapped up that notebook". "Young officer Chase".

"This case is closed".

"Pastor meet us at the station".
"We don't want to make a scene". "You can pay a fine or do the time".

"Whatever you do just leave Ms. Heather and Paul alone!".

By this time Janice was well in conversation with the young officer Chase.

"I like your uniform".

She said as he walked her out to her car.

The crowd outside shouted

"False prophet, must go!"

"Wolf in sheep's clothing!".

As the pastor went to his car the police had to disperse the crowd who was ready to attack and bring him to their own justice.

He drove out escorted by the police. Shame was a understatement of how he felt.

Then other church sisters started making complains to his wife or his soon to be ex-wife.

Chapter 41

Love is coming at you

The dignitaries of the Church were informed about Pastor's action and the most Godly and and righteous thing to do was to contact Heather.

The head Archbishop himself apologized to her and said if she wanted to withdrew her membership he would understand. But they knew Heather was a strong person.

They knew that she didn't give up easily.

"I am so sorry Evangelist Johnson".

"I don't know what got into the pastor".

"Let us know if there is anything we can do to make you feel better".

"Also your bishop told us about your awesome work for the lord".

"And how you have been humbled and show strong faith throughout your adversities".

"If there is anything at all please let us know".

"You're truly a woman of God and we are happy to have your expertise as a member of our decision making team going forward"

"I don't know what to say".

Heather said blushing.

"Just say yes Ms. Johnson".

"We won't take no for an answer".
The Archbishop said

"It's ok let me think about it".
Heather said.

Take all the time you need ms. Johnson and we are sending a cheque in the mail for you.
Treats yourself and your kids.

"God bless your heart".

He said as he hangup.

Heather was sitting next to paul on the couch and they can't seem to stop. Staring into each other's eyes.

Then he blushed and then she blushed.

(Corinthians 13: 4-8)

"Heather".

He said to her.

"Did you believe I hit the Pastor?".

"It's possible".
She she joked.

"Because I know you would fight for my honor".
She replied with a smile that could start world peace.

"Because you're the woman I have been dreaming of.
He said. With a smile that carried deep and raw emotions of love and affection.

"There is this management get together at the Knutsford Court hotel".

"Would you do me the honour of being my date?".

(1 Corinthians 7:3)

"Why don't you go and asked Janice!".

She teased him.

He laughed out loud.

"What?".

He said. Playing along.

But Heather was just pulling his leg to see how he would react.
Now he was tickling her side because he realized she was shy when he did that.

The kids were asleep or so they thought because the Malcolm boys are still not giving up on her daughters.

The texting and calling has been low key. But they sure do connect. And one of the twins was thinking of going all the way with her boyfriend.

As for Peter Ms. Jennings is back on her medication. She had calm down quite a bit.

And he was liking her now for who she really is, well dispute the obsessiveness of course.

He too was thinking since mom and Paul are now in a happy place. He too should go out on a limb and find his own happiness.
Let's review their last conversation.

Ms. Jennings: 'Hi handsome".

she texted him.

Peter: "Hey gorgeous lady. What are you up to".

Ms. "Jennings: I am grading papers".

Peter: "Do you need help?".

Ms. Jennings: "Sure but not with grading papers'. "Lol".

Peter: "Lol what's that?'.

He asked playing fool to catch wise.

Ms. Jennings: "you know what time it is lol?".

Peter: "Yeah it's almost 8pm lol".

Ms. Jennings: "I am going to spank you'.

Peter; "Yes teacher".

Ms. Jennings; "I will pick you up at 9pm".

Peter ok: "Let me make up a getaway plan".

Peter came out in the living room just after Paul had chased Heather around for his keys that she was keeping hostage until he agreed to sleep over on her couch.

Heather come on. I need a good sleep. OK sleep in my bed and I will sleep on the couch she teased him.

"I don't have change of clothes". He laughed

"Then bring a bag next time she toyed with him.

"OK I will give you two more hours of my time".

"Then I am going to start charging if you demand more".

"OK how much per hour?".

She messed with him again.

"I don't know maybe I can give you myself for free'.

He held her and stared in her eyes. Letting her lose all train of thoughts. Her mind buffed like a old 95 windows computer software.

But she held it together before her feet got weak and she felt like surrendering her all to him.

"So you're coming with me to this Gala".

He asked her.

"What if I said no?".

She touched his masculine face and admired his eyes. They look like they contained magic.

As he looked Into hers and saw a future of splendor; white picket fences, green lawn. And a least a two year child calling out for daddy.

They lock in, almost close enough for a kiss and then they heard Peter coming.

"Sorry to disturb you guys'.

Well this was good moment for Peter anyhow.

"I need to return this book to my classmate Davion".

He said.

"How long will it take?".

Heather asked.

"Less than an hour I think".

Paul replied.

Paul looked at him and could read his countenance.

"Be safe Peter".

Paul said.

As he rushed out the door seizing the opportunity.

He had to meet her at mall as usual.
He took the roller blades she bought him.

He was a good skater as well.

When he arrived she has just pulled up.

"You change your car".
He asked her.

"Yes I needed a jeep".
"Bigger more room".

"Mmm"

"It's nice'
He added looking around.

As she reached over and kissed him.

She drove out to the Port Royal Area. A secluded spot. They had been there before only this time.

They went all the way.

Paul eventual left after a game of
of friendly dominos.

He hugged at the steps where the moonlight cast down a dazzling glow that lit her eyes.

She leaned into him.

"I am going to miss you'
She said.

"I am going to miss you more"

He replied.

Before they knew it. There was a effortless kiss.

The stars twinkled like they never did before.

As he walked home his heart was happy and for Heather hers was about to explode.

She realized Peter had not been back yet and she called him no answer.

Peter had just put himself in a web. Most teenagers will do this. It's the thrills. of being a teen and the mind is not fully developed and if they are not educated about sex, love and relationships. Then that's where we have a problem.

It's not a taboo topic anymore. You love your children and want the best for them. Talk to them. Be open and have decision. Don't only punish then when they are wrong. Guide them.

(2 Timothy 3:15)

There is no such thing as a bad child. But there are misguided children. Who make decision without thinking because they have not had the platform from an adult point of view to express themselves. You think about what you want for your child. But have you ever asked your child what they want for themselves?.

And figure out how you can help them achieve this?.

(Proverb 22:6)

Chapter 42

Be a man about it

Heather called a few more times and still he did not pick up. Peter did not pick up.

Her prayers have painted the walls red. This time he would be safe and he would have a good explanation.

For sure tonight he may be surprised by her more than any other night in her life.

She was thinking of talking to him. But she had done that what like two times already.

It was close to 10pm and she had work the following Morning at 7am.

Paul was keeping her company via text and calls.

"Don't worry he will be home safe".
Paul said.
Being a voice of comfort

"But at least he should have answered your calls".

Peter was ok, sure enough. As Ms. Jennings drove to Halfway Tree and bought him KFC and showered him with other gifts she had bought the day before.

She is sort of playing the this for that game. Peter was too blind to see it.

He was hoping to take it home and share it with his family.

But time lapsed a bit and two hours had passed since he left home.

Heather check the time like every half hour.

The sounds of gunshots rang out and her heart dropped.

But somewhere in her subconscious and her faith in God she hoped it wasn't Peter.

Due to the war between rival gangs lately the community was not a play haven for kids and the working class anymore. It's either you get off the streets before 10pm or be caught up in the in a war affair.

Ten minutes after Paul had hang up with her. She heard a rumbling at the door.

A little scared at first, then she quoted The Lord Prayer.

She called out for Peter three times but there was no answer. The looked through the keyhole. Just to see him walking into the yard with the KFC bag in the his hand.

She left the door unlocked and sat on the couch and waited for him.

He arrived. Looking quite himself. New headset "beats" a small bag marked Levi jeans, a new jeans pants she was assuming it was.

"Where are you coming from this hour of the night Peter?".

She asked getting up and standing to face him. He was taller than her she had to practically look up in her face.

"I called you and you never answered".

Her anger was building Like a car merging on a highway.

She raised her hand to slap him. But when she looked at him she saw herself at sixteen doing the same things that he has done. Finding love in all the wrong places.

She felt like her hand was held by a higher power. And the prayer she prayed earlier had well been answered.

(Genesis 33:5)

She prayed for her kids safety, for them to realize that she only wants the best for them. But at the same time they are rules that they must follow. In order to stay alive, to prosper to avoid the same struggles she went through.

Her hand fell in the form of a hug instead.

"Peter what can I do to help you".

(Psalm 113:9)

She asked him. Tears just flooded her face and she can't help to know that she love him and won't be able to go on
If she lost him. He watched her face and his conscience almost choked him like bad cough.

"Where did get these things from Peter?".
She asked him almost stamping her feet. She knew the beats were expensive, she have seen the ads.

"Where did you get these". she asked him in a calmer tone. Undoing the hug and pointing on the bags.

"Don't even think of lying to me". She scolded him. As he held his head down.

"Hold you head up Peter and speak so the world can hear you. Never look down", "defend yourself". She told him.

"Ms. Jennings mommy".

He answered knowing in a time like now she could just see through him.

He felt like there is was fire lit beside him. And wonder why he can't seem to tell a lie.

"I won't tell not take them". She said wiping her tears.

"If that's the kind of man I raised you to be". "Then the shame would not be yours'. It would have been on me".

"The kind of man who seek out the weak and needy and prey upon them".

"Or maybe it's the other way around". "Maybe it's because I was still growing when I had you". "Maybe that's where the mistakes came him". "Because my date were like a way to food on the tables."

"Maybe you think I was too drunk to remember. "But I do."

"I was just hoping you will be able to forgive me for not having enough time to give you enough love then". "Now you seek love in older women".
"I am sorry."

"I love you son". She said looking in his eyes.

Making him want to undo all the wrong he has ever done.

"I am sorry too mom". He said.

"I do remember the days when we didn't have nothing to eat and it was only cucumber and salt"

He said hugging her and crying.

"I am just confuse mother".
He said

"Trapped with grown up emotions in childhood dream".
Trying to save someone". "When I myself is In need of saving". He teared up and hugged her.

"You have to think of yourself first". "The moment a new youngster come along she is going to go after them".

In fact Heather is right this not the first time that Ms. Jennings is going out with a youngster.

Only Peter showed more interest and he is not demanding for much.

"Peter you have to know what you want son". She sat him down and counseled him. Giving him the opportunity to ask and answer questions.

(Matthew 21;15)

He told her because he was failing English language that's when Ms. Jennings offered to help and things sprung from there.

"I can help you with English". She informed him.

"I thought you were only good with business subjects?".

He uttered.

"I never told you this but I was offered a government scholarship in English when I fell with you".

He laughed and repeated the word fell. "Mommy sound like you know your stuff then man".

"OK all I am asking is that you return all these gifts tell her you can be friends but you don't want the complication".

"Peter your job right now is to learn all you can to be a better person". "So you don't have suffer like me". "So your kids don't have limitations to things". Like how you guys are limited.

"You think I don't want to buy you beats earphones or Jordans or any meal you want to eat?. "But I can't afford it now".

"Don't be caught up in greed it can lead to stealing. She coached him.

"Learn more about the bible, hold your head up for your sake and mine. Don't disappointed me or yourself.

She sent him for his English language book and proceeded to help him.

They came to a nice compromise that he would avoid Ms. Jennings otherwise Heather would come to see the principal and even the entire school board.

The next Morning she greeted Paul in a decadent office dress and a nice sophisticated blazer.

She looked so well.

He was looking sharp too
In a dark brown shirt and a khaki pants and a nice tie.

"Good morning manager".
she held his hands

. "Good Morning Angel".

He responded.

They hugged and waited for the bus.

They talked about the gala that was coming up on the weekend.

He can't wait because there is a fire in his system and he needs to get her for himself. Forever.

Generally teens who date older persons are looking for love, financial or emotional gains. There might be a missing link at home. The absence of one parent or some physiological issue. Though it can stem form peer pressure as well but the basis still take on one of the issues mentioned above.

Talk with your teens see where their heads are at and how you can help them make the right decisions. Sometimes one hurt can cause a lifetime of misery. Keep loving and guiding our children.

(Psalm 8:2)

Chapter 43

'What I need from you is understanding"

The girls were left to attend school under the supervision of peter.

Who was a drill Sergeant whenever he was in charge.

He rattled on their door and woke them up.

"School let's go let's go!!"

The girls kissed the teeth and act up, just not directly in front of him.

He runs a tight shift.

"Justin come eat this hurry up". He told him".

As he brushed his hair and put some lotion as his face.

The girls were fighting over the washroom. As if it was the latest addition to the house.

"First come first serve Peter shouted out.

As he stood in the passage to ensure they comply.

Then Natanya got in and there was peace.

Natasha was simply having another bad day she wanted to see her boyfriend.

The little texting was not enough and she was planning to meet him after school.

Though Natanya had cautioned her about the staying out with him and the storm that Heather may kick up if she found out.

"Natanya I have to see him today."

"Stop try to tell me what to do!".

"We already plan this".

"We are just twins you're not my mother".
Natasha was getting upset.

"I want Peter hear you and tell mommy you see"

Natanya said.

"Him act like him not going on him with things too".

A close to angry Natasha replied.

"You don't see the KFC bag on the table".

"Him a go hard man".

Natasha said.
Trying to justify her 4pm plan.

"Listen you're on your own you hear that".

"Because if mommy work 7am to 3pm". "The woman must reach home by 4:15 the latest".

"So when she ask me for you i will just tell her you gone with your boyfriend!".

"You wouldn't do that to me man".

Natasha said

"Okay you will see".

"A jealous you jealous because Trenton slow.

"Him not making the big move like Trent"."

"Power to the big twins".

Natasha showed off shaking herself doing the latest dance moves.

"Yeah man chicken merry hawk deh near"

Natanya told her.

"You sound like mommy".

"A freedom time now."
Natasha said

"I don't see why I should old up myself".

"Is what get in your head?".

"Just try make when school over I can find you at the busstop".

Natanya told her.

"Well if I am not there consider that I have a ride home"

"You too hot" Natanya told her as they headed out the door for school.

After school Natasha did go about her business leaving her sister to trod home alone.

She was cloaked up with Trent in the his parents lexus Suv. This was a again unknown to them.

Loads of teenage and some adult stuff happened.

"Just know you're the only girl for me". "You're beautiful and there is no one like you".

"You have my heart anyone else they are just renting baby".

"I want to marry you and we grow old together".

A few of the things Trent told Natasha to get her to submit to his request. He manipulated her young brain.

She gave in.

She was dropped off around 4:4 4pm while he played some Jay-Z music in the van.

A few of the Heather's church people say her getting out of the car at the mall. The music was blaring and the attention was undeniable.

Heather got a call with regards to this after she had lunch with her favorite guy. Paul.

Heather brought lunch today. Some mashed potatoes and brown stew chicken and mix vegetable. For drink she had some tang with ginger a good solution for the scorching summer sun.

Food she had saved from the previous dinner.

"Mmm" Paul said

"Tasty it's true that the food taste better the day after".

"He added.

He could just look in her eyes and see that she cared about him. They shared almost everything together.

"You fit in just right he said to her. In my life at work your the real deal".

He blush was a rainbow and it coloured her face.

"Thanks you're quite the man yourself so charming, ambitious and caring.

Women like a man who is self driven who wants to go somewhere in life. Same for the man if his wife is busy with work that will motivate him to find work as well if he is a real man.

"All I ever wanted from you was understanding but you meet and exceed that".

"Now I feel like I could just float in the air". 'With you as the wing beneath my wings".

When is the next baptism he asked her.

"The next one is three months away what are you thinking".

She asked him.

"Thinking maybe I will just a give my life to lord".

"What's else is there in the world I have done it all". "I am open and willing to give him a try"

"I am very happy for that."
She said blushing.

He was blushing too.
I hope it has nothing to do with me she light up.

"It has everything to do with you. "I think god made you for me"

Paul told her with his sweet charming voice.

This decorated her evening. With a bright white sky with golden horses. Her mind went for a ride.

Her smile was an Oscar winning one. If the had such a category.

"You're making me seem so powerful". He answered with a smile that could power an electric train.

"I will am definitely up for the date to the Gala".

She said.
Finally confirming.

As they finished up lunch under the same tree every day at the same time. The vibe was so right. You could take a picture of the atmosphere and and two hearts looped together will appear.

After work it was the usual routine they went home together.

When she got home Natasha was not there.

She asked her other siblings to if they had any idea where she was but nothing sounded promising because she had received the call about what the Church sisters had witness. Another bit of shame on her path.

She wanted to at least assessed the situation. But no Natasha.

She finally came returned home at 5pm.

After she got dropped off she went to see a friend. To do some home work.

Heather checked her books and she had some homework done for sure.

But in Heather's mind and spirit something else was wrong.
She was no longer shining like the little diamond she was.

What did you do today Heather asked her.

She rambled on about school and everything else.

"What did you today?".

Heather asked her again.

She forgot that she can't lie to heather anyway.

"Who dropped you off at the mall".

Heather dropped the bomb on her.

Oh it was a teacher.

Heather shook her like she wanted to take the truth out her mouth.

Heather then told her to stand in a corner holding one foot and one ears with opposite hands.

That's lasted for almost an hour.
Before she started to cry and volunteered to tell the truth.

She did not go into details but Heather had a mental picture of what took place.

Come with me Heather said we are going to the station.

She was hesitant.
He is much older than you Heather said with her eyes filled with tears.

She was hoping someone had enough sense to be safe about the act.

The shame that she felt was like a truck load of wet sand stop and unloaded unto her back.

At the station Heather had a conversation with Natasha.

Was it safe she said yes.
"Why did you need to do this?".

I don't know mommy she said with her head held down.

"Can't you see he is taking advantage of you."

"He said he love me".

"When you want something don't you lie Natasha?".

"Just like you are doing now?".

"Boys lie Natasha boys think about the here and now". "Good men think about the future".

Heather was firm and would not show any ounce of pity toward the Malcolm boys well with Trent per say. She had have it with them and Natasha oh boy Heather was going keep a leash on her.

Things were beginning to stabilize at the home so she didn't see the need for this.

Teens are curious yes. But without proper guidance things can go way out of control.
She should have to face this now.
And God knows she talked to them. If Natanya can heed to the warnings why can't Natasha?.

(Proverbs 22:6)

Natasha is having this larger than life personality. Based on what Trent was telling her.
Marriage, money, Love, and together forever all the good stuff.

She was thinking by committing herself to him this would have made her the number one his chart. But if there are other numbers on his chart. What is she doing there anyways?.

"When last you read the bible?".
Heather asked her.

(Ephesians 6:4)

She was yet to respond.

She likes the attention. She thinks she doesn't get enough at home. It's been awhile since she heard she was beautiful. It's been awhile since she felt loved.

Girls generally mature faster than boys physically, physiologically and mentally.

Their first love should be their father and way he governs them will direct them to the kind man or what a man should be like in their life. Without that a step dad an uncle or a big brother with all the good qualities may fill the cap. Or she will move on to next guy who appeared to be responsible and have stuff that makes life easier for her. Like a car, home or business. Because ladies like men who are in control. Hence woman or submissive beings once all the elements are in place.

Natasha idolized Trent and see all these things in him.

But he just putting on the show. His mind too his young. He is not fully developed to know exactly what he really wanted. He is just being a teenager. But he should at least find someone in his age group. Well then again girls is age or looking for someone in authority. Well not all because if children are raised right then all the elements may come into play perfectly. They make a full mistakes but finally they will get it together.

Children who feel their parent(s) are too aggressive towards them. Will find outlets to heal. They may start running away. Or keel the wrong kind of friends. If they think it's a happy home to come home to where they get hugs and kisses and get told that they beautiful, special, loved. Instead of you weren't planned. Your unwanted. You are a bad seed. The black sheep of the family. If one child is given more love and attention than the other. Simply because his or her dad provides for the family. Then watch this child action. Pure rebellion. And even for years to come unless the circumstances changes. You will have a child who will carry emotional baggage for years to come and it may alter their productivity. Also watch what we do or say around our children. Children live what they learn. What kind of examples are you setting?.

(Deuteranomy 6:4-10)

She liked to experiment. Dare herself. But it's not even a full day after and she was already in trouble.

More so that she forgot to put the phone on silent and it went off.

This triggered a few slaps from Heather and the phone was handed into the police as evidence.

(Proverbs 13:24)

"Did he force you?".

Officer Riley asked her.

Chapter 44

How deep is your love

How Heather felt was beyond devastating. Her mood a sorrowful river that was stagnant.

Disappointed. She felt powerless as a parent.

(Romans 5:6)

She was feeling as if she didn't want to take away someone else's child's future. But justice must be served. She can't sit and watch older people manipulate her children.
What kind of examples would she be setting.

(Deuteranomy 1:28)

Yes, it's an unjust world but either you use the methods given to you are lay down and die.
With God's grace Heather won't let that happen.

Natasha said that they were safe about it.
That's another load off her shoulders.

Now she is working on the preventative methods. Though she knew she can't stop it but she can try to show Natasha the pros and cons of this pleasure and pain world that she was about to embark up on.

Soon after the report was made officer Chase and a few officers from a neighboring station went to find Trent.

"This is not going to be a talking to situation".

Officer Riley made it clear to Natasha and Heather.

"She is underage". "You Heather may need to take a parenting class and well as your self Natasha may need to do some therapy". "Here is a councillor's information. You can't miss any dates".

"Will he go to jail?". Natasha asked.

"Possibly it depends".

"You said you consented but still you're underage". Officer Riley layout.

She started to cry.

"But we love each other". "He is my boyfriend".

"You need friends your age Natasha and you don't have complicate things by having a boyfriend now".

"You have so many years for that".

Heather told her.

(Jousha 1:6)

"Mom can you just drop the charges".

"Once it's reported Natasha it can't change".

"He will do this again and again until someone stops him".

"Natasha this not his first time".

Officer Riley told her.

"Just a few months ago we had a similar incident". "I can't go in details but just so you know you're not the only love of his life".

"These older men (boys) will say anything to get with a younger girl". "For some of them it's a thrill". "A count down".

Then they are those who are immature and want to be with someone in the same mind frame.

Chances are that those who have kids especially a daughter and still date young girls are not effective father's. But if the role should be reversed then there might be a fight.

These again are boys not men. Boys who wasn't raised right.

Those who don't know the value of a woman beyond her beauty and good shape and sex appeal.

Some thinks is because they are handsome and rich they can buy love and having the hottest freshest girls. In their minds this make them stand out, it empowers their manhood.

It's is purely psychological.

The truth is they lack confidence to stand up to a real woman who will make them look small.

In this day and age women may wonder why they can't find a stable minded or a serious man who goes beyond physical attractions. One with a goals, ambition and ability to love and not cheat.

The maturity level will stop all this.

It's a predator's world in the undeveloped minds. It's a hit and run until they are hungry again.

But then they are the few good ones. Who are hard to find because she looked past him because he is a cleaner, security guard a rubbish truck driver.

Then she wonders why am I so unlucky.

Behind most people with financial gains and good looks is a undeveloped mind. It could be the ability to gain but not keep or love because they think of everything as material easy come easy go.

Material don't need emotional connections. They are there to serve a need. Once the need is satisfied then the case is closed.

They maybe able to impress younger people with a materialistic mind, emotional setbacks and those with financial difficulties.

Natasha was crying hard like she was about to lose herself.

"OK"
Mr. Riley said

"Let me prove something to you but you have to put the phone on speaker".

"Call him" Mr. Riley said.

She dialed his number. It rang to voicemail.

"Try again". He said.

Then Trent finally pick up.

"Hi"
She said.

Mr. Riley was coaching her. "Can I see you later?"

She asked him.

"I am busy now maybe I will call you later when I am free".

He just hang up no goodbye or nothing.

"See?". Officer Riley said.

"How would he have acted in the past", "before this happened?'.

"He would have ran to see me"

She said feeling used.

Now she got a part of the picture.

She felt so violated but her mother was there and she hugged her and comforted her. Mother are Always there.
The good ones are.

Paul came rushing into the station.

"Heather I heard you where here is everything alright?'.

'Yes I am ok it's Natasha".

Natasha ran into his arms and hugged him.

Feeling the love of a father (a man) who cared.

"It's ok Natasha you will be ok we will get through this together".

The words from his lips acted like therapy to her aching heart.

"We will find him!".

Officer Riley concluded.

"When are you two getting married".

He said. Looking under his glasses

Just out the blues and put a smile on Heather's face. Just as they bid their goodbyes.

"Soon".

Paul said as heather walked away.

"And you will be invited".

At home things started out slowly and everyone riding on the mood. Until Heather burst out in worship and prayer.

"Lord I come to you again because there is no other help I know".

"Let the devil take his flight away from my home and leave my family alone".

"I bind all evil forces great and small".

"Let my kids be able to be satisfied with what I can give them".

"Lord take away greed, impatience and impure thoughts from their minds.

"Lord let them look and come to you because all other roads leads to destruction".

"Lord let them be strong enough to avoid peer pressure".

"Lord grant them wisdom and understanding".

"Watch over everyone in this house help me to be an advocate for your ministry".

"Bring Paul to your throne of grace and bring all these kids home to you and wipe every tear drop from our eyes".

She went off into unknown tongues.

"In your name I leave all my troubles'. "Amen".

The house never felt so at peace like the demons had got the eviction notice and they all left.

Leaving Heather and her family at peace at least for now.

"That was powerful a prayer"

Paul said. Wiping her sweat.

"You should be a pastor". He said to her.

"The Church may not be ready for a female Pastor yet".
She added.

"Any thing god sets on you". "He will make it happen". He said to her.

He embraced her. As the kids stood around and she touched each of their foreheads.

And quoted.

"Salvation belongs to the Lord". "Your blessing is upon thy people Selah!"(Psalms 3:8).

Chapter 45

How to control the home

Things calm down in the house and dinner began. Well Paul started it.

Heather made a final speech.

"Anything in this house given to you kids that I did not buy please return it".

"You all are going satisfy with what I can afford".

"What we can afford". Paul pushed his head in from the kitchen area.

"OK' Heather almost smiled what we can afford.

"If anyone want to have a special friend I need to meet the special friend and their parents".

Heather said.

Again Paul butted in again "we need to meet them".

The kids liked it well that Paul keep saying we not only is it funny. But it makes the deal much easier to buy into. A little cheap psychology. Well not so cheap, because at the same time he was pulling Heather into a little soft web. Making their liking for each other more formal.

She smiled as the kids giggled.

'Mommy are going to marry Paul?".

Natanya asked just like was in a different mindset.

"I don't know maybe when you all settle down and stop giving one trouble after a next".

"Then l can try and life a little".

She said.

But she was making them look at the facts at how she has been dragged from one extreme to the next and still she holds on. Knowing that God holds her hand.

Knowing the body heals faster than your mind. That when you get a cut and it heals and maybe if the make disappears your mind will always remember where the cut was.

Similarly your kids will remember good morals that you have thought them.

Like sitting and talking over things with your kids. Forgiving and moving on. (Luke 17:4).

"Mommy I am sorry I never listen to you and now I feel bad".

Natasha said going back to subbing.

Her sister hugged her and spoke.

"People do make mistake Natasha".

"But are you just going just sit there and say I made a mistake or you're going to use it as a landmark and try and think and do better next time".

Natanya is on the right track because number of persons use the blame it on someone else game. They never did anything yet or it's never their fault and so the mistake is not theirs and so they never learn from it and so they keep making it again and again until it becomes habitable like lateness are smoking are giving up on your goals are letting what people have to say hurt you so bad you want to give up. It because you don't know yourself. Are it's simply because you don't know God or you don't believe when he said;

"No Weapon Formed Against You Shall Prosper".

(Isaiah 54:17)

Heather continued.

"I am not asking you to live for me am asking you to keep out of trouble or just stay in the right lane".

"until you can drive your own lives".

"Right now I am responsible for all of you until at least 18 yrs old after that you will still be my kids".
"and I will help you where and when I can".

"Children all you need to do is to learn that's all for now is that's so hard".

"I may get mad at you at times it's called tough love".

"But I love each of and everyone of you".

"I may pay Justin more attention because he is younger and he has needs that no one else has"

"If you need more love Paul is right there".

"We are a team". "We are struggling because not everyone of us are team players".

"Peter I need some help here son".

Paul called out.

He went in the kitchen area to assist Paul.

He was trying to get Peter in the kitchen as well to learn to cook.
So he can be a man who can help himself.

"Just show some respect for the work I do for the lord". "Come to know him and you will see the difference he will make in your lives".

(Mark 12:30)

"So what rules you want change and why?"

The girls looked at each other.

"Mommy can you make it easier for us to come to you with stuff like personal problems?".

Natasha said timidly.

"Sometimes I feel afraid to approach you because I don't know what mood your in".

Natanya added.

"I can work on that But you if you don't step out line I don't have have any problems".

Heather responded.

No sooner her phone rang they caught Trent. He was at another girls house Alicia when a cop saw the van parked and called in the license plate.

"Can you bring your daughter to identify this the accused".

Head Officer Riley said over the phone.

"OK sir I will". Heather answered.

Again she walked back to the station Paul accompanied her.

Leaving Peter to tend to the cow foot in the pressure cooker and some seasoned rice.

When they got there. There three other girls. Two of them were friends and school mates of Natasha.

"What?".

Heather said when she saw the faces of the girls crying each of them don't want him to go to jail. But their parents saw things differently.

All three girls pointed him out as his parents and brother wept.

"Have mercy"

His father shouted out.

"Be quiet'

Officer Chase.
cautioned him.

Head Officer Riley spoke.

"Now this would not have gone so far if like I warned you parents about keeping your children safe especially the girls".

"And more so if you girls had listen to your parents".

"I hope your eyes are opened now and you will listen".

"We can put Trent away but we can't put your pain away".

"Only you can do that".

"By making sure you only act on your feelings when you know you're ready to deal with the consequences".

"I Hope you all take advantages of the counselling sessions".

Heather went over to the girls and the mothers and offered to pray for them.

She could see pain was reflective of her own and her daughter's.

The mother formed a little bond and exchanged numbers.
Heather too was ready to gain soul for the Lord's kingdom for the lord. This is an example of how you turn your pain into passion. If you find three people who are struggling in the same situation as you. Then you can reach

out to each other and find solutions are ways to deal with issue for a group a blog and help others.

The case was going to trial. Since the 7pm newscast parents have been calling in. Some the moral less ones want to make a deal for their daughters. Some just want to get some money from a sad and unhealthy situation. One mother view was that "they still kids and he shouldn't be charged". "Because the mothers left their girl children careless and that's what kids do".

Many callers on the program lashed out at her.

Stating that even though you may try and give kids all they want and leave yourself sometimes without. They will do what they want when you're not their.

You can only be civil with them, show them what will happen when things go too far.

The police officials said since he had been warned many times and have multiple charges. That he should be charged as an adult because the Jamaican law sees a child as anyone under age of 14 years. A minor is anyone under 17 years. So now that Trent is nearly 18 years old, life is real.

The days that followed were pressing and media tried to get Heather's view on the situation and making her story a little less private.

It's was lot of praying and reaching out to god for his help.
The family started to pray together more. God was watching over them.

The gala was few days away and she had just received the cheque in the mail from her church. She prayed before she opened it.

It was 20g cheque.
k. Her heart almost leaped.

She knew at least 15g will have to go her savings because she was practically living off her little savings and god bless Paul. This was actually her children saving if anything should happen or the just in case situation.
(Proverb 13:22)
Because she would have gone broke.

Just one more week from her payday. They money she got from her bus preaching she gave back as donations at Church.

And the pastor was buying ladies bag. She smiled at how God payed her back because he will never let the righteous go without bread. (Psalms 37:25)

Life was getting better she and Paul were getting closer.

Everyday lunch keep them talking and bonding and sharing ideas, thoughts and even little gifts like he made her favorite peanut porridge for lunch.

She will hide sandwiches in his work bag so he will be kept feed. Make natural juices and feed her family with high protein foods such as nuts, milk, eggs fish, vegetables and beans. Healthy family healthy minds.

"I want to take you shopping". Paul said.

"Why?".
She asked him.

"For your gala dress".

She smiled.

"I am making something".
she told him.

"You can sow?" He asked her.

"But I never saw you do that".
He said.

"Because I always make time for you".

She complimented that she liked his company.

OK he said thanks you.

You know how special that make me feel. He said.

"You're special Paul very special and sweet and smart and handsome and kind".

"And I love you".

She said.
Out loud from for the first time.

He felt afloat, his feet elevated off the ground.

He looked at her and she at him.

"Heather I love you too".

He said as his eyes and face showed off a certain glow and his smile just made her feel defenseless against his charm and is mere presence made her filled with completeness.

And they had a slow lip kiss and she felt the softness of his lips against hers.

The evening had came and gone. the sun played a game of hide behind the evening clouds.

And then the night came and passed. It's Saturday, the day of the Gala.

Chapter 46

Heart and Soul

When Paul saw Heather she made him tear up.

She was stunning.

"Oh I can't let her see this".

He said. He held back the tears.

She was singing the same tune.

"He looked so debonair".

His good friend Larry would drive then to the ball or sorry the gala.

They looked so red carpet-like.

Paul wore a black jacket suit with a white and grey inside shirt, sleeve cuffed face neatly shaved and outlined. Eyes sparkling and his smile a glimpse of his magical soul.

For Heather she wore a dress she designed herself.

White satin with grey and white lace piping the edges. She made a small train and when she walked she looked like a queen.

Her hair well made up by her daughter's.

Her eyes just dreamy and the flower that he brought her complimented them their natural beauty as couple.

They smelled and looked like hollywood. The kids watched and some nieghbours watched on.

"They look lovely".

Natanya Said.

Peter took a few pictures.
The they all joined in on a few. They looked like a nice family.

They were truly blessed to have each other.

(Matthew 5:3-16)

They arrived at the hotel and Larry opened the car door for them, like a chauffeur service.

They looked so fetching on each other arms. The air seemed to stood still as they walked and when all eyes behold them. They smiled and they had their pictures taken.

The dinner was delicious and the entertainment was a blissful outside taste to Heather's usually indoor pattern.

George Nooks performed. "Ride out your storm".
Then "I can't stop loving you".

Heather song along and so did paul.

They had such a great time together. Then Paul had to make a speech representing his department and work they did.

"Usually I would be shy to get up talk in front of a large group of people". "But when one person have become your world. It makes work easier".

"In our department we receive and transfer good to the other departments and ensure their quality quantity and follow appropriate procedures". "I work with twenty five other people to make this project work effectively". "And they all work hard".

"Let's hear a hand for them".

"Tonight is a very special night for me as well not only that I am proud to be the man manager of these loyal, hard workers. He paused.

"I found have the woman of dreams".

The crack came in his voice and softness of heart was visible.

Loud cheers came from his department

"You go paul". "It's about time"
"Come on!"

A few coworkers cheer him on.

"If I may I call Heather johnson to join me on stage".

Shocked she rose to her feet and ballroom lights hit her fancy dress as she walked gracefully to the stage.

She looked like royalty.

The cheers and whistle rang out loud.

As George Nooks serenade then with "Be my woman"

"Heather from the moment I saw you my heart chased after it's own beat".

"And from that day forward you
keep knocking me off my feet".

"I have fallen in love with your every move and now I can't breathe without you".

"Just like music you're my groove"

Whistles came from the audience.

"I want to be your man and your everything". "I just want to know if you will accept this my proposal ring".

He went down on knee and reached for her hand.

"Heather will you marry me?"

(Mark 10:9)

The moment was surreal. the audience held their breaths, the band stopped playing and her tears came and so did his and members of the audience.

She raced through her mind and couldn't find a moment that would have allowed her to say no.

"Yes!" "yes!".

She said and the audience cheered they had a wonderful after dance.

Form the music of Celine Dion "For I am your lady"

She can't help looking at her ring because it was a set and it was exceptionally gorgeous.

She clinged to his arms like flowers to vase and his smile never left his face.

The radio station had tune into the gala festivities and pastor heard a recorded version of the proposal he through the radio off the counter where he sat making an appeal for the Church not revoke his membership.

He was still learning day by day and god his still showing him mercy. He paid the fine and avoid jail time.

They fed each, other they danced, the talked. She was happy he was intoxicated with love, joy and still he was the perfect gentleman.

He walked her out to foyer where flowers were perfectly tendered to and small fountain trickled in the background.

"I want to marry you so bad he said to her".

"I am so weak".
she said.

"I am not".

Paul answered.

"For when you're weak I will be strong".

"Giving you the strength to carry on".

"I know you will do the same for me".

He told her.

"He made her feel to just fly away with him".

"I have never felt this way about someone before".
She told him.

Her lips so cute and he kissed her.

She kissed him too.

Then they stopped and thought "oh we are not married yet".

They both laughed when they explained to each other why they stopped the kiss.

Oh she have prayed for her prince charming to come along and the love of god answered.

(Psalms 103)

"Big wedding or small?". He asked her

"Medium is ok".

she responded. Showing her good business face that made him smile because he can tell if she totally agreed.

He held her hands and the talked and planned things out.

They relaxed in each other arms and let me moment seeped him because God has taken them this far.

Paul is now ready to take the vows to follow the lord.

But the Church needs a new leader and there is someone who is rising up against the person who God has designed for the job.

(Isaiah 59:19)

Chapter 47

The road to happiness

Paul was so happy and it radiated off Heather as well.

At work they are know as the Wife and husband even without the final weeding day.

"Where do get money to buy this expensive ring?".

Heather asked Paul.

"It's actually an upgrade I payed a little more on the one I had planned for the ex".

"Things went sour so I gave it to the best".

Heather was very content but she wasn't acting like she already owned Paul because this will make him feel closeted and this mirrors the way the marital relationship would be like.

After a proposal it good not to make the person feel overwhelmed by you. Just like a visa pass it can be revoked are short lived.

She have always made herself look beautiful and she kept him grounded well, they both kept each other grounded.

A couple months later the Church had decided to remove the pastor from front line duties until he completed his counseling sessions.

He wanted anyone but Heather to get the position of pastor. Because once she got that role. He knew she was so good that it may never need to be discussed for a reinstatement.

Now he has teamed up again with Rita and Mavis. And they are still plotting against her.

The decision is usually made by the Head of the board but they get the Church involved by putting in ballets on for each member's vote.

A large container was set up like a drum and the members cost their independent votes.

The committee will count the ballots. But Mavis was on the committee and her job was to hide most of Heather ballets so David could get the post.

Heather wasn't into that as much she was more concerned if God saw her fit for the path. The baptism was also coming up soon and she wanted to ensure Paul was ready mentally.

Also she was trying to see which of the kids she could convince to take a leap of faith and as a result inspire the others.

They have been doing a lot of talking and she knew Paul was man and and that things more faster in a man's mind.

"I hope you're good at waiting".

Heather said to paul.

"I have been waiting a while you don't hear me complaining?".

He joked at her knowing what she meant.

"Just checking".

She mentioned and made him smile.

"If it was for me alone I would be married tomorrow".

He said.

Chasing her around his garden the first time she came to visit his house.

She loved how everything was in place. He was neat and clean. His family pictures hang their on the wall. Happy days with his ex wife.

"Sorry he said I should have taken these down".

(Hebrews 13:4)

'That's OK no rush things take time".

She replied.

Heather was also sensitive about her status in his life. She sure wasn't expecting he still had his ex memories tagged to him.

But though she is not expecting him to drop all memories she was hoping it was just in his mind.

"I am sorry Heather".

He said holding on to her hands.

"I just forgot to remove them that's all".

He tried to comfort her.

As she walked to patio."

"I said it's ok".

She said sounding dry.

He wasn't sure how to take her answer and he went inside.

She stood outside on the patio. He slowly packed the pictures away.

If she was to be the head of his life.

Then he has close the door emotionally with his ex wife.

Chances one can easily get over the physical relationship after it's over. But emotionally it's harder. He may still be hang up on the good times they had together even the bad ones.

Heather may have had too many bad ones to be hang up on.

As time progress they will learn to live with each other's past. Putting things into perspective and mold together.

Some reasons why some couples don't reach the altar after a proposal.

He or she has been there before and knows what a damage divorce and even a Bad marriage can cause.

He or she may have lost interest because you stop taking care of yourself. No vivaciousness or glamor, charms or sparkle because you think you have won then over so you have stop the show.

(Corinthians 7: 3-5)

The actual show starts when you have got their interest. And you're sure that those little butterflies are real. You're not worried because you don't trust then or you believe they are hiding something those are red flags.

Timing though is everything. It takes time to see someone's true colours.

(Romans 14:1-23)

Paul gently held her and made sure she looked in his eyes and he told her he was sorry.

She looked him in the eyes and saw that he would not lie to her. That his feelings were in fact in here court and she could play them as long as she loved him.

It almost time for the new pastor to be announced.

They are casting their ballots at the Church hall. And though pastor was not allowed to participate he had his workers well assigned to make the victory fall into his hands.

(Romans 8:35)

Chapter 48

Trials are training

As soon as Paul had made her feel confident again.

Her phone rang it was Peter.

Justin was having a seizure it's been awhile since he had one of those.

Justin as a mild case of epilepsy.

She rushed out and Paul went with her.

When she got there he was on the floor with the pillow under his head like she taught them to do whenever this happens.

He was shaking and foaming from the mouth.

She has been aware of this since he was age three.

That when she developed extreme patience and motherly empathetic skills.

She saw that he would need more attention. His father slowly drift out of the picture.

Like most alpha males without understanding. He never said this out loud but it was obvious he didn't like weakness. Like most man who didn't want to represent a abnormal child. And that is just heartless. But God give those kids the best moms.

But no child or anyone is a weakness. Everything in life is for a reason. Everyone gets what he can afford. No one gets more than he can bear.

(I Corinthians 10:13)

From Jason's experience she has learnt how to care for someone to a point where she anticipate their needs and always pre plan ahead of time to make it easier on herself when crisis comes.

She knows if it happens in public that his information is written and attached to his bag.

She was hoping he had would have grown out of it.

His siblings watched on helpless they can only do so much and no more.

She just has to watch him and make sure he doesn't go into a unconscious state.

Sometimes she wished he has an outward deformity and not one she can't predict when it's going to happen.

For this reason she wanted to take up nursing. But she was waiting until the girls have acquired their cxc subjects and move on to work and upper six.

Paul saw the way she cared for him and can tell that's a real woman firstly and then a real mother. He can tell just by this that his sons will be cared for by her.

She need to seek out role models for him. Someone who have overcame or have accepted his/her challenges.

The first stage to deal with anything is accepting it for what it is.

Knowing that people will talk because they have to and that's what they do. If they are not productive.

Set small goals for your child to accomplish. Take them out on little adventures. Show them the happy part of the world sometimes.

She knows she has to be flexible and use common sense. He needs air to recover and they have already placed him on his side and Peter had timed the seizure. The usual 60 sec.

What Heather have done was great a support system for Justin each person is well aware of what to do incase this happens.

Now Paul is becoming aware of this part of his illness.

The main problem with most parents and particularly those with special needs kids. Is the constant worry that lead to anxiety and all the worst things are happening in their minds but not in reality.

As long as people who are administrated to your kids are informed about their health conditions then all is in good hands and god hands as well.

Make sure your child knows where to go and what to do in case of trouble.

Who to trust and who they go with and when.

Keep close contact with educators and doctors about your child's development.

Research and find ways to aid your child development. Don't limit your child's achievement and put him or her in a category. Teach them how to motivate themselves. Be mother and father or father and mother as much as you can if you're single.

All is important to your child is that you love them. They can go to bed hungry tonight because mommy and daddy loves them and they are taught that Jesus loves them.

Only special people get special task. Each will be repaid according to the work they did.

"You're so good at this Paul told her'. "I thought you were a nurse if I did know you well".

"A mother/father is everything when the time is right".

She answered him.

He is ok now she told him cleaning up the the area.

She preyed a small prayer and touched Justin's forehead.

(John 3:1-2)

In her love life too she was now happy for those trials of those bad exes. Who had fight, mistreated, misunderstood her and even those who abandon their responsibility. Where are they now?. She asked herself as God was talking her from pain to passion.

She is ready to have them see their kids anytime because there is so much growth that God had bless them with. For everything is a lesson in life and until you have learnt from your mistakes you will keep repeating them more miserable each time.

Now that she had found a good caring man who is willing to not only help her fight her battles. But he wants to love her and make her happy.

The following Sunday at Church the ballots were counted and Mavis did her job.

They were about to announce the the most favored person to to acquire the pictorial post was "David". Sister percent of the members shouted. "No way!". "what?"

The head bishop was in shock and ordered a recount. And a thorough investigation.
Because he had numbered each card inconspicuously and he notice the numbers were adding up in sequence.

(John 4:17)

But that not the only secret there was a camera in the room. That he ordered to be reviewed by the technicians.

The baptism is next Sunday and the Church needed the right pastor to dipped and replenished souls for the Lord's kingdom.

When the result should be heard and the wolves in sheep's clothing are revealed then they may be some firm disciplinary action.

Because it's easier for the camel to go through the eye of a needle than the rich, the unrighteous and a lair to enter heaven.

(Mark 10:25)

Chapter 49

Too close

Heather wasn't even aware that something like that would have happened to the ballots boxes.

She was thinking that this only happened in elections. And not in the Church.

The rumor had started by Janice that some ballots were missing and that the count may not be accurate.

Janice was still coming on to play and Heather was not liking it.

Because she knew that Paul had been on this waiting list. And men do have needs.

The last conversation they had about waiting.

Was when she help him to shave his face. He was shirtless and she made a comment.

"Very nice muscles".

Heather teased him.

"Well closed your eyes he teased back".

"Then how am I going to shave your face?"

She asked him.

"Well you have a point".
He said smilingly as he lathered her face with shaving cream and they played a little.

He kissed her and was a little bit more forward and that's when she cautioned him.

Janice with her happy go lucky self was a threat.

She wanted help with kitchen supplies to her car and she was delegating and directing Paul to help her with it.

She eyed him and waited till he was away from Heather and whispered to him.

"Can I borrow you for a second?".

she said was sure he was a easy stow away.

But he spoke out.

"How are you Janice?".

It was so profound it startled her. He kept no secrets.

Janice has gotten to realized for herself as people started staring at her and this made the situation awkward.

Not more awkward than being asked to wait while the bishops try and solve this case of the the missing ballots.

Now the technicians has reviewed the hidden camera, and have made a copy for the bishop and the other officials.

Will Mavis take the fall alone?.

They gathered everyone together. Eighty percent of the Church stayed behind to help or to see who was at fault. "Who cheated the game?".

The bishops and elderly as well as the deacons all watched the video slowly. Seeing four people entered the room with the ballot boxes.

They can tell Mavis apart because she was wearing red tie head. And her huge dress like she was a part of a cultural festival. The counting began and there she was stuffing ballots in her head dress and stomach. Being careful to make it look like a hitch or movement to ease into a relax position.

The bishop was levied. He trusted her. He thought she was honest and God fearing and was holding up the banner of christ.

He stormed out of his office and almost marched her in. Well he had the Janice called her to office first and then he lashed out on her.

"Who put you up to this Miss Mavis?". "Because this is just not your doing?".

She was quiet, head dropped and she didn't know what to say or who to say."

The other dignitaries watches on as he basically scolded her.

He drilled her

"I can do one of two things show the video to the entire church!".

"Or you can tell me who are you working for". "Or with".

She felt like a student who was about to face detention. She just can't tell her parents.

"We can give you a simple written warning and you can go for counseling".

(Matthew 6:15)

The head bishop continued.

Usually he would have been more humbled but today he was disgusted with all the little crooked things that goes on behind official's backs.

He wanted to make a fine example out of someone because if pastor was still behind this then is goose was cooked but only this time it was sunny side down.

He continued to lecture Mavis.

Who was rolling her fingers, one over the other. Like a cotton wheel. She was drenched in guilt.

"You see Miss. Mavis we don't want to chase anyone out of the church".

"We are hoping that these counseling sessions will help you or us forgive ourselves and forgive others."

(Matthew 6:14)

"See the true meaning of being right with God".

(Isaiah 53:6)

No body or no where in the writing of God it said people of faith don't make mistakes, don't keep hatred, malice. Be conceited and sometimes over really act. But it's the way we seek forgiveness for our sins. Our own confessions to him shall set you free.

"Miss Mavis for the last time who put you up to this?". He bellowed with his loud coarse voice. And made a 225 average weighed lady trembled.

She wasn't even worried about herself. It was the pastor that she was more concerned about.

If she would stop get those discount grocery cards. Or if she won't be able to get her own ham and sorrel this Christmas.

But will all eyes and ears tunes into her she better not lie. Or she better not be the only one playing this dangerous came.

She said it but not loud enough

"Say so that the others can hear you!"

It was the pastor she announced and a they audience began to talk among themselves saying they knew this would have been his work.

The bishop was so distraught he asked then to get the pastor right away.

The pastor who have voluntarily missed the
This Sundays service in a bid to hide his dirty dead.

What the bishop had in mind was to let him announce who the winner was. Then he had to explain why there was a discrepancy in the first place.

Heather had enough of Janice play for fame around Paul. She waited for her to enter the church kitchen area.
Then she approached her.

"If this is not the gorgeous Heather Johnson".

Janice gave out in a tone. That could be taken as your not yet married to him. So don't even think you own him.

"Soon to be Mrs. Phillips".

Heather highlighted her and flashed her ring.

I want you to take your eyes and plays off him".

She announced clear to Janice.

"You can't be serious Heather with your past", "thinking that a man like Paul will go through and marry you!".

(1 John 1:19)

She threw her psychology class work on Heather's mind to see if she can break her down.

But Heather had caught because just yesterday she had thought about how her past was always training her for moments like this.

That's easy Heather said.
Because he will be marrying me because my past as trained me well enough to keep him.

She was cooked up in her own stew.

But Heather was not done yet.

"What about your past janice?".

"I have never been married but you have".

Heather annoyed by digging up her past.

"You care to share any tips?".

Janice stood like an empty frame.

Then Paul came rushing in.

"Honey they are about to announce the winner the ballots have been recounted".

"Come on!".
He hugged her.

"I have been missing you".

He said.

She hugged him back and replied.

"I missed you too".

He hurried her along.

"Let's go pastor is about to speak".

Chapter 50

Tell it all

Pastor was almost forced upon the pulpit. Quite the reverse of his usual rampage and chanting after he would sprint up the magnificent stairs. Made of ceramic tiled flooring, huge large wall and fancy windows.

The house of the lord he has been pastor for close to thirteen years.

The curious faith seeking community hardly go to Church because he never comes out to greet them. To Share a word with them.

If you want to see pastor you had to go to the Church. There was a fee to sign documents if your not of his liking, faith or church. There is a fee for funerals more if the deceased was killed violently.

Some events were unrecorded in the journals and he wasn't very popular among the members and officials of the church.

His poor wife is trying to be strong and of good faith still go up to the house and cook for him and make sure he goes clean. As far as love is concerned she is having a hard time coming to grips with that.

She shunned his earlier advancement about two days ago. And since the young followers have heard of his latest scandal no one wants to play in his little dirty games anymore.

He final got to the microphone with all the elders and bishops and deacons behind him.

(Ephesians 4:30-33)

The choir had a song going.

They sang it low and meaningful. Smooth and their voices gelled together like butter on warm bread.

"For I have touched the helm of his garment and his blood made me whole". "Oh it his jesus". "Yes it's Jesus in my soul".

He appeared dazed. The choir went lower and slowly faded in the background.

"Church I am here to tell it all". "That I have tampered with the elections by asking someone to remove ballots from a certain name".

People gasped and awed.

One lady was having a prayer and worship moment. She shouted out for Jesus lord have mercy she yelled.

"Say the name!".

A member shouted out.

"HEATHER I am sorry for doing this to you".

"You're the new pastor of this church".

"I didn't want you to have this power but there is no man as great as God".

He started coughing. It sounded like he was having a moment of weakness. But no one has ever seen this man cry.
Not even his wife.

Because he too holds the doctrine that men should not show emotions.

He went on.

"I am so sorry every trap I set for you". "Against you and Paul because I was selfish and saw you as my own and wanted more than what you could offer".

(Colossians 3:8)

He was coughing more rapidly.

He was getting short of breath.

He tried to go on.

But his words became stutters.

He tried to hold on to the podium. Then the bishop came to his rescue.

"He is having a heart attack". He shouted.

As people tried to come to his rescue.

Heather was there and cleared the space for him to get fresh air.

They called the ambulance and his wife comforted him on the way to the hospital.

He went into a unconscious state. With all the odds stock up against him. He still saw Heather's face as he rendered first aid to him.

He was seeing a light and he was hoping this this was not his judgement day.

The Church in the meantime prayed for him and Heather read out the rest of his speech.

"For I have been less than a man of God when I first started to deceive". 'I found myself excited by material things, sexual immoral desires". "And I have accepted them and made them manifest through me".

"I had the thoughts, but it was my will that have acted upon on them". "For anyone that I have treated unfairly or unjustly", "I am sorry". "Please pray for my forgiveness and God is faithful and just to forgive me".

Heather ended and she asked the church to pray for him.

She introduced herself and made background checks on plans they can improve as a church.

"I didn't come prepared with a full sermon".

"But I come with words I am preparing for the women's conference this weekend".

"I hope with the Divine intervention of God I can bless your souls".

She prayed and began.

The fact that she had never said me or I. She kept referring to we. Made the church more leaned toward her leadership.

She has plans to make a class for married folks from which they can learn from each other. As well as the unmarried so they can make the transition into a happy marriage.

She noted that one of the leading cause of divorce is that people didn't take the time out to plant roots in their relationships. And when it rained. And soils were washed away they had nothing to stand on.

"Also greed and sense of entitlement can cause a lot of harm". "You belong to me. You can't go anywhere".

"Everything you have is mine".

Those words fuel faster divorces.

"Amen".

A lady gave out from the choir.

"No one is putting women just in the home".

"It should be co-parenting so the children can be balanced".

"Don't say it's a mother's or a father's job leaving it up to one person".

"Making it overwhelming and tiresome".

"Marriage will also lean to one side of the parents are family of a partner is too involved".

"Limit involvement in other people's lives and watch out for your relationship and the great inputers".

Finally she went on to say.

"I thank all those who have voted and believed in me".

"I give Paul a great deal thanks next to god he is a tower of strength.

She held the pulpit exposing her shining engagement ring.

"Pray for us as we mean well for each other in Jesus name".

"It's been a long day and we want to send you all home safely".

She prayed and dismissed the congregation.

She said as they listened to her articulation. They saw her poised and her ability to lead them to a better group of Christian people.

When she stood on the pulpit the light shone on her. It was like she was a gift from God the pulpit no longer looked darkened.

With so much on her mind. Justin being not well, work, Paul, the girls and the Malcolm case.

The fact that the previous pastor was in the hospital. She was praying for the strength to be the best leader of the flock.

(Hebrew 13:7)

All she needed now was to attend some pastoral studies to nipped this blessings under her belt.

They escorted her to her office where she would be working from as a pastor.

It's cozy but she needed to add her little touch to it. That's a ladies thing. Make it more personal. She smiled as Paul stood there behind her as she related to him the changes that she wanted.

"Congratulations". He said to her.

"You knew I would have gotten it all along she said to him".

She said smiling at him.

"What is yours it can't be for anyone else he encouraged her".

"Keep working hard and stay focus and pray and fight and struggle and you will survive Heather". "Because that's all God wants you to do survive and show off in his glory". "I am right here for you when you need me".

Paul said holding her hands.

But it was more like she was thankful and grateful for changes that have already come on the name of God.

I thank you Paul she said and rested her head on his shoulder.

Still this is only a landmark leading to where these two can go in God's grace.

(2 Corinthians 12 8:9)

Chapter 51

Working Together

Heather was fashionable dressed for her women's conference held at the conference center.

How she got this recommendation was from preaching on a bus. And her information was passed on to the local MP.

Paul had offered to take her to the conference. He had a little surprised for her well this is one of many.

Her dashing mint Green skirt suit embroidery with silver patterns and her matching big church hat. Her unique design.
Made her looked morning fresh.

He offered to meet her at the bus stop as usual.

She waited like five minutes and she did not see him. She had to take a couple hours off that Friday morning to deliver her speech.

Marlene had recommended she go and take up the challenge. Even though they have not seen each other often. Marlene knows that other things was occupying her time, like paul who honked a car horn across the street.

She was about to call him and make a little lover quarrel. Because she did not expect him to come in a car.

"Hello nice lady may I offer you a ride?".

He rode his window down and yelled to her.

His voice pulled her in and she looked again carefully.

He spun the car around and stopped at her feet.

He went around and opened the door for her.

There is a joke that says whenever a man does this for a woman either the car was new or the lady was new.

Today the car and Heather was new.

He had took it out with help of Larry and Mr. MCKEAN. Brand new Honda Accord.

Heather entered almost in shock or was it tears or maybe a little of both.

She smiled and reach over and kissed her cheek good morning.

"Where to Ms. Daisy?" He teased her.

"Paul". She said shocked.

"I like it". she smiled.

"It suits you well".

she rubbed her hand across his cheek. A blush came over his face.

"I got a huge discount because Mr. MCKEAN knew the dealer".

"Also Larry fix cars for them as well so it's a double discount".

"GOD Is truly AMAZING". She said.
As she emphasized on the words in capital.

"I love how progress you're Paul"

she hugged him.

"Behind every good man there is a good man".

"You're a good woman Heather he reminded her".

As he started the car and the new engine and smell fused together made it felt like a jet plane.

"You are going to learn to drive". He coached her.

"Definitely".

She answered as he open the sunroof and the wind toyed with theirs smiling faces just off the cement company road way.

She felt at ease and in the hands of a great man. She silently thank god for his mercies. Blessing and also for all the trials.

They got to the conference center which was not that far from work. He had to sign in and make sure his staffs were on the right track.

"I will be back before you start man".

He teased her.

"You know that I am your support". He told her.

She was about to speak from a biblical, theoretical, and spiritual point of view to ladies and gentlemen who are ministers of nations building and decision making of the Jamaican society.

A little nervous was all natural. But her prayer weighed tons for when she smiles. The natural allure of God's love comes from her heart and she never just smiled from her lips. Because where there is god there is love.

She watched him drove off and she knew she loved every ounce of him. He looked so dapper in a suit he wore to support her.

She went inside and looked around a little she has never been in this setting before.

The people seemed so sophisticated and over the top. Not so much in attitude but in status.

She ran through her speech then checked in with the receptionist.

She carried that Christian look as well that glow that make her stand out.

"You must be Heather". She said

"My how do you know?". Heather asked her shocked.

"Thou ought preceded by thy blessings".

The pleasant young lady told her.

"Bless you". Heather said.

"And all that you touch shall manifest and multiple".

Heather could see so much of the young lady in herself and wished she had heed to her calling sooner.

They opened with a nice cultural dance. Paul caught the end of it.

He held her hand as they sat through the proceedings.

She wasn't sure if she should go all gospel gangster on this crowded or to throw out point and knock each of them so hard that people would believed she knew their life story.

Paul had went ahead and made her some business card.

He put them in her handbag and she just manage to unravel the misery he wrote that was so unique and clever.

Heather Johnson-Phillips. Pastor, Councillor, Wife, mother and friend.

(Isaiah 40:31)

On the flip side it read.

"Life is a relay and when you get tired", "Jesus will take your boton". "He will not only take you to victory but sustain you and bless you".

"Only if you believe".

Her contact information was attached.

She almost teared up but she looked too gorgeous for christ today to spoil her glamour.

The moment she was introduced and walked on to the podium. Her present held them.

She began with her greetings.
She fired them up with her jokes of wanting to become the next female president of Jamaica.

She spoke of how she admired the female president (PM) love that like herself she came from humble beginnings.

"I stand among distinguished ladies and gentlemen only because we all distinguished by the creator". Made special for his purpose at this time at this moment.

"Many of you shoes I may not be able to fill in many capacities but with God all things are possible and all depths can be reached.

"Women today should uplift themselves and take the entire family with them". "Yes including the husband's".

"Don't take this as ruling the man of the house".

The audience laughed.

"But encourage them to talk more, bare their feelings and be support system for whatever they wish to do".

(1 Thessalonians 5:11)

The audience Clapped and cheered.

"She is good".

One minister said.

"Very good".

Said the other".

Her confidence soon settled and she gave it her all.

"As leaders of this great and striving nation".

"We need to help our younger generation by leaving the legacy of peace with them".

"Giving them skills will encourage work".

"The HEART TRUST and the National Youth Service have some vital programs that will help to foster this".

She went on.

"We need more infrastructures that looks after the nation children". Better motivators and music makers."

"Songs with clean motivating and uplifting music like Bob Marley real life music"

They cheered her on.

Paul watched her and felt proud.

"I won't take up the entire day I promise as the audience laughed and Clapped again".

On the subject of love.

"If we want a better world a better country".

"Then we have to show love".

"The peace we need all start from our homes".

"Teach each child to love the other".

"Teach then to say I'm sorry".

"Teach them how to forgive move and move on"

"There one great big book that everyone can learn from".

"Politicians", "mother's", "father's and even our generation to come".

She lifted up her bible.

And showed to swaying it around back and forth.

"The bible".

"Let it be our guide".

They Clapped her and some men whistled.

She met with a number of dignitaries and ministers. She felt very pleased with the work she did for the lord.

She polished it up well.

She handed out her cards and people wanted her to speak elsewhere.

Paul waited for her as he always did. Hugging, pushing and supporting her. She was doing the same for.

They had a great lunch.

She made a deal with a top merchant from the USA.
Mr. MCKEAN was happy with her progress.
For years they tried to get this Company to ship with them.

Thanks to heather they got it.

He wanted to reward her but he was thinking of what was sufficient enough.

(Colossians 3:23-24)

Chapter 52

Mindful thinking

Heather was glad she had so much bliss and life was looking better.

Her gift from Mr. MCKEAN. A pay increase and she is now a permanent staff. Leading up to a management role, if all goes well. She is now called the "client specialist".

She beamed like a ray of sunshine.

"Did you start your driving lessons yet?".

Mr. MCKEAN asked her as she was about to leave the office for the day.

"I will start this Tuesday sir". She answered. She was never on a first name basis with any of her bosses clients or work associates.

"Thanks for everything Mr. MCKEAN". "This is for you".

She handed him a gift bag.

After she left and he opened it. He found it to be the holy bible she also left a note.

"Read this book and god will be there for you always". Thanks for all your help.

She was hoping and praying that he would read it and god may touch his heart.

She realized that the kids weren't as rowdy as they use to be and they were starting to be more civil and the space was also getting too small.

Paul had invited her several time to move in. But she had a bigger goal as she discussed it with him.

"Let us try and get a bigger place that way everyone will be comfortable".

"Your boys can come over whenever they want and we can be a big family".

"Have you picked a date for the wedding yet? He asked her.

Just offering her a bunch of roses. A mix of red and yellow.

She couldn't help the big blush that fell on her face.

"I was thinking some time near the next three months".

she answered.

Sounds good he said.

But Paul wanted it a little bit sooner no pressure but he was feeling a bit depressed (sexually).

A feeling any human can understand but it should not be so readily on the mind that it overwhelms you.

It's almost been 6 months and still he remained on par.

"I know Paul".

She said admitting to the elephant in the scenario.

"Don't you think my mind is wired as a human too?".

She asked him.

"I know just a friendly reminder". He punched in.

She smiled.

Well it takes three days for a man to be ready mentally and physical for the closed bedroom activities. And usually when there is a great deal of chemistry then we could be looking great at more closed door per week.

Then one may ask what is chemistry?. It' don't have to be sexual. It's emotions that are build up over time. Her smile, feel and also those bonding moments and connection that's makes you want to see this person and can't get tired of seeing them.

Women are wired to go for a longer waiting period maybe a week or so.

For two people to wait for each other. Especially for a marriage to happen that's a commitment.

There are other things beside hopping in the bed. How about A movie A game, a date night.
Somethings like that.

Bet your going to argue that the closer you get to each other. The more intense. But the commitment to wait also proves if you are a good person or not and will help to make future decisions if the cheating issues should ever arise.

Everything is for a reason always remember this.

Many may say do it now or later if the person loves you they will stay. It's not so in general and more not according to the bible.

How to identify potential users or self pleasers?.

When the deal is always on their terms. No flexible whatsoever unless it involves them getting alone with you.

(Amos 3:3)

They generally say 'I did this' even when it was a joint effort.
Look at how they treat people who are not close to them.

They are usually very private about most things because they tend to overstate their accomplishments and lifestyle. Hence they are pretenders.

The constant need for intimacy and once it's over a call is placed to you days or weeks after with repetition in mind.

Their attitude, thou stem from behavior or mental disorders. Such as Trauma, hurt or some form of abuse or abandonment. These are just a few of the examples. It may be also that they have adopted the behavior and is making a trail of broken hearts.

(Proverbs 27:6)

A toxic relationship is never healthy. Where you have to face insults, belittling, manipulation and worst abuse. Physical or verbal.
It will reign on you for years. The best solution is to get out of the relationship.

Heather knew Paul was none of those persons. But she also has a religion to protect and a better futuristic relationship.

We all know the flesh is weak but faith is stronger.

He then drove off, on the way they did groceries together.

He was eating full time at her place now.
Tending to the kids and molding them.

Now Natanya wanted to introduce Trenton to the family as her special friend.

But is Heather ready base on the court battle?.

Trenton was a more pleasant boy than his brother. Most of his actions was just to please his brother. Like leader and follower. Now his brother is on house arrest and his hardly talking to anyone.

Because he believed his parents should have bought his way out of this one like they did for everything else.

But the saying is true that money has limits to what it can buy.

But he sure do love Natanya. And they won't give up on their young and contained relationship.

Chapter 53

The truth about love

"Love don't see physical only the eye does"."

Just as god don't matter about your hair", "face", "clothes or what you own".

"As a result of praising him and honoring him". "He will allow to live comfortable and give you peace of mind".

Paul was talking to friend Larry who was asking his approval about this new lady he was seeing.

Larry outgrew Paul by and inch or so. A slimmer built and a junior to paul by 3 years.

They sometimes confided in each other on a woman basis or general decisions.

"Yes man Paul encourage just come to Church even one Sunday".

The conversation involved Ann-Marie. She was a little new in town.

He showed her picture to Paul.

"She looks really good man"

Paul acknowledged.

He then left Larry place and drove back Heather's.

Where they had a talk with Natanya about this early love situation.

"Yes Netanya we understand that you like him".

"Not like mommy love!"." I love him".

"Lord Jesus have mercy".

Heather whispered under her breath.

"What are you doing in love at this age?".

Heather asked her".

"Mommy we have been texting and talking for almost a year now".

"He is not like his brother I promise you". Her eyes were filled with tears and Heather could see her heart beating.

"Natanya they travel a lot he may not even remain in Jamaica".

"He will mommy he said he won't go away unless we go together".

"I just want you to keep focus on your book Natanya".

"Did I tell you I got a promotion already and a raise?".

"The affectionate Natanya jumped and hugged her mother".

"I prayed for you mommy. "I read my bible and prayed".

"God is good". Natanya said.

But this didn't stop her debating that Heather should meet Trenton.

"Mommy he is kind", "patient," humble and he respects me.

Natanya that sounds deep Paul added. Before he was just listening.

"Natanya your eyes and feeling may have fallen for a Trenton".

"Because you see him as a father figure or someone you can talk to".

"I am here now. I can help you find the comfort you need".

Paul said hopping this was what she was missing in her life. But then she was feeling real deal.

Natanya was feeling the blues.
She had recently received a letter from Trenton and he professed his undying love for her.

She listened to Paul and even though she was learning to love him as daughter loved her father. The letter she showed them. Had moved a blot from each of their hearts.

It read.

"Moonlight city
Sunlight gate
Love notes like this needs no date.

Hi babyface.

I know we can't talk anymore on the phone. So I will go back to old school love.

Because when I think of you I feel like so powerless as a boy. I should have said man because that two days away. I was so hoping my brother would have came to his senses and at least apologize to your family. Though it wouldn't change what happened but it can sure restore some respect.

I started reading my bible as well and I am praying that our parents will see eye to eye and don't let the past stop me from loving you.

When you're not near me my heart seems to stop. I am not just saying this. I get nervous when I think of you. I know you may think this is just a note to get your attention and maybe get you alone and do whatever. But I am not that kind of guy I am a lover. I just want you and will wait on you forever.

I just need to see you for my birthday and I will be alright. No expectations.

I know you have feelings for me too and hope you will not let them all slip away.

I feel like together we are a tree and you're the root.

(Ephesians 3;17-18)

I want to stop writing but I can't end without saying what I feel is real. We are like the fight your parents had with the church. You're my Heather and I am your Paul. It's though I can give you all my love and you don't have have to return it. Because I loved you first.

(Ephesians 4:2)

Please I know it going to be hard but just talk to your parents and see if they will let you come to the party.

I love you.

Lots of hugs

Trenton.

Trenton is not just writing he is indeed feeling the powers of love.

Those little butterflies that drives you crazy almost like you want to have an heart attack. When your not with that person. When you felt like giving that person your all and they don't have give much in return. Because whatever little they give you will accept. Because your giving is a form of sacrifice. That real love right there. That is why it hurts when they get up on leave. Sometimes it's not that your love is not enough. It's because they are not at the level to receive that love. You are too real for them and they are scared because not everyone can receive or give love. Love is a sacrifice like the love of God.

(1 John 4:10)

The fact that he and Natanya has started reading the Bible is very good. Now If he his guided properly then things may work for them. If they take things slow and wait for the future.

Four years is not a big square to measure the surface area until she turns eighteen.

Heather was having a hard time coming to grips. With her been so young and with happened to Natasha she sure couldn't have a repeat.

It was when Natasha who had put Natanya up to asking their parents. She was hoping Trenton and Natanya make it to a nice future.

She came of the room and finally spoke.

"Mommy I know this none of my business but Trenton and Trent are two different people".

"I use to say Trenton was slow because he was more into love and bonding"

"And he wouldn't not be like Trent".

"With the forward questions and promiscuous behavior".

"If my opinion counts in say let her go at least for an hour".

Now Natasha had greased the wheel and now the decision should come from. Mom and dad.

OK girls give us some time on this one. Paul said hugging both of them.

They have grown to like him alot. They are at ease when he is around and they find themselves learning to love a man without any form of expectations.

"What you think Paul?".

Heather asked him.

It's kind of hard. But I could drop her off and pick her up.

"Better yet let's meet the boy frist.

And then we decide"

"Agreed?."

"Ok".

Heather said trusting his judgement.

They got the girls to gather again.

"We have decided to meet this Trenton first".

"And then we will decide from there".

Paul responded to the girls as heather was still not in the one hundred percent zone yet.

But she trusted his wisdom.

As the girls happily went to their room.

Her phone rang out, it was Pastor's wife.

"Heather it's about pastor.
"He-he is awake".

She stumped over her words.

"And he need to talk to you can you come to the hospital now please?".

Chapter 54

A Parent and a Leader

Heather rushed over to former Pastor's hospital bed.

Luckily Paul had his car to make it easier.

"Pastor? ". Heather said touching his hands.

"No you're the pastor Heather!".

"I want you to pray for me and add me to list of people to be baptised on sunday".

He said in a weak tone.

"That's the right thing to do".

Heather agreed.

"Now I don't care about shame and if they want to say I am bad person".

"Because God told me to Repent and he will forgive me and all my past will be washed away".

"Takei it easy".

Heather told him".

"I will baptised you".

Heather replied to him.

Tears ran down his to back of head. As lay on the bed looking up at her.

"I fought you so much Heather but still you never gave up".

"Because I never had to fight you alone".

"God was always fighting for me".

(Mattew 5:9)

"Bless his name".

Heather said.

She felt deliverance coming his way. For he was wrapped up in greed and confusion and she laid her hands on him.

"Father I bind the enemy in the name of Jesus".

"Cripple every plan and let us take home the victory".

"I pray for healing for the sick and call out for mercy".

"I plead your blood".

"I give you thanks.

"for you said whatever is written so it shall be done.
Amen".

Ask and it shall be given.

Knock and the door will be opened.

"We ask for healing", "We ask for love".

The prayer was so powerful, that other patients and their family asked her to pray for them.

God was with her and she was with him.

Paul also watched her learning from her how it's easier to give than to receive and how God make your enemies your footstool.

(Psalm 110:1-7)

Because who could have been (more mightier) than the pastor.

And now he quivers at sound of the voice of God through Heather his chosen vessel.

After left the hospital and headed home it was disgusted that Trenton would like to meet with them at 7pm if they had the time.

They agreed and wait for him.

(1 Peter 5:3)

"Being a parent is a complex matter joy, pain, worry and more importantly love.

Parents are truer to their kids than they are to themselves.
Simply the case is we want the best for our children.

(Titus 2:7)

A parent who abuses a child in most cases is a child themselves. Who is trying to be a parent.

Sometimes their history, (the way they were raised.) Frustration and abandonment and stress itself. Can cause parents to get off on their kids.

Like when the father ran away.

When the neighbours complains.

Develop methods of how you deal with your kids.

Don't embarrassed them in public. It may work before the teenage years. But it may drive a wedge between both of you after that.

Children have feelings too.

Children will test you to see the number of things they can get away with.

And keep adding until they break the glass ceiling. Like staying out late or overnight.

(Proverb 29:15)

"The get a inch and take a yard" (Old school game)

Not everything deserve punishment or the corporal punishment the belt. How about a little taking to?.

Not a scream fest. When we shout on top of our vocal cords, to show how angry we are.

"But did the child get the message all?". That child sees an adult(parent) with lock of reasoning.

Who have just mirrored the behavior they hope to correct.

An (adult) parent who can't control his or her anger.

Yet you want to correct their behavior.

Sit your child down and explain what's wrong with what they did.

How it can affect them.

Explain why you are upset.

Give examples but never compare them to anyone. Apologize when you have misjudge them.

Teach them to Apologize as well. Give them hugs and lots of I love you and tell them they are important.

Paul and Heather waited for Trenton to come and visit them.

When he arrived he drove his parents lexus jeep. He dressed modestly and was filled with charms and good mannerism.

"Trenton you're too old to date my daughter".

Heather told him.

"She need to focus on her schooling.

"We don't have things as easy as some people".

"I understand", "but I want to be Tanya's friend as well".

"I will wait for her 18th birthday so we can be more than friends".

Paul intervened.

"We have read the letter you wrote her we think it's too much for her age".

"But we like that your humble and willing to wait for the future". "But right now it's too much for a near 15 year old".

"I probably went over my feeling". Trenton said.

His eyes were sincere and he kept good eye contact.

"At that party will there be alcohol", "smoking and will there be any adult there?".

"There will be two parties sir".

"The one for my brother maybe that the party you just described".

"Because I was planning something simple".
"Just cutting a cake some friends and family".

"And if Natanya was there that would make it more special".

"She won't be coming". Paul said.

As a shock ran through Natanya face.

'She is underage and we are of a Christian faith".

"We are not saying you're a bad person Trenton".

"Your intentions are good".

"We are just saying give her more time to grow up".

"If you were meant for her and she for you we can't stop it".

"I am now the pastor of the church you can come there for worship if you want to".

"And build a life with God and see how and where he directs you".

Thanks Ms. Heather I would like to attend".

"How is your brother doing?"

He is not bad just worried about his troubles.

"I was hoping he would have sent his apology".

"But he didn't"."

"So I am sincerely apologizing for him". "Hoping you". He paused and corrected himself.

"We all can mend our differences".

"Natanya I will do what you parents suggested things real slow".

"I don't want to disrespect their home or because of me you break any of their rule".

"I will wait for you and I will see you at Church on Sunday".

They could almost hear the tear in his voice. And how serious he was about what he was saying.

It reminded Paul of when he first met Heather of how determined he was to get to know her.

He gave Natanya a small hug and shook Paul's hand he embraced Heather and told her congratulations on her becoming the pastor.

He then drive off as Natanya ran to her room crying.

Heather went after her.

"Let her be alone for a while".

Paul said.

"it will soak in, she needs time".

Similarly to when he was heart broken. He know because he had felt it. But haven't we all. That's what experience does it teaches.

It's was Saturday and it's the twins party already the streets where lines up with posh cars and out of town teenagers. Who had came to this every year affair. But each year they are one year older and for a few the troubles get bigger.

They even had a artist line up.
it was more of a dance than a party.

Heather and Paul was praying and preparing for his baptism.

Natanya was up in her bed having a tear fest. But she will soon see the value in this lesson even if it will take years to unfold in her head.

The music was loud and half the town could hardly rest until 2pm that night.

Chapter 55

I am coming home

I surrender all, I surrender all, all to thee my blessed saviour I surrender all.

(Israel Houghton)

This was song by the choir as Pastor Heather made her way from her office. Which was breathtakingly refurbished.

Earlier Paul had covered her eyes and lead her to the office.

Where he had replaced and painted the shelves. He had removed the old book shelves and gave an open concept. With a small seating area with a nice picture frame. And clean fresh white walls.

On her desk was a stunning orchid plant that brought the office to high class look.

Her name spelt out in gold on a plaque on her desk.

'HEATHER JOHNSON-PHILLIPS PASTOR'.

when she opened her eyes and behold this magical beauty her tears fell from her eyes effortlessly.

"Thank you." She said choking on her words.

"I really appreciate this". "It is so beautiful".

She said hugging him.

She rested her head on his chest and she could feel his heart beating.

"Are you ready?".

She said to him.

"To be baptised?". He asked her

"Sure I have never been ready for anything in my life".

"The number of miracles I have seen god performed in your life".

"I am ready to get all the blessing god have in store for me".

"I believe you"

"I can feel your going to have a great future with God".

"Because when all fails Jesus his the only one that remains the same".

(Hebrew 13:8)

Deacon williams. A female as well, lead the praise and worship, welcomes and did the introductions.

"I welcome all visitors and hope you change your status from visitors to members in the future".

"Bring your friends", "husband's and kids". "Bring everyone".

The congregation clapped.

"Today I introduce a lady", "I have admired". "Her strength is like a mountain".

Her suffering were like the days of job. But she persevered. She said it many times that she is not perfect and and she is no stranger to mistakes and mishaps.

But she is thankful for those mistakes and mishaps because they are her testimony.

Ladies and gentlemen rise like christ has risen and welcome. Our first female pastor Heather Johnson she paused. "Should I say Phillips?".

As the congregation rose to their feet and welcomed her.

Heather stepped onto the pulpit and into the church's view. She was not wearing black clergy gown. Like the one the former pasture wore.

She wore a white one. This made her looked angel like. They all had dropped jaws and awe sounds coming to meet her glorious look. Some even continued clapping for a minute before she spoke.

She signaled Paul to join her.
At the podium.

He was a little shy and his handsome face carried a glow that made them just stand out whenever they are together.

"Good Morning church".
SHe spoke.

The Church yelled back a powerful. Good morning and their smiles and eyes were happy.

"Today is baptism day".

she continued

"And as the newly appointed Pastor". "I get to baptised my husband".

"Isn't that heavenly?"

She asked.

She wanted all those who had condemned her to hear.

The Church cheered, whistle and clapped.

"How do feel being baptized by the woman you will marry?"

She gave him a chance to speak

"Good morning church".

He responded.

"It's a privilege to be baptised by the woman of my dreams".

"After today I can stop dreaming and just live the life that God has prepared for me, for all of us".

The audience cheered.

"I have never found as much joy as I have found with Heather".

"She is a great mother, she will be a great wife and she will be the best pastor."

"Keep praying for us while we pray for you".

"In Jesus name"

"Amen"

Pastor Heather took the mic.

"Church let pray for the souls who are ready to march in the army of righteousness".

"Lord you call me to be a shepherd and here I am", "Lord use me".

She paused.

"Can I hear the choir sing".

"Take me to the king". Please and thank you.

"I feel his power in this place".

"Paul do want to join in?" Give Paul a mic please and thank you".

Paul started as the choir waited for him to join in.

"Take me to king I don't have much to bring".

The choir listened to Paul and when he hit a note they clapped.

"The truth is it's time to stop playing these games. We need a word for The people's pain".

He song and some shouted out "Jesus" it was Natanya.

She was getting a touch for the hands of the almighty.

Trenton sat beside her and he was flooded with tears.

Heather went down to the congregation and got Natanya. God had answered her prayer. All she needed was one child.

"The truth is I'm weak, options are few. I am trying to pray but where are you?"

Several person cried out for mercy.

As god made them whole.

She prayed quietly and the choir song as Paul lead them.

"Take me to the king"

Chapter 56

The water is trouble my friends

Heather stood at the door of the church and the light that shone in was a spectacular heavenly glow.

And the church eyes followed her wherever she goes.

It was like she could perform miracles. She prayed at the Church door for more people to come and recognized that God is the miracle worker.

The choir and Paul had changed songs and was now singing.

Lord I Give You My Heart.
(The Anthony Evans version. Look his songs up). They will bless your soul.

"This is my desire to honor you".

Paul song and the choir backed him up. His vocal range was impressive, he had great control of his voice. Whenever he hits a note or exercise his vibrato. He sends chills and goosebumps all over the listeners bodies.

"Lord with all my heart I worship you".

Paul song putting meaning to the song.

The former pastor was in a wheelchair and he turned to watch Heather who knelt on a pillow at the baptism pool.

The pool was to the left of the huge service hall and once the drapes were pulled back you and the wooden cover removed you could see the holy water.

Her prayer was so profound.

"Lord let this water be troubled".

"Take these souls home and keep them".

"Lord I do nothing here by myself".

"I am just your vessel I am ready lord fill me".

She went off into unknown tongues.

People trembled and most were crying and some late comers showed up. It Was a full church.

The ushers got them seated on extra chairs brought from the storage area.

Paul continued to sing and the choir backed him up.

"Lord I Give you my heart I give you my soul I live for you alone.

She prayed.

"Lord send your servants to the waters".

"Give them a Clean wash from their old selves make them white as snow".

"Deliverance lord".

She prayed.

"Every breath that I take every moment I'm awake.
Lord have your way in me".

He went low and deep and his tears came but he song it all the way through. Because he is receiving his ministry as a singer. With a voice that can change emotions break down wall and break chains.

The more He cried and song the more people cried out.

There was like a fire in the house of God. When he hit some high notes and his tears just streamed down like a fountain as he song and walked over to pastor Heather. As she reached out for his hand like they have always done for each other.

He was leaving all behind. His sons watched on from the balcony. She song along too and tears filled their eyes because at last their dad will be happy.

Heather teared up too but she held it together. For Paul the joy was much too real.

She gave him a moment to finish his song.

His testimony, his last walk of the uneven yoke.

He repeated the chorus.

Lord I Give you my heart….

The entire church including the former pastor was crying as he melted the core of their hearts.
It felt like tiny particles of angel duty sprinkle all over them.

He went low and faded out as heather.

Heather started.

"Paul Phillips. Do you accept god as your lord and person saviour?"

"Yes pastor". He answered

"Repeat after me".

She told him

"I will worship no other god but him"".

"Things i use to do i will do them no more".

He repeated every word and sincerity hugged every word.

"I Heather johnson pastor with power invested in me by the almighty god I hereby baptised you in the name of the father son and holy spirit".

She dipped him.
And his gown soaked with water and when they lifted him from the water he felt like a brand new man.

It was Natanya next, she insisted she was ready to go.

And Heather dipped her too.

The choir song out.

"The water is troubled my friend step right in".

"God almighty power is moving ever hour".

Then it was the former Pastor's Time.

He had difficulty maintaining his balance.

"Leave him".

"Because If he believed in god as much as god loves and has forgiven him he will take up his bed and walk".

(Mark 2:11)

She said.

"Because today the devil his once again defeated".

"For the blood prevails.

"The blood of the risen lamb".

"Pray with me she held his hands".

"Because you're still holding on to who you use to be".

"God has forgiven you".

"I have forgiven you".

"We have forgiven you". The Church has forgiven you.

"The problem is have you forgiven yourself?".

"Father look down at your servant and change his frame of mind". "Give him the will to know that all his forgiven and he has a clean white sheet to walk on".

"Restore his health lord and place him on his feet and your solid rock".

"Because all other grounds are sinking sand".

"Bless him lord".

"Let him walk to the destiny you have for him".

"Let him walk not to his own destiny but the one you have prepared for him".

"He slowly got up".

"Trust in the lord Paul came back out in his new suit".

"A new man with a new life and he song".

"With all of thine heart and lean not to thy own understanding".

He went up to the choir and blend voices together. And while they song. Heather prayed.

She asked the church to pray. And he slowly took one step after another.

She lead him to the pool and dipped him.

The light flickered over the pool and some people gasped.

Paul and the choir song.

"But in all thy ways acknowledge him and he shall direct thy path".

The light stabilized and pastor came up shouting and crying.

"I am free".

"I am free".
He shouted.

"Glory be to God.
I am free".

The choir continued signing.

Paul raised another song.

"GOD IS TRULY AMAZING"

Heather baptised twelve people in total some she never even seen before.

But everyone wanted to see the new lady pastor who was once a Don among rebels.

Who God have called out of bandage.

Who God has brought from valley of the shadow of death.

Heather did her little after ceremony.

Where all of the twelve people she baptised held a lit candle.

"For this is the light of the lord", she said to them'.

"No matter how you see darkness".

"There is light inside you all of you she pointed to the congregation".

"And you can".

"Use that light and change one person at a time".

"That light is love".

"The love of god".

"Am closing now'. she said.

The choir hummed.

"Come into my heart".
"Come into my heart lord Jesus".

She looked around at Paul and he at her.

She could tell he was comfortable where he was and he is cutest singer she had ever seen.

He nodded at her and she at him.

"Bless your name lord".

They both said in their minds at the same time.

"If ever you forget what to say when you pray".

"Always remember".

    "The Lord's Prayer".

    "Our Father", "who ought in heaven",
    "hallowed be thy Name",
    thy kingdom come",
    thy will be done",
    on earth as it is in heaven".
    Give us this day our daily bread".
    "And forgive us our trespasses",
    as we forgive those
    who trespass against us".
    And lead us not into temptation",
    but deliver us from evil".
    "For thine is the kingdom,
    and the power", "and the glory",
    for ever and ever'".

"Amen".

(Matthew 6:9-14)

(Luke 11: 2-4)

Chapter 57

Have You Forgiven Yourself?

"Earlier asked have you forgiven yourself?"

Heather continue her closing argument.

The low humming of the choir held her voice like a golden pin on a white cushion. The harmony was so rich, that it was priceless.

"We all pray for forgiveness.

"Yet because we carry the past with us some much".

"It's just follows us everywhere".

"We lose our confidence because of this'.

"We hold ourselves back".

'What happened to the little girl or little boy who wanted to be a teacher", a doctor".

"A lawyer", or a nurse".

"Oh yea he is sitting right there!".

"She is sitting right there!". "listening to me".

"But because he had made a few mistakes.

(2 Timothy 4:7)

"Glory be to God she held her stance in the spiritual moment".

"Preach it".

A voice called out from the congregation.

"Because she had made a few mistake".

Heather preached.

"She gave up".

"Yes yes". Some members Shouted in agreement.

"I need a witness"?

Heather shouted.

"Did you hear me?"

She yelled.

"Why are you giving up on yourself?".

She screamed the question out at the congregation.

"It's because you have not forgiven yourself".

"And you think you have failed".

"You only failed if you didn't try".

"Can somebody get up and try".

"Will you put your fighting glove on".

"Get in the ring called life and fight for your survival".

"Fight for your financial independence".

"Fight for humanity".

"Heather was so inspiring and her words hit the congregation like a unexpected hailstorm.

They worship God and cheered her on.

She feed them his word.

Her well organized choir song low behind her voice.

Like a boat a sail on silky waters.

"I almost gave up".

"I felt like I just couldn't take life anymore."

Them some shouted in a loud towering voice.

"Mercy please".

The holy spirit was searching healing and fixing thing on the inside of the church so the outside that's always so pretty and with fake smiles and nice hellos can match the inside.

Heather was indeed the vessel. And God was using her to Transform his church.

To break down the hatred, the deceptions, the lust, the pretentiousness.

Heather continued preaching

Most of us are like
"Like doubtful Thomas"

(John 20:24-29)

"You have to have your own experience to believe it".

"Why you do think I am standing here today?".

"Because of the grace of God".

Her voice was so powerful. It barred through the speaker and those who stayed home could hear her ceremony through the outdoor speaker.

Several passers-by stood and listened to word of God.

"It's because he was merciful enough to forgive me and I was strong enough to believe in him and forgive myself".

"That is why I am standing here today".

"You want to go the position posted on the notice board".

"But your afraid because of your past".

"You came work late sometimes because you couldn't help it".
"Because those days he had no one to take care of your kids".

"You limit your capabilities".

"You're not talking to your family members because for last year".

"Because they did you wrong".

"The way you responded to it was not right either".

"So now both of you are waiting for each other to make the first move".

"Forgive and forget" move on".

She preached and the melody behind her reminded the congregation of the good old chruch time.

The good old chruch days when it was ok for people to be themselves.

Where there was one lady who would dance down the whole place.

"Because that was her praise to god.

And that lady or young man like Paul. Who could just sing one line and you're ready to confess your sins.

That church mother who you can confide in and she would tell you what to do.

The old church, that even if you went barefooted you wouldn't be judge. Your praises and presence would just bless someone else and make their burden lighter. Because you choose God over your pride.

"I almost let go". I felt like I couldn't face life anymore".

The choir song low and passionately.

"Forgive yourself don't hold on to the memories".

"No wonder you can't sleep at nights".

"Thinking about 500 people who did you wrong and how you are going revenge them".

"Then you saying you can't get a break through".

"Because you can't go forward if your mind is in a backward gear".

"Sometimes it's not easy to just forget".

"But you keep adding onto your memory and clogging your mind".

"It becomes overloaded' there comes depression and anxiety the friends of the devil.

(Philippians 4:8)

"Rebuke him". She yelled.

"Keep your mind active by working", "dancing", "singing" "playing and exercising making yourself healthy".

"So the lord can use you".

"Who wants to drive a broken car".

"Show me your hand if you want a broken car?"

No hands went up. She was so logical and Paul was enjoying this.

"Worst if the engine won't last".

"Because it's corroded with the past milage it had no oil change".

"It's trapped in the memory of past time".

She spoke and it was as if she was reading their minds.

"Forgive yourself".

she preached. Doing her closing sermon.

"Forget your past troubles".
"Avoid the roads you once took that lead nowhere".

'Avoid and caution and still pray for those who have wronged you".

More importantly love yourself as christ loves you.

"I going to ask our bishop and trusted faith banner holder".

"In the army of christ to do the closing prayer".

She asked.

The Bishop came up

And he began.

"Before I do the prayer".

"I just want to first call back Mrs. Phillips to be to the pulpit as well as Mr. Phillips".

"What do think of these two people".

The congregation cheered "Amazing!". "God sent!". "Powerful!". "blessed!.".

Were among the cheers that rang out from the congregation.

Let pray for them the bishop said.

"Father in your wondrous and highly exalted name".

"We put your servant before you".

"Who Already to have blessed and chosen".

"Mr. Phillips song like the songs of David".

"And pastor Heather is wise and article beyond her years".

"We watched her struggles lord and she has passed her life's test".

"Keep her lord and give her strength to hold up your banner as the first female pastor of this church body".

"And send many more after her".

"For women too can do just as great a job like Ruth," "Esther," "Mary" and "Naomi".

The woman at well.

"Come see a man who told all these things of myself".

(John 4,4:42)

"Feed them lord from your well that never round dry".

"Thank you for these souls who have chosen to march with your light".

"many more will come because you have only just began".

He went off in a spiritual moment.

"Bless all in the hearing of my voice".

"Send people from near and far the message from one to another".

"That' you can only be free when you free your own mind".

"Free it of all negativity and follow your commandments".

"We asked for your blessings".

"Cover everyone and their family safely". "Who will joinery home and those who wish to stay and partake of our dinner".

"Bless the food and the cooks and may be done to honour".

"Bless your holy name amen".

After the service the after dinner began.

Where anyone can eat from a buffet of delicious meals.

This was a part of Heather's plan so that the Church and the community can hang together. And mix and values will be past on. That no one is better than the other and Christianity still makes us humans.

"Will our wedding be as big as this".

Paul asked Heather.

She smiled.

"I don't we can feed as much people".

"We can't but God will".

He Said as the went with their meals and sat with just random folks, they talked and ate and and had a wonderful Sunday evening.

But just around 5 hours after dawn, the following Monday.

The faith of Trent's future hang in the balance of the justice system.

Chapter 58

"What circle are you in?"

Heather went home with joy in her heart and Paul on her arm.

Life was way better, way better than it used to be.
It is way better

(1 Peter 3:8-12)

She could just marry Paul right away. Like the next day.

But there is a lot planning that goes into a wedding.

Most people will think life start after the wedding.

It's more like the life before determines the wedding.

Tiny little butterflies circled her heart and her emotions were high.

she was in a good place and Paul as well was ready to marry the woman of his dreams.

They already know about each other.

The feelings were mutual they wanted to just make that connection and tie the knot so that they can move on as a happy couple.

Because the bible said two is better than one because one falls down the other will help him /her up.

(Ecclesiastes 4:9-10)

Peter was still playing around with Miss Jennings.

She had not stopped texting calling and find ways to meddle with his mind.

He didn't even spend all day at Heather's baptism.

He left early, just shortly after he had something to eat.

He had to meet up with Miss Jennings again. The devil sometimes look for secret place to hide, to hinder and to distract.

His only mission is total Destruction.

He has two warriors to fight against now and Natanya his not as simple as she looked.

He was cut of her mother cloth and devil will be ready and waiting to test her. Because God does not test anyone it's their own thoughts that are convinced to fulfill their desire and the devil will make it easier by putting the ingredients you need right at hand. But the choice is always yours.

What God does I'd give you the strength, wisdom and courage to walk away from it because sin brings death to the soul.
"What circle are your thoughts in?".

(James 1:13-18)

What Circle are you in?".

"Do your friends tell on you?"

"Can you show me your friends and I'll tell you who you are?".

Sometimes we are in the wrong crowd and that's why the wrong things happen

Peter is probably an example.
If Heather don't reach out to him and not in just in time.

Things are looking good for Netanya.

she seemed to have the right intentions the right attitude and she had made the right choice by getting baptized.

It was not the same with Natasha.

she still feeling the after effect of being with Trent.

It's emotional coaster coaster ride in her brain.

Because she don't want to hurt him.
But she has been hurt herself how does she get rid of the pain?.

Again the question is

"What Circle are you in".

"Are still finding love in all those horrible places like you did before?".

If you always fish in the same pond what kind of fish do you expect to catch?"

"How many times are you going to make the same mistake?"

Then you say to yourself you have no luck.

Natasha is in the circle of pain. Some people will avenge pain with pain.

Sometimes to get rid of pain you have to show love, sow seeds, forgive and forget.

"What are we going to do about this trent situation?"
Heather asked Paul.

"I'm not a hundred percent sure but at least we should let him feel it a little bit"

He replied.

"If he doesn't get a taste of his own medicine", "he will keep repeating his action".

"He keep hurting other people and making a ripple of hurts". "As he goes along he need to be in check with himself and his emotions as well as other people's emotion"

(1 Thessalonians 4:6)

"Maybe he need psychological help or just a good dose of Jesus".

"Again the question is what Circle are you in?".

Some people will not admit when they need help.

And a build up of hurt spiral into very dangerous territories where the mind is bombarded by all the hurts and the physical body and the raw emotions is it only outlet.

For a crackhead is not just a crackhead.
it's the drug of choice he/ she uses to hide the pain.

"A sex addict has chosen a drug of choice to hide his or her pain. A repeat of what emotions break down they may suffer.

A Gunslinger has chosen his the drug of choice and uses it to hide his or her pain.

Remove the weapon and you mind a little person inside.

There is one remedy for all this pain.

One remedy and only one and Heather had preached about him.

Paul sang about him.

His name is Jesus the the son of God the king of kings and Lord of Lords.

"So now what Circle are you really in?".

Because in life all we need is someone to look up to.

someone to hold your hand when you're falling.

someone to love you when nobody else does.

someone to help you get over your problems,

Your mistakes and your mishaps and there's only one person that it's possible to do all this.

there's only one person who can take on all the burden of the world.

Because he made the world.

In the begin was the word and was was God.

"Again what Circle are you in?".

"I think it's best to go with the lowest sentence they can find for him".

"I don't really know what to say Paul".

Heather added.

"I don't know".

Paul said.

'I think he needs to go to some rehab or some school to learn discipline or maybe like a boot camp for a reality check".

Good decision she agreed.

His eyes was set on her, as they only had one more hurdle to cross and that was to get married.

They case was the only next big thing on their minds

Justin was doing ok as far as his health was concern.

Because all those prayers Heather prayed had not gone in vain.

(1 Corinthians 16:1)

She did not have an ulterior motive like many others who would have like to gain money or a buy out.

Her main goal was a path of redemption for trent.

She grouped her family together and she warned them.

"Be careful of circle you're in".

"Ensue your friends respect you and are loyal to you and you to them".

"Don't be anyone's friend for what they have".

"Also do the right thing at the right time and if you don't feel you fit in".

"It ok to leave and find where you belong".

She went on and ended with this prayer.

"For these are my children lord and hopefully they will listen to me".

"Keep them under your wing lord".
And protect them from all danger".

"Watch out for the friend they keep and keep them in check".

(1 Corinthians 15:34)

"Bless them and keep them from harm".

"As a mother I reach out to you".

"Be around my house and keep everyone who goes to and from it safe".

"I leave an in your name amen".

The Monday Morning had removed it's curtains. And before the roosters would crow.

Heather was up and about.

At 830 am everyone squeezed into the car and headed to court.

Trent's big shot lawyer was there and so was the crown prosecutor.

The jury and judge Headstrong was the one preceding.

Mr. Malcolm was nervous that even his feet were shaking.

Trent's mother was more embarrassed than nervous.
She felt as if she had raised a monster.

It was Natasha's time to take the stand and give her story.

"Did you consent to have relations with this man?".

Mr. Hightower. Trent's lawyer asked her.

With all the anger built up inside her.

Heather hope she wouldn't lie and just tell like it was.

Chapter 59

"The judgement of mankind"

The Children's advocate office representative was in attendance. It couldn't have been for Trent because he was officially eighteen two days ago.

"Did you you give consent for Mr. Malcolm to do everything he did to you?".

Trent's lawyer rephrased the question.

Natanya was the third of three girls who showed up.

A few of them took 'the under the table buyout' his father offered.

Natasha looked at Heather because she feared if she lied Heather would stop her.

"Yes I gave consent".
Natasha said.

"He was my boyfriend at the time or so made me believed".

"Are you hurt by the fact that you're not his girlfriend as you believed Ms. Lawrence?".

Trent's lawyer Mr. Hightower was a very witty and big shot lawyer. One of the best.

He specialized in cross examination. Where he questions you to a pulp. He is tactful and usual he sets the prosecutor witness into a hambush. And stoned the with questions. Until he gets what he wants to hear.

Much like how Satan plague the human mind. But he can't get to you unless you let him.

Thus when we let our defences down.(Lack of prayer.)

Taken on more than we can manage.

You can say no sometimes.

Don't be the scapegoat for everyone.

Escape to free yourself.

Keep building yourself up.

Seven natural remedy for a healthy life are:

A). Love. This is the most important. To keep us going. From whatever handle it cometh. If it's real like the love of God embrace it.

Not only do we need love but we also need to give and show love.

Half the people asking for love don't even know what it is to give love.

They always want and never gives.

People who are Just selfish for everything.

Avoid those people.

MR. Hightower always look for loopholes in his opponent's witnesses or even the questions asked.

Just like how the devil always operate on your weakness first.

He was playing on Natanya anger as the reason why she came fort and told her parents.

"Ms. Lawrence can you tell the court", "at what age you started a friendship with Trent Malcolm?".

Heather raised her hand.

"Yes Pastor Johnson?".

The judge asked her.

"Can the court please refer to my daughter as Natasha and not by Ms. Lawrence please.?"

Point taken.

"Please use Natanya councilor".

The judge ordered him.

The public crown. Prosecutor. Is the one representing the complainant or the victim.

The Jamaican justice system was adopted from the British system.

Whereas its crown's right to protect its citizens.
Make them equal or whole in the case of a contractual situation.

Incase like this it's up to the crown to prove that Trent was guilty beyond a reasonable shadow of a doubt.

But in a small claims or civil case it is the preponderance (more of common sense, More evidence.) Will determine the who wins the case.

The crown Crown meaning the Queen or representative thereof.
Most likely the PM.
Governor General.

(Leviticus 24:17-22)

What Heather pick up on was very clever and it comes with her anointing.

The crown prosecutor missed it twice.

Calling Natasha "Ms". Invites her to feel and act like an adult.

Because it gave her that opportunity as well to argue with the defense while showing the court that she not that innocent at all.

There are different tactic a lawyer will use to get you to show your true colours.

"You lied to you parents right Natasha?".

"And you (he points the finger at her like she was his daughter. Fueling her with hatred for him.

"You cut class and you went and force yourself onto Trent?".

She could just tell him her mind.

He continued looking in her eyes if she would lash out. But Heather was looking at her. With that look that we all get from our mothers.

"Because he is rich", "has a car," and he is popular".

(John 13:16)

"You had to have him".

"Didn't you?".

He pounded on the table and startled her.

He nailed Natasha with piercing augment.

Her face looked as if she wanted to burst out into tears.

"Objection!"

The crown prosecutor said.

Oh Finally he is working

Saving Natasha from telling off the defense lawyer. In the bitter rage he had dragged her mood in.

"The councillor badgering the witness".

"Councillor be careful they are children".

The judge reminded him".

The crown prosecutor is clearly identifying that the defense prosecutor is putting the witness under extreme strain pushing her to our Breaking Point.

But Heather maintained that look.

And Natasha simple said no that's not how it happened.

She gave them the exact version of what happened. So did the other two girls of which one recently found out.

She was with child.

Her mother cried and sobbed. And as her daughter took the stand she cried again.

Because was she hoping of all her girls this one would amount to a hill of beans.

Mr. Malcolm said they will take responsibility for the baby. But for the mother of this girl. She his doing the eye for eye situation.

Trent was nervous like a single white fowl in a coop. Not knowing when it's his time. and what it's going to be his driving him to sweating wreck.

He was drinking water like a camel.

Now it was his turn to take the stand.

"How many girls have you dated at that school?"

The crown prosecutor asked him.

"I am friend with them".

"I never dated any of them".

Trent answered.

"So is this a case whereby you sleep with all of your friends?".

The prosecutor asked him.

It is clear that Trent don't even know what a friendship is. He is mixing up the signals.

(Poor parenting).

He is confused about boundaries and expectations.

I don't he responded.

"How old were you when you met Natasha?".

"I was 16 going on to 17"

"Have you two ever dated?"

The crown prosecutor his more calm and is using a tick tack method. Where is allowing Trent to lay out the foundation and build himself up to show he was unreasonable in his doing.

We talked on the phone.

You mean this phone.

With these text and voice recordings.

"I love you I miss you" that's considered dating Trent.

The Crown Prosecutor showed the video of each girl. Saying exactly what Trent told them. Before he had his way with them.

"Did you love Amy of these girls?"

The crown prosecutor asked him.

"We were just friend".

He answered getting upset.

"So you lied to them?"

Trent held his head down.

"Do you know that they are under age?".

He didn't answer.

Answer the question. The judge ordered him.

"Yes he stated. Bringing himself to a pause and reflecting on what he had done.

"Counselors your final arguments".

The judge asked. Making note of what Trent had just said.

The defense went first.

"Lady and gentlemen of the jury".

"What we have here is a situation of teenagers young minds exploring".
"There intentions was simply wanting to have fun". "But it was a little miss handled".

"All the girls gave consent to my client".

"He did not hold anyone against their will".

"They are drawn to his charisma", "wealth and good looks". "That's what young minds look for".

"This is a case of expectations not being met".
"They wanted more he could offer".

"Trent Malcolm may need some corrective counseling but not jail time".

"I rest my case".

The crown step up.

"Did you lie to these girls yes?".

"That's was Trent's answer".

"Did he manipulated them?".

"Did he used them?".

"The answers would still be yes".

"Ladies and gents of the jury".

"The man in question has several reports made to the police".

"Public mischief". "Soliciting and engaging in sexual activities with minors".

"Rehabilitation", "counseling and even some jail time is necessary to set this young man straight".

"If he should become a productive citizen".

"How many young girls life's does he need to make a mess of before he is taught how to be responsible for his actions?".

"The justice system is not to condemn people or make their lives a living hell". "It's a way of reformation". "A way to train people rethink their actions and how to effectively live in a civil society".

"Does Trent need reformation?"

"Does he have the wrong ideology of responsibility and morals and even simple relationship?".

The Crown Prosecutor continued.

"Trent is still trainable.
In fact he is a twin like Natasha whose twin has been recently baptised".

"Trenton the twin of Trent is friends with Natanya".

"Why are we "NOT" having the same problem with the other sets of twins.

"Let me just rephrase that".
Mr. Benson representative of the crown continued.

"Why can some people be law abiding citizen and some cannot?.

"I rest my case".

(Like 6: 37-42)
The jury will get an hour to deliberate.

"Is there anyone would like to add anything before they make a decision.

Heather raised her hand.

He asked her to come to the center and state her name and give her comments.

"I am Heather johnson", "mother of Natasha and I am pastor".

"I would just like to add that no child is innocent in all this".

"And that this is just a wake up call to what could have been worst".

"We as parent need to pay more attention", "show more love and spend time on morals responsibilities and common courtesies". Like "Thank you". "I love you". "Good morning". Etc.

"Tell your child why he has to wash the dishes".

"Because it's a form of responsibility that keeps the house functioning". "It's something that will teach you that whatever role you're given to play".

"It must be taken serious from now up until you have your own children".

"Then you will teach them as you were taught".

"I too have made mistakes with the upbringing of my children".

Heather said.

"But I am taking the Power back".

"By letting them know I love them".

"And I am sorry for times when I weren't there from them".

"But I am here now".

"And that Jesus the son of God will always be there for them".

"Whatever the decision the court arrive at". "I am hoping to be able to minister to him and talk with him sometimes".

"If his parents would allow".

"Also I think he will do well with some form of therapy rather than a locked away situation".

"I well keep you all in my prayers and hope that you will all pray for each other".

"In Jesus name".

"Thank you".

"Thanks for those kind and thoughtful words Pastor Johnson".

"We reconvene in the next hour".

He pounded the gavel.

(Mattew 7: 1-5)

(B) Laughter.
Do things that spike your laughter. Watch a play a movie or even cartoons.

Let out your inner child and live, love and laugh. Laughter is good for the soul. It release stress and lessons wrinkles. If it's a positive laugh, then go for it.

"A joyful heart is the best medicine but a crushed spirit dries up the bones".

(Proverbs 17:22)

*C to G will continue in other chapters.

Chapter 60

The verdict

Paul just sat there sad this youngster is throwing his life away.

How much can one blame his parents though. Don't he has a mind of his own.

Paul was almost thinking out loud. He could not come to grips of why someone would like to put themselves in a situation like this and to be dragged from one end to the next.

Sleeping on the cold concert and all those, all those things that a company the prison system.

He look around the courthouse and remembered when they were on their way in. There were several young men lined up to be tried.

Some maybe even for murder.

What is happening to our youths?", "to our nation?".

Are we the same nation that Marcus Garvey, Paul Bogle, NOT forgetting Nanny of the Maroon. And all the other great warriors fought for.

So we can be free to kill each other.

Even the killings of children women the elderly. Oh Lord please have mercy Paul said in a low key.

"For so it is written so let it be done".

Natanya was busy busy with little Justin who is still trying to gather why they are there.

Peter a few times wondered what he would do if he was in Trent's place.

They don't talk much after the attack.

And this may even make it worst because Trent's as friend who are gun handlers.
Well so does Peter who grew up with Odane who is the Don of the rival gang of young Mexican. A name given to Trent Spanish Amigo who heads the a tough gang called "peppers".

He was thinking out of the box. Because though he believe in prayer he has also seen reality.

Where a Christian lady her Don gargon son in law was killed. After his enemies kicked off her door where he was staying. They went after him and she protected him. Causing her to meet her untimely death.

Seeking protection before you need it is a good ideas he thought. He sat next to paul in the second row of the huge he could tell by the floor ruggedness it had have a lot of traffic.

He looked across and saw the two other girls. They look so innocent but yet they are caught up in all this misery. But like I am any better he thought to himself.

That's when Ms. Jennings text him.

"Can I book you for tonight?"

He read it on smile because that's a game they are playing.

Oh what danger may lurk when this verdict is read.

The jury a group of 12 citizens chosen at random based on the voters list and or license plate system. People chosen generally has no run-ins with the law.

Usually they are mature people of good standing responsible citizen.

They returned first and then the judge came back to his elevated seat. He wore the

The the black robe and those white wigs repenting the monarch an Jamaican flag and a British flag stood on either side of his desk.

The bible was highly respected in the court as well. It's use as an sworn in tool. To help to deter people from lying. At the same time showing reference to God almighty.

The judge then took his seat and called the court back to order.

The Malcolm mother teared up because her son's fate is about to unfold upon him. Now she was thinking what a mess up job they did as parents.

(Proverbs 24:17)

"After almost an hour of deliberation".

"How did the jury find the defendant?".

The judge asked.

The lady in the middle who look like a school teacher or an administrator read. The result.

"The jury find the defendant guilty!"

"With a 8, to 4 count your honor".

There was gasps and oh no.

"Silence the judge pounded the gavel".

"The court hereby sentence Trent Malcolm to 2 consecutive years of community service".

"In these same calendar years you must fulfill three different therapy including anger management. Personal and people relation family orientation. And other training programs".

"Including checking in at your local station once every month".

"Failure to do so will result in a full sentences that range between 7 and 10 years in prison".

"You seem to have too much time on hands. Mr. Malcolm".

"These two years we will keep you busy and see if that will help you develop a better mindset".

"That's it".

"This court is adjourned".

"That's not a bad deal".

Trent's lawyer said to him.

But he was levied.
And two of his groupies were in attendance and they looked at Heather's and all the other families with hatred that brought Trent to justice.

Paul find himself tense when they walked by him. Because one said.

"We will take it to the streets".

He was hoping that Peter did not hear that. But he did and he took good note of it.

(Luke 6:27-30)

Heather bargain with the Malcolm's to visit and minister to Trent.

But they said it was up to Trent who immediately dismissed the motion.

(Romans 12:20)

Heather and her family left knowing that Trent needed more than rehabilitation, he needed God's love.

At home Heather was slowly making preparation for her marriage and was hoping to be the first to make her own dress. She was looking through magazines and seeing what she could combined to make that dazzling dress that will make her look like the most sophisticated bride ever.

She ran into Paul when she passed through the living room.

He friendly invited her to come sit with him.

And they talked and cuddled and made all those important details that would make their wedding special.

"Your eyes are so beautiful".

He said to her.

Touching her soft face.

"Your voice is so soothing".

She told him. And made him blush.

They sat there listening to soul music.

Unaware that Peter was out with Odane making plans in case the Malcolm friends. attacked.

(Exodus 23:22)

Chapter 61

"Wedding Jitters"

It's official they are sending the invitation the invitations.

You're cordially invited to the share in the merger of Heart (Heather) and Paul (Soul).

At main square Church
Saturday June `20th 2015.

Ceremony commencing at 2pm.

Reception follows at the church Hall. At 3pm.

Come and see the miracle of God's love.

The wedding was set for three months from the date they received their invitations.

A whole lot of time to prepare because by now churchgoers are already calling it the anointed wedding.

The shops and dressmakers, tailors, stores where seeing increase in business. The whole town had interest in this wedding.

Heather's ministry was taking off as well. She has Been asked to do workshops and many motivational speeches all over. She uses the contribution towards the church her ministry. And more importantly the love of God.

Paul singing was coming along as well. Himself and the choir had attended two funerals and have blessed and inspired souls and now they are sometimes contracted to perform.

The thought of Heather and owning their own and a bigger place is a constant topic.

Because Paul wants them to move into his house and then look for a better place together.

They are both strong minded people. With strong family values and soon we will meet there other side of their relatives as the wedding fever build up.

The sometimes have their little lovers quarrels but nothing too serious to harm their precious relationship.

The Church is calm and going good with after school program going on to help kids and young adults with their homework, counseling is offered and sometimes dinner program are available. It was such a blessing. Natanya was so invested in this and Trenton went along with her. Always supportive and waiting for her as he had promised.

Natasha was getting Trent out of her mind slowly. But now Ryan is now casually talking her up. She liked him.

Peter came back home in time but he didn't come back home empty handed.

He has everything he needed. If and when an attack should happen.

Heather was wondering why she was feeling so beside herself why she was so perplexed when trouble was brewing right under her nose.

The family as soon jumped one year together since the additional of Paul and occasionally his two sons.

Now there mother is telling it around town that Heather is working some form of science on her.

She is also making it known to anyone who will listen that Heather is successful because Paul is helping her.

There was so much going on in and around this marriage planning that it can't be contained.

Work was getting more ethic for the two it's the summer and those barrels are coming in.

Still Heather maintained talk time. Family time school and homework time with her kids. Paul sitting in on most of the activities as well.

A tension was building inside Trent. He had started the community service nine to five each day. First he was repainting the library that someone had spray painted. Then he had to repair the broken door. He had boundaries of where he could or could not go.

He hates doing all this when he could be hang out at the beach it summer and the schools are out.

He was levied.

He warned his brother Trenton.

"Stay away from that girl. In case of fire I don't want you getting burn!".

(1 Peter 5:6-7)

He hated Peter more that he heard that Odane and Peter are new acquaintances. It's like all he saw was darkness. Whenever he thought about the number of people he has on his hate list.

The counselling is barely sinking in and he can't wait to get out of it. He was having all this revenge build up and he got this mental list that he wants to avenge.

Heather's dress half done was already a spectacular to behold with beads and lace and long train. It's full white with gold piping on some parts.

"I love it"
Her friend Marlene said.

"You deserve every ounce of happiness coming your way because you have battered, "fight and you have kept your faith in God".

"I respect you so much. And I would be happy to be your maid on of honor".

She embraced Heather. Knowing she has been through a lot.

The days when she had to hold credit to feed her family. Her credit was always good anyways.

How wonderful Heather was. To those who knew her well.

Her dress was half finished and she was already having wedding Jitters. "Should she go through with it?"

He notice how Peter was behaving like he had something to hide.

The war was brewing up. And Paul ex-wife was still throwing spades.

Paul too was having second thoughts. It was his second time. He wanted to make sure he has got the right package.

It's this feeling about always wanting to do something and the moment you get close or it. You feel like giving up. You now feel like you can't go through it.

That's fear. The problem with fear is that is is inevitable just like being impatient. We don't like to wait for other but they should wait for us.

Some people with hostile or rough parenting, those who were humiliated and downgraded as a child may carry this fester along with them. (Blacksheep). When we wonder why they never try and why can't they go anywhere. They are hurt. But working with God and their inner self can fix it. It's Fear of failure.

(Isaiah 35:4)

But fear comes when you're not prepare if you didn't not gather all the tools you need to win. Then you are afraid of failure. What's bad is if this is your second try. Then people are thinking if he/she should have not learned their lesson. But each case is different. Keep trying.

You love differently each time around. And having a few broken hearts is a good thing. Because they teach you what you DON'T want ever again.

It teaches you what to stay away from. "But do we ever learn?".

Well some of us don't. Because we are fishing in snapper ponds and expecting to catch a salmon.

To overcome fear make sure well educated about the subject. Take your time cover all the steps. Check it again, ask for help when in doubt. Pray and move towards what to pray about.

Get in an attitude to face your fears head on. Stop delaying and proceed towards what God has called you to do.

When you know it's god who gave it to you. Is when you look back and see all the reasons why you shouldn't get it. And still you did. Set smaller goals for yourself and try to achieve them one at a time leading to the bigger ones.

Control your fear by knowing all you can about what you're fearful of. Knowledge is power and god gives us knowledge.

*seven nature medicine for a good life.
C* Sunshine get as much as that early morning sunlight as possible.

Sunlight help the body to produce vitamin D. The sun is one most direct way of getting vitamin D. Remember when as child (baby) our parent walked us in the sun in early mornings. This was one the reasons.

Sunlight help the brain to make a hormone called serotonin which is responsible for feeling relax being in a good mood and being more focus. So, go and enjoy the sunlight but don't overdo it. It's natural it's our gift from the almighty

But Heather sense something wasn't right in her spirit and she was praying and singing about it.

(Matthew 6:34)

It's roughly after a couple months after the trial before they had this big brawl. Peter and two of Trent's friends it was close to heather wedding day. A month shy to be exact.

Peter was coming from his hidden rendezvous with Ms. Jennings. He also had a drink with her. And was a little lit up.

The boys started by making statements towards him. Such as "preacher's bad seed. "Teachers pet". Boy toy and the list goes on.

He manage to not answer until they ran up behind.

One hit him. And he turned around and he hit back they ganged him. He fought and got away ruining into his yard toward the side and returning with a pistol in his hand.

One the guys pulled one too and gunshots rang out.

(Psalm 34:4)

Thank you for reading. Please recommend this book to anyone who you think it be be of amazing benefit. Share The love of Jesus Christ

May your faith and hope weigh heavily in God almighty.

Look out for Just as I am (2) The Marriage.